LADY ANNE
and the
HAUNTED
SCHOOLGIRL

Books by Victoria Hamilton

Lady Anne Addison Mysteries

Lady Anne and the Howl in the Dark
Revenge of the Barbary Ghost
Curse of the Gypsy
Lady Anne and the Menacing Mystic
Lady Anne and the Haunted Schoolgirl

Vintage Kitchen Mysteries

A Deadly Grind
Bowled Over
Freezer I'll Shoot
No Mallets Intended
White Colander Crime
Leave It to Cleaver
No Grater Danger
Breaking the Mould
Cast Iron Alibi
A Calculated Whisk
Sieve and Let Die

Merry Muffin Mysteries

Bran New Death
Muffin But Murder
Death of an English Muffin
Much Ado About Muffin
Muffin to Fear
Muffin But Trouble
Double or Muffin

A Gentlewoman's Guide to Murder Mysteries

A Gentlewoman's Guide to Murder
Some Touch of Madness

LADY ANNE
and the
HAUNTED
SCHOOLGIRL

VICTORIA HAMILTON

BEYOND THE PAGE
PUBLISHING

Lady Anne and the Haunted Schoolgirl
Victoria Hamilton
Beyond the Page Books
are published by
Beyond the Page Publishing
www.beyondthepagepub.com

Copyright © 2024 by Donna Lea Simpson.
Cover design and illustration by Dar Albert, Wicked Smart Designs.

ISBN: 978-1-960511-71-3

Chapter One

December, 1786
Bath, England

"I don't think I can do this, Alethea," Lady Anne Addison said, fingering the diaphanous *robe en chemise* her seamstress had made for her in advance of her wedding to Tony, Marquess of Darkefell. It was December. The wedding would be in three weeks.

Unless she jilted him. The way she felt that moment it was a distinct possibility.

Her friend, arching one eyebrow high, said, "Misgivings about marrying that man? He's not my type, my dear, but even I can see the attraction. The man is a mountain of smolder, like a hot, glowing ember waiting to burst into a bonfire whenever he looks at you. He can barely restrain himself from grabbing you in a *most* inappropriate way."

Anne grinned. Her fiancé didn't always restrain himself, but she was not about to share those most private moments even with a close friend. "I wasn't saying I don't think I can marry Tony; all I *think* about is marrying Tony. Or more precisely, what we can do *after* I marry Tony." Irusan, her enormous cat, eyed the *robe en chemise* material with interest and hooked one claw in it, tearing the delicate fabric. Anne shooed him away. He huffily retreated to his velvet cushion to sulk, turning his back on them. "My father and Jamey arrive in Bath tomorrow. I don't know if I can be in the same room as my father and my mother. They've been estranged so long. My mother is so . . . and my father is . . ." She sighed, plopped gracelessly down on a chair and covered her face with both hands.

Her father and brother would be staying with her fiancé rather than in her grandmother's home, where she and her mother were living. Her brother Jamey, with struggles of the mind so profound he required careful assistance, was a handful. Disorder agitated him, though he did his best to behave. And in this move to Bath and the weeks before Anne's wedding, there was guaranteed to be tumult.

Fortunately, a married couple traveled with him. Dorcas, the woman, and he had a special relationship. Early on she had set boundaries for him, and he behaved for her better than for anyone.

1

Still, the trip would upset him, as would unusual surroundings and living in strange quarters. Seeing his mother for the first time in years would be trying. In short, the chance for trouble in Bath was weighted heavily in favor of catastrophe.

Anne's mother was not equipped to deal with him, nor was the break with Anne's father healed, by any means, though letters had passed between the two. Would she see Jamey? Would she see Anne's father? She had promised neither, becoming agitated and taking to her bed at the thought. Her nerves, she cried in anguish. Her poor frayed, fretted, ragged, unraveling nerves!

Anne sighed heavily.

"What are you thinking of, my friend?" Alethea asked. She stretched out her long legs, gowned in lovely blue brocade, and examined her own wedding ring, symbol of her marriage to Bertie, her friend and, she would say, her saving grace. "Or do I know?" She eyed her and nodded. "I do *know* what you're going through. I recall even your brief time at school was chaotic for you, managing your worries about your mother and father and Jamey. I don't envy you the next weeks of distress. But it's not all up to you, Anne. Your father and mother must manage their own relationship as best they can. It is your duty to think of your husband-to-be and your wedding."

"Ah, yes, the *wedding*!" Shuddering, Anne rolled her eyes and collapsed back in her chair. "*There* is a topic guaranteed to make everything worse. It's the event my mother has looked forward to her whole life, according to her. And with me marrying beyond anything she could have hoped or planned—she never imagined I'd catch a marquess—she is determined to parade the event before the bon ton. If she could, she would trundle me to London to be married at St. George's Hanover Square. Tony, fortunately, refused, saying London was for others, but not for him. He will do his duty in the House, but not in the church."

Alethea snickered.

"St. Swithin's, thankfully, remains the site of our exchange of vows," she said of the lovely church just up the street from her grandmother's Paragon townhouse.

"Wherein you will promise to obey his lordship," Alethea said, with a wicked gleam in her eye.

"I'll do as I always have," Anne retorted tartly.

"By law he can do what *he* will."

Anne sobered. "I am wagering my whole future happiness on his promise to give me freedom, Alethea. Am I foolish to think him different than other men?"

"I don't think you foolish at all, my dear friend." She put her hand over Anne's then swiftly removed it. "I don't know him well, but what I have seen of your man, I like." Energetic as always, she jumped to her feet and put her hand out. "You need a distraction. You're hungering for a problem to solve. Accompany me on a walk? I have someone with whom I'd like you to speak."

"Who?" Anne said, eyeing her friend with concern. Alethea did not go out much right now; her and her husband's marriage had been subjected to scandalous rumor, and both were fragile still. She grabbed her friend's hand and allowed herself to be pulled to her feet.

"Do you know Miss Sophia Lee?"

"I know *of* her but have never met her. I'm acquainted with her sister, Harriet. We are contemporaries in age and have met with pleasure at lectures and readings, as our taste in literature agrees. We've thus corresponded on occasion about what she and her sister are writing."

"You know that they have a school quite near you."

"Of course, in the Belvedere Villas on Lansdown Road, a lovely building. I left my card there upon arriving in Bath, but I know how busy Harriet is. *The Errors of Innocence* has come out this year, and she's now working toward having a play, *The New Peerage*, produced at the Drury next year," Anne said. "She's promised me a first-night box, as she said I inspired her in my letters. She did write me a brief note thanking me for the notice of my arrival in town, but she is engaged most days with the school and other concerns."

"Both sisters are very taken up with work and school affairs."

"I don't take her inability to see me amiss. We are acquaintances, not close friends. She wishes me well and wrote that perhaps we can see each other over the Christmas season, when lessons will be suspended." Anne frowned, searching amid the clutter of clothing draped about the room for her spencer. "She's in quite the dither about the school from what I understand through mutual acquaintances."

Alethea nodded, her brows arched with a knowing look. "Your feelings are hurt," she said.

"Not at all," Anne insisted. One of her friend's more annoying traits was that she thought she knew what people were feeling every day of the year. "In case you have forgotten, I have been busy myself with fake werewolves, ghosts and gypsy curses, and even in Bath with murder investigations and such nonsense," Anne said.

"Of course, Anne. I don't suppose you know, though, that Sophia is a dear friend of mine, one of the few I trust. She has been quite as busy as her sister and writes as much." She fished under a pile of stays and shifts, pulling out Anne's spencer and handing it to her. "Perhaps while we walk I can explain their preoccupation with the school. Sophia is presently having trouble with one of her students, Miss Faithful Collier. The child is quite a silly chit, the kind who believes in ghosts and haunting and mediums. You know how that goes," she said with a smile.

"Yes, like the victims of our fraudulent mystic," Anne said. The one she had exposed as a swindler.

"Sophia is worried, and with cause. The child tried to do away with herself."

Anne, startled, stared at her friend as she pulled on the spencer. "Maybe you should begin at the beginning."

"Walk with me while I talk. Please speak with Sophia. It will do you both good."

"I will, if only to get away from my mother. There is no safe topic of conversation with her. If it is not my wedding, it is the marriage settlement negotiations with the family barrister. And if it is not that, it is my trousseau, thus the impossibly fragile *robe en chemise*. Tony will tear that frivolity apart in two minutes on our wedding night, unless Irusan destroys it first, behaving like a little lion."

The cat's ears twitched and he looked over his shoulder at them as Alethea smothered a grin.

"Lately the only thing that distracts Mama from talking about my wedding is worrying about getting robbed."

"Oh, those awful break-ins lately!" Alethea exclaimed, shaking out her gown, smoothing it with her gloved hands. "We are altering the new house because of it. Bertie is having a German-made safe box installed to protect valuables. Thank goodness we are moving from our poky little hole-in-the-wall. Where we are is far too easy to break into, being so private."

"And what good are the magistrates? None at all."

"There are only two of them, Anne, after all. One is quite harsh and has had many thieves up on charges, though it always seems to be the cutpurses and market pickpockets rather than the jewel thieves. Magistrate Brereton, his name is. I know his wife. A lovely woman. We've been friends, though her husband doesn't approve of our friendship, especially not lately with the trouble Bertie and I have had."

After the inevitable bustle of getting ready—the December air was chill and required the help of Anne's maid, Mary, with muffs and boots as well as the requisite hat—they walked up the Paragon, then turned left onto Guinea Lane. From there they would walk up the steep incline until they reached Lansdown and turned to their right, strolling Lansdown briefly until they came to Belvedere House on the right. Before they got there Anne wanted answers. "You tempted me out for this walk with the promise of conversation and an explanation of your mysterious hints about Miss Sophia Lee and her troubled student. Speak."

"Miss Faithful Collier, daughter of a barrister; good enough social standing. He prospered in his second marriage in particular, the youngest daughter of a viscount, Faithful's mother, you know." She paused, then added, "The girl's older brother, son of the first wife, took training as a solicitor."

"I sense a slight in your tone, as if the young man has degraded his family."

"I *intended* it to be an insult. No man—or woman—should bring their family *down* in consequence. It is the obligation we bear, to *lift* our family, not submerge them. A barrister may be a gentleman, but a solicitor never will. It gets worse; instead of making the law his occupation, the son is now a clerk in a shipping concern. He failed even as a solicitor." She frowned and shook her head. "There has been trouble there with the son, gambling debts, or misbegotten seduction or such. The family's trajectory is firmly set on a downward path."

"How discriminatory you are."

"Are you a Leveller?" she said, referencing a very old movement. "I hadn't thought it, and you the daughter of an earl."

"Maybe it is *because* I am the daughter of an earl that I have learned to view men and women in the light of their own qualities, not their family's inheritances."

"Perhaps. I assure you, I am not discriminatory, merely a realist. You are fortunate, but mere misses like myself needed to be careful lest we bring our family down a step."

Anne wasn't sure whether Alethea was joking or not.

Her friend glanced at her as they strolled. "I'm quite serious, you know. I say nothing at all about the *quality* of the person if I condemn their station. Their value as a man or woman is entirely separate from their position in society."

"About the girl . . ."

"Yes, about the girl. Her mother — "

" — the viscount's youngest daughter — "

" — is dead. Her father is a tyrant, her brother looks down on her — "

"He looks down on *her*? She has the higher status over her brother, yes?"

"Of course, but has illogic ever stopped the ignorant from looking down on the intelligent, or boors from looking down on the cultured? He is a man, ergo, he is the superior. The son is a rotter, a wastrel, from all evidence, though I cannot say where Sophia got the information from. Gossip, likely. She is widely connected through the school, but also through her writing and meets with all sorts of people. Because the family is descending, poor Faithful will likely do no better than to marry a dreary law clerk without higher aspirations."

"How awful that all she can expect from life is marriage to the first decent fellow who deigns to ask." If her father even ensured the fellow *was* decent, and not merely willing to take responsibility for her forever after in exchange for a marital moiety — in other words, a dowry. Anne paused on their ascending walk to catch her breath. The frigid weather caused her lung condition to trouble her on occasion. Gazing at Alethea, she said, "You seem very engaged in the whole affair. Do you have a connection with this child?"

Alethea moodily stared up Guinea Lane. On their right was a low wall interrupted by an entrance onto a walking path into a park. "I am become tender in my old age and current troubled situation. I have nothing to do and am bored."

"That is not the extent of it, my friend."

"I have met the girl. She's sensitive, nervous. Unhappy. Motherless. I feel a kinship, I suppose, both of us rudderless boats on storm toss't seas."

This was the closest Alethea had come in the last few days to referring to her self-imposed status as a social outcast. The skies had become as gloomy as Alethea's mood, with a cold wind sweeping down the street. They continued their walk, past a maid scrubbing a front step, who cast a wary eye at the sky and hastened her scrub brush to her task with alacrity. They turned onto Lansdown and Anne's companion stayed her with one gloved hand on Anne's arm.

"What is it?" Anne asked, examining her friend's uncertain expression.

"Faithful is an imaginative girl. Please don't belittle her for it."

"Do you think me a monster?"

"I know your opinion of flights of fancy."

"On the contrary," Anne said lightly. "I delight in folly. I will indulge tales of brownies and elves, fairies and gnomes living in the hedgerow. As long as humankind does not try to blame their own misdeeds on the faery folk, I shall indulge it."

"Let us see if you put that philosophy into practice. She claims she is being haunted by the ghost of a dead schoolgirl who led her to the roof and told her to jump. Or the ghost of her mother." Alethea frowned and shook her head. "The tale has become confused."

Anne thought, *or maybe the girl is confused*, but she did not say it aloud. "How old is she?"

"Seventeen."

"Seventeen! From your description I pictured a child."

"Wait until you meet her, and you will understand why I described her so."

Together they passed a shrouded lane that led, Anne knew, to the park they had passed when they strolled Guinea Lane. Belvedere House was a pretty villa set back from the other residences on Lansdown. With eight sets of windows along the front three stories and an attic, it was symmetrical and pleasing to the eye, a pretty break from the townhomes beyond them, stolidly towering over the street in conjoined dourness. Anne looked up to the top of the building, a distance of forty or so feet, and wondered, would the girl have died if she fell — or leaped — from there? "Was it from the front or back she was about to leap?"

"Er, the back, I suppose."

A pretty maid let them in. Alethea stared at her until she colored pink and curtseyed, with a flourish of her skirts and a brassy, pert expression. She handed the girl her card, which was swiftly carried away after she showed them to a reception room off the hall, bidding them await the mistress, if they pleased.

"That girl will be trouble for my friends," Alethea said dourly, taking a seat near the fire and pulling off her gloves.

"What do you mean?" Anne asked, sitting near her. "She seemed perfectly polite to me."

"You do not have the experience with maids that I do, engaging them and firing them," Alethea said, staring at the door through which the maid had left the room. "She is the sort who is unhappy with her position and will find a means to change it."

"How is that bad? Shouldn't she try to better herself?"

"There is your society-leveling streak again. The means by which she will try to escape it will involve a man, flirtation, sex and money to keep her in style."

"You can't know that." Anne got up and strolled to the window overlooking the street, watching a man and woman walk by. Around her the house was active with the sounds of students moving about upstairs. A child cried somewhere. Serving staff in another room clanked and clattered, setting up luncheon, or clearing away. The place smelled of fish, floor polish and the indefinable scent of a score of girls and women.

"Never mind my gloomy reflections," Alethea said. "I apologize if I sound ill-tempered. I have been plagued by staff problems lately. The new house will require more servants, and it's hard to find good staff when you are a pariah. You have been reticent since I told you our mission today, and of young Faithful's tale of ghostly visitation."

"I don't know what to say," Anne remarked, strolling away from the window, touching a pianoforte, admiring a painting mounted on a silk-covered wall. She turned to her friend. "It is an incredible tale, and I'm not sure what I am to say except, *indeed?* I have been ordered to eschew ridicule, and what else do I have in my arsenal of speech?"

Alethea chuckled at her friend's arch reply. "I didn't say you could not be cutting to me, I merely suggested kindness toward Faithful."

"The girl was found on the roof outside of a skylight or window in the attic of the building and appeared about to jump to her death," Anne mused aloud. "A disagreeable way to go, since I'm not convinced she would have died, merely maimed herself. When questioned, you tell me she said she had been led there by a ghost and told to jump. Are we sure she was not dreaming?"

Alethea raised one brow.

"I'm serious, my friend. Or sleepwalking? A clandestine meeting gone wrong? Mischief? I can think of a dozen explanations that don't include ghosts, but that a girl might attempt to cover up with a wild ghost story." Fixing her friend with a speculative gaze, she said, "Or she was looking for attention. Girls on occasion invent wild stories to make themselves stand out, or to cause a stir."

"Let us wait for Miss Lee."

There were voices outside the door, one low and melodious, one shrill and complaining. The melodious tone altered to commanding, and the shrill voice quieted and stopped. After a moment, a lady swept into the room.

Anne had met Harriet Lee at the Drury Lane theater in London and they had struck up a friendship and correspondence, but had never met Sophia Lee. She examined a pretty lady of mature years, medium height, high arched brows over piercing eyes, and tidy figure. Her clothing was moderately fashionable, with a cinched waist emphasizing a high bosom concealed under a linen tucker. She bustled forward, hand outstretched, as she examined Anne minutely.

"This is your friend, of whom I have heard much," she exclaimed to Alethea. "I am to offer felicitations on your upcoming wedding, I understand."

"Thank you." Anne took her hand and the two women examined each other. "I am acquainted with your sister Harriet."

"Harriet is closer to being your contemporary than I." Miss Sophia Lee was her sister's senior by seven years and had taken on the care of her siblings at thirty. Her duties had perhaps resulted in her manner, which was brusque, commanding, and confident. Anne liked her the better for it. "Our other sister Anne is almost exactly your age."

"A sister namesake to me! Where does Miss Anne Lee live?" Anne said with a smile.

"Why here, of course. She's about somewhere. We rely on her, for she is responsible for many details of the curricula. Sit, ladies, sit," Miss Lee commanded, waving a hand over a grouping of chairs and a settee. "I have tea coming in a moment if the mindless girl remembers."

Sophia and Alethea sat on brocade chairs lined up to face each other like soldiers on parade. An upholstered settee created the bottom of a U-shaped seating arrangement. Anne took a seat there.

"I know your friendship with Alethea and Bertie," she said with a warm glance toward Anne's friend. "I am grateful on their behalf. Good people should not be mistreated. And I watched from afar and applauded as you evicted the charlatan and her retinue from Bath," she said of the mystic Anne had exposed. "When this current trouble occurred, I thought of you. I don't mind saying this incident leaves us perplexed. My sisters and I have dealt with over-ardent girls, but Faithful . . . I had not expected this of her. She's a Bristol girl, sensible, intelligent, not a silly dreamer like others her age. We're not far from Bristol, of course, but with no mother resident, she goes to one of her classmate's homes in the summer. One in particular has grandparents living in Bath and Faithful stayed there for a few weeks. We had her here last year with no problem, but this year something has changed. This fright, her almost . . . er, falling from the rooftop has alarmed me. At the very least, I would appreciate your advice on how to get through to this chit that there are no ghosts at our school, nor any such thing as ghosts."

The directness of her appeal to Anne was uncommon. Not many ladies were as straightforward. It was a novelty, and one Anne rather enjoyed. However, Miss Sophia's pause before saying "falling" was telling. She was not sure what she was dealing with, and the uncertainty was unpleasant to her. "Are you sure there are no ghosts in your school?"

Miss Lee stared at her as Alethea snickered. "I assume you jest."

"Not at all." She watched the other lady for a moment, then elaborated. "I have been a witness to a ghost, you see. Or what was meant to be a ghost. Is it possible the girl is seeing or experiencing an illusion? She's too young to be as cynical as I have become to what my eyes behold. What I saw was a machination, but there are other possible explanations. In short, she may not be lying or even imagining. She may have seen what appeared to be a ghost."

"Ah, I understand you now," Miss Lee said. She glanced to Alethea. "Perhaps you should meet the girl and tell me what you think."

Chapter Two

The maid brought a tea tray and set it down on a low table beside her employer. "Kate, will you fetch Miss Collier?" The girl curtseyed and flounced from the room as Miss Lee glared after her with a narrow squinting gaze Anne noted but did not comment on.

The three women conversed over bowls of tea, Alethea asking questions about Sophia's literary plans, until a pale girl entered the reception room. Slim and tall, Faithful Collier appeared surprisingly childlike despite being seventeen. Maybe it was her clothing, for she wore the unadorned white dress of a very young girl, and her hair was loose, curly and billowing exuberantly from a pale blue silk ribbon tied at the nape of her neck. Or maybe it was the wide guileless blue of her eyes, the pink bow of her mouth. The girl was pretty but carried herself with no self-conscious air. Anne had expected Faithful to be timid, frightened, even. Instead she appeared defiant, her mouth set in an obstinate line.

Introductions made, Miss Sophia said to the girl, "Miss Collier, I've been concerned after the incident on the roof and your astonishing contention that you received ghostly visitations urging you to self-destruction. Lady Anne has experience with these matters and would like to speak with you."

There could hardly be a worse introduction, Anne thought. The girl stood mutely, hands folded behind her back, staring at a spot above Alethea's head. She had been mishandled and would not trust easily, Anne thought, having been in similar situations. She cast a look at her friend.

Alethea stood. "Sophia, could we speak in private?"

"Of course, Mrs. Birkenhead. Let us repair to my study."

Once they were gone Anne said, "May I call you Faithful?"

The girl stared. On closer inspection her enormous eyes were rimmed in red and underlined with dark circles. Her clothes were plain, with little in the way of ornamentation, and ill fitting, the overskirt drooping on her as if made for a heavier girl. She had recently lost weight. She nodded at Anne's question.

"Please sit." The girl obeyed, perching on the edge of one of the chairs. "You say you were bidden by a ghost to leap from the rooftop. Is that true?"

No response.

"I will not ridicule you, Faithful, I promise it. My sole aim is to help you." She didn't move. Something must break the silence. "Come here. Sit beside me, please."

She did as she was told, her weight making barely any indentation on the sofa. Gentling her voice, Anne said, "Faithful, you can talk to me. I promise not to tease or ridicule you, no matter what you say. Were you told to go up to the roof to jump off?"

She hesitated, then nodded.

"Who was it?"

"A voice, at first. Then I saw a ghost in the mirror, you see, and it bid me follow. We climbed the stairs—"

"We?"

"The specter and I."

"You saw the specter and it moved with you?" The girl stiffened and clamped her mouth shut. "I am not making fun. I want to understand, Faithful," Anne said. "Tell me what happened. You saw a ghostly apparition and it ascended with you."

She shook her head slowly. "Not exactly. A light preceded me up the stairs."

Mirrors, perhaps? Light reflected? "The stairs to the roof?"

She shook her head. "There are no stairs to the roof, my lady. I was led to the servants' floor."

"Had you been up there before?"

"No, my lady. I did not know the way. The light led me to a door, and the stairs."

"Did you hear anything while this was happening?"

"A voice, saying I must obey. Follow the light." She shook her head, pressing her lips together in a firm line. Tears welled in her eyes. One spilled over and trailed down her cheek. She dashed it away impatiently.

"Tell me, Faithful." The girl shook her head. Anne thought she had likely learned that telling the truth led to mockery. "I *vow* I will not laugh." The girl was silent. "I always keep my promises. You can tell me all."

There was a tension in the girl's slim frame, an agitation in her very stillness. She burst out, "I . . . I started hearing a voice—"

"Was the first time at home?"

She shook her head. "Here. At school, a few weeks ago."

"Where did the voice come from?"

"It was . . . oh, it was in the air. I cannot *say* where it came from: everywhere and nowhere."

"Was it clear, muffled, one voice or many?"

"It was clear at times, and not at others. One voice, at first, but . . ." Faithful tilted her head and looked into herself. "Sometimes there was also a *whisper*." She glanced at Anne. "And now you shall say I am imagining it. Or I am going mad."

"I won't. Let us continue. There was one voice but whispering also."

"Sometimes."

"Was it female or male?"

"One voice, a girl's."

"Did you recognize it?"

She shook her head, but her eyes said there was more to be said.

"What is it, Faithful?"

"At times it sounded almost like my mother," she whispered, her breath catching on a sob.

Oh dear; the poor child. Girls could be cruel, even toward a motherless girl. "You lost your mother years ago, but you remember her voice. How would you describe it?"

"It was soft, sweet, loving." She smiled through tears. "She would call me her *darling dove*."

In other words, the voice sounded like any voice tempered to be sweet and loving when whispering phrases remembered through the mists of time. "I'm sorry, Faithful, truly. I'm sure it helps having friends to talk to about your mother. Do you talk about her often?" Anne asked.

"I did at first."

And probably told her friends about what her mother called her, how her voice sounded. Anne started to see a pattern, how what Faithful had said in the late-night conversations girls have had been turned into a weapon with which to trick and torment her. But why? "What about the image in the mirror? Was it female, or male?"

Female, Faithful said, as far as she could tell, and she only saw her once.

"When? And where?"

"In our room. It was evening, and the other girls were late going up. They lingered behind in the music room, where we had been working on an amateur theatrical we are planning. They were all whispering and laughing." A thread of bewildered annoyance threaded through her tone, but there was a note of aloneness too. "I was tired, and I was finished with my work."

"You went up to the room alone. And then?"

"I got my brush—"

"Was that your habit?"

She nodded. "Every night. I brush my hair one hundred strokes and braid it, tying a ribbon around the end."

"And . . . ?"

"My brush was on top of the bureau. I glanced at the mirror and . . . and that's when I saw it!"

"Saw what?"

"The face." She was trembling all over. A sob caught her voice as she exclaimed, "It was horrible, a figure covered in a ghastly torn veil like a . . . like a shroud! She laughed and pointed at me—the hand was a skeleton's hand—and said I was a fool. She said I would be visited by others. I must do as I was bid or I would d-die."

Someone was taking despicable advantage of this child. "And then?"

"She disappeared, and I heard only a voice."

"Saying . . . ?"

"Saying to beware. To tell no one or my family would be cursed."

"Your family would be cursed? You father and who else?"

"My brother, my lady."

"Do you like your brother, Faithful? Do you see him much?"

She shrugged in a way that revealed more than words. "I . . . I don't see him much, though he has been in Bath a few times lately. The voice said they would suffer under a curse that would devastate them forever. My mother had been punished, the voice said, for being immoral, and I was headed down the same path to destruction."

Anne bit her lip to keep from exclaiming against such offensive humiliation.

"I was to listen for instructions." It finished, she said, with ghostly, mocking laughter.

"Did the instructions come?"

"Any time I was alone."

"What did the voice tell you to do?"

Trembling, she looked like she would not answer. Finally she said, "It made me do awful things!"

"Like what?"

"One time it was to creep into the servants' hall and put salt in the sugar cellars. The next time it told me to pour vinegar in Miss Dankworth's bedside water glass."

Schoolgirlish pranks. "Was it always the same voice?"

Faithful nodded.

"You didn't recognize it?" The girl shook her head. "Did you tell anyone about the voice?"

"Alys Edisbury, my friend. I tell her everything. One of the other girls learned it and made fun of me. It was horrible. I can't bear it!" Her voice had risen in tone, hysteria creeping in. She rocked, twisting her hands together in her lap.

"Who was the girl who made fun of you?"

She shook her head, unwilling to tattle. If another girl knew, it was likely because she was the guilty party hoaxing poor Faithful with a cruel joke, though it sounded to Anne like more than one girl was in on the hoax. "Faithful, where is the bureau where your brush is kept?"

"Inside the bedroom, near the door."

"And the bedroom is where?"

"Bedrooms are on the third floor by the staircase."

"Are there other rooms up there?"

"Yes, my lady, the other student bedroom, the Misses Lee's rooms, offices."

At the top of the stairs. The timing would have to be precise. Anne imagined the "ghost" was another girl dressed in a gray veil, glaring into the mirror, frightening Faithful to the point that she was frozen in place. Roommates know each other's habits. The girls would have known that she brushed her hair in the mirror every evening the moment she went to their room. The trickster was able to flit out the door in a split second, as Faithful finally turned. "And when you turned, there was no one there."

"No, but there was this ghastly laughter, mocking, floating." She shuddered. "After that, the voices haunted me whenever I was alone."

"And started making you do things to the staff and teachers?"

She nodded. "The voices started saying other things, too. They taunted me."

"What did they say?"

"I would go mad, like my mother did."

Startled, Anne said, "What do you mean, going mad as your mother had?"

She turned away and rocked back and forth, choking on tears. "My mother had to go to a madhouse. She was going to hurt me."

"Who told you that?"

"My father. He had to protect me from her," she whispered. Her eyes large and tragic, filled with tears, she clasped her hands to her bosom and stared at Anne. "Am I going mad?" she asked. "Please, my lady, help me. I don't *want* to kill myself."

Anne gently pried her hands apart and took one in hers, chafing the cold fingers. "I'm going to be stern with you, Faithful," she said, holding her gaze. "Listen to me, and listen well. You are not going mad. Tell me what else the voices said."

Faithful's gaze slid away, her mouth firming and her shoulders setting in stubborn lines. "If I wished to avoid becoming like my mother, I must do as I was told. To make it all stop, and to keep my family from being forever cursed, I had to follow the ghost to the attic."

"The ghost voice didn't tell you it wanted you to jump?"

"Not then," Faithful said. She followed instructions to locate the stairs and go up to the windows that opened onto the roof. The window was unlocked. She opened it. Shivering, she admitted sitting on the windowsill and looking at the moon, praying for courage.

"Were you going to jump, Faithful?"

"No! Not . . . not at first." Tears now streamed down her face. "Oh, that *voice*! It drifted upward, my lady, like a . . . like a vapor, soft, insinuating! Like the ghost of poor mad Isabella in *The Haunting of Isabella S.*"

"You've read that book?" Anne had read the novel, a typical (and enjoyable) tale of Gothic castles, a maiden trapped in a faraway country, and the ghost that possessed her.

"We all did. Miss Hopewell was reading it and she loaned it to Julia. We passed it among ourselves, us older girls, anyway."

There was the genesis of the ghostly presence, the kernel of an idea the trickster had used. "You heard the voice even as you were at the window?"

"Yes! Though it was muffled. The voice told me that to make the haunting stop before something terrible happened I *had* to do what it said, you know, to jump! I didn't want to, truly I *didn't*."

Anne wanted to hug the girl, but there was a fragile reliance and a flow between them, one she did not want to break. "What happened next?"

"Miss Lee found me. She brought me inside and took me to her room, wrapping me in a shawl until I stopped shivering."

How did Sophia know Faithful was on the roof? "And what do you think now? Have the voices stopped, or do they keep on?"

"They have stopped. Perhaps showing I would do it stopped them?"

It was more likely her tormentor was frightened by what happened and had backed down for the moment. There was no guarantee it wouldn't happen again, though. She must arm the girl against further torment. "Faithful, I want you to listen to me," she said, with as much kindness as she could when she was shaking with anger. She took both the girl's hands in hers. "Despite what others have said, the voices are real."

The girl nodded. The voices had always been real for her.

"It was a cruel hoax, a trickster using the configuration of the staircase to make their voice heard. Have you noticed that sound travels oddly near the stairs?"

"I suppose so."

"That's what has happened. If it happens again—it may, or it may not—you *must* not let them see they are frightening you. Say, '*I know you are trying to trick me. Stop it now!*'"

"Who would do such a thing?"

"Who was the girl who first started making fun of you for the voices you heard?"

Faithful looked away, mute.

"Won't you tell me?"

She shook her head. "I . . . I can't."

Prodded, the girl was unmoved, stubbornly shaking her head and looking away. Anne released her hands and sat back, thinking. The girl was afraid of reprisal, most likely. "May I speak with you again before I leave?"

Faithful nodded, then stood, curtseyed, and fled back to her class. Alethea and Miss Sophia rejoined Anne. In response to the schoolmistress's question, Anne explained her theory and said, "I suspect the scheme was inspired by a book the girls have read, *The Haunting of Isabella S*. There is a ghost in the book, and a young lady who is haunted. I've read it, harmless enough fare if one takes it as entertainment. Faithful saw a ghostly apparition in a mirror, an old trick, one mystics have used for centuries. In this case I believe it was one of the girls with a veil thrown over her standing behind Faithful when she, following her routine, went to get her hairbrush from the bureau. After that it was voices only. Someone is tormenting the girl, likely one of the other students."

"Not *one* of my girls would do that," Miss Lee said adamantly.

Anne shared a look with Alethea. The woman may not know her girls as well as she thought. "Miss Lee, I do have a question. How did you know Faithful was up on the roof? She says you are the one who stopped her."

"It wasn't me, it was Anne who found her. The little girls had already gone to bed, but the older girls were gathered in the music room rehearsing for our Christmas theatrical."

"That sounds like fun," Anne said. "What are you doing?"

Miss Sophia colored faintly and looked away. "We are planning a ghostly Christmas tale with musical performances throughout. When we were young my sisters and I would perform a theatrical for our father every year. As an actor he was never much impressed, but we tried." She smiled and met Anne's gaze. "It keeps young minds engaged, we believe. Some of the girls are particularly good. Fanny will be our sprite. Henrietta our ghastly ghoul; she's a very dramatic girl. Julia is our lovely young lady, haunted by love. Faithful was to be our naif ingénue. She has a delightful singing voice. Something upset her that night, I don't know what, and she went upstairs while the girls put away the props."

"Props?"

"Oh, you know, the skeletal hand that reaches out beyond the grave . . . that nonsense."

Skeleton hand. It was all coming together, the silliness of youth, inspired by a romantic novel and a ghastly play, to play tricks on the vulnerable Faithful. Urging her to jump, though, took it to a more mean-spirited place. "Go on."

"Faithful went up first. The other girls went up some time later. Miss Alys Edisbury, missing her friend, went to Anne's room. I don't know why she didn't ask Miss Hopewell, but the teachers are often occupied helping girls at bedtime. Anyway, Anne explored and found a door ajar that should not be, which led to the next door that should not be open, to the window letting out onto the roof."

"Did they see anyone else?"

Miss Lee shook her head. "She found Faithful and brought her inside."

"May I speak with the other students?"

"Why?"

Anne hesitated. The schoolmistress had openly stated none of her students would be cruel to one another and she was dismissive of Faithful's sincerely held belief she had been haunted. She must hear the truth and not view her students through a distorting rosy-hued lens. "Whether you will acknowledge it or not, girls can be cruel and tease each other. This, though, is an insidious intimidation going beyond what girls usually inflict on one another. Faithful will not expose the culprit or culprits, but I want to follow the trail. Perhaps I may speak to the ones with whom she shares a room? Who are they?"

Miss Sophia named them: Miss Fanny Patterson, a twelve-year-old vicar's daughter from Cardiff; Miss Henrietta Greerson, fifteen, granddaughter of local magistrate, brewer and landowner Mr. Brereton; Miss Julia Halliday, seventeen, who hailed from Burnham-on-Sea; and Miss Alys Edisbury, fifteen, another Welsh lass from further west than Fanny, closer to Swansea.

"Ah, Alys Edisbury, Faithful's bosom friend, as you said, and the one who alerted your sister to her absence from their room. What about the teachers? Where do they sleep?"

"One in each of the girls' rooms. It helps to keep the peace, we find. In Faithful's room is Miss India Hopewell, who teaches etiquette, stitchery, and religion. The other female teacher who is in the littler girls' room—we have girls from seven to ten—is Miss Carlotta Dankworth. She teaches composition, penmanship and introductory geography."

"What about the arts?"

"Mr. Marcus Russell teaches drawing and painting. Mr. O'Brien teaches pianoforte and music theory. Mr. Durrand teaches dance and tutors French for those parents who wish it. They all live in lodgings, of course, and come in for lessons. All three also teach at a local boys' school and have private pupils."

"What do you, Harriet and Anne teach?"

"I teach history and conduct examinations. We are very strict about reporting to the parents their daughters' progress. Harriet teaches literature and composition for the upper girls, and assists with testing the younger girls."

"And your sister Anne?"

She shifted. "Anne does not teach, though she tutors. She writes class material, marks papers, creates tests, and . . . etcetera."

"I would like to see them all."

"Certainly. What excuse would you like to give for questioning them?"

"We need an excuse?"

"I suppose not."

"Let us proceed." The benefit of a title, Anne had found in her life, was that no one was surprised when she behaved as a tyrant, demanding special service from even a school. "Students first."

Chapter Three

The first girl, Miss Fanny Patterson, was a tiny, fey, winsome girl of twelve years, well cast as the sprite. And yet as Lady Anne met her gaze, she was startled by an ancient ethereal wisdom in the child's eyes. Or was that an impression encouraged by the child's resemblance to one of the fairy folk of myth? "Do you get along with the girls here, Fanny?"

She smiled and nodded.

"Do you like your teachers?"

"Yes, my lady," the girl said, her voice a whisper. "Except for Mr. O'Brien. He shouts when I am stupid at the piano."

"Are you girls all kind to each other?"

The girl's expression clouded, but she nodded.

"You are?"

"Mostly."

"Does anyone tease the other girls?"

She cast her eyes down and said, "She doesn't mean it, I'm sure, but Henrietta *is* sharp, at times." She would say nothing more.

Miss Julia Halliday was a young lady of almost eighteen years, the same as Faithful, and would be leaving school in early spring to be presented to London society, she volunteered. Her godmother was sponsoring her, for her family did not have the money or position to launch her properly. It was clear by her meticulous plans, which she laid out at length and in detail, that everything depended upon that debut. She must make an impression and capture interest. There would be no second Season, she implied, with a worried expression. It would be an anxious time for her, as well as a joyous one, and Anne felt great compassion for her, and all the girls like her, who must make the most of their one opportunity. A man could find his way through diligence and hard work, allied with a winning personality and intelligence, but an impecunious young lady must dazzle in her Season or fade into obscurity, trying her luck at the lesser watering holes.

Julia was excited and ready for it, a shade passing over her face as she said, casting her glance about the sitting room, "It is time I am out of this place. I detest studying. It's foolish. I will need none of it when I marry, after all."

She cheered up after that comment and was chatty and vivacious. Mostly she talked at length of art, painting and in particular the art master, Mr. Marcus Russell. How clever he was. How wonderfully talented. How good-natured and intelligent and . . . no sense could be drawn from her. No sense can *ever* be drawn from a girl that age in the throes of passionate first love, Anne thought.

She had to discover what was behind Faithful's trouble, and the first step was to get Julia to speak of the other girls. Mendacity might be required. "I was speaking to another student of Mr. Russell's. Faithful Collier said he —"

"She is *not* his favorite, no matter what she says!" Julia blurted, her cheeks pinkening.

Taken aback, Anne was silent.

"She *isn't*. Faithful is very sweet, most of the time, but she is childish. Not like me. Not grown up, you see. She believes our art master is in love with her. Mr. Russell explained it all to me when he told me why he cannot go on walks with me anymore. He must lead by example, he said. He must show Miss Collier that he will not play favorites." She glanced about, leaned toward Anne and whispered, "She was trying to tempt Mr. Russell into taking her away with him."

Taken aback, Anne was speechless for a moment. None of that seemed remotely like the girl Anne had met and spoken with. Jealousy threaded through the young woman's voice. Anne was about to ask about the ghostly haunting when the young lady spoke again.

"Not that it matters. She's no longer his student, you know. Her father won't pay for her art lessons. She's a little odd, you know, Faithful is," Julia whispered, leaning forward and staring at Anne. Her eyes were slightly protuberant, giving her an avid stare. "She believes in ghosts. The vicar should have a talk with her, tell her it's blasphemous."

"Maybe someone is trying to trick her into believing there are ghosts," Anne said.

Julia paused for a moment, her gaze hooded, lids heavy, eyes shaded with guilt, but then shook her head, tossing curls back. "No one would do that."

She knew about the trickery; Anne was certain. "How do you know that for sure?"

An insouciant shrug, and the young lady said airily, "Faithful is sweet, but she's immature for her age. Not like me." A practiced smile curved her lips and she looked yearningly into the future, glancing at Anne, then away again. "I so wish to have a home and a family. Even Mr. Russell has told me I am *very* mature. The most of any girl here."

Anne dismissed her and sat in thought for a long moment after she had left the room. If Miss Julia Halliday was by any chance behind the ghost hoaxing of Faithful, it would be because of her jealousy.

It was time for the next girl. Miss Henrietta Greerson was a sly girl of fifteen, an age on the boundary between teenage silliness and adult observation. Anne watched her carefully, remembering Fanny's lisped confidence that Henrietta did tease on occasion, and also recalling that she was to be the "ghoul" of the play they were putting on.

When asked about the other girls, Henrietta said sharply, "Some are very stupid."

"Stupid?" Anne said, startled.

"They know nothing," she said airily. "Vacant silly children."

Eyeing her, Anne tread warily, saying, "I'm surprised to hear it, given the excellent reputation of the Misses Lee's school."

"Oh, the teachers are all right. The girls are foolish, though."

"How so?"

She smiled with a superior air. "They fancy themselves in a romance with one of the teachers, when anyone with eyes can see she is fooling herself. He treats her no different than any other girl."

Maybe she *had* crossed that invisible line, because her petulance sounded a lot like jealousy of Miss Julia's flirtation with the art master. Or . . . did she mean Faithful? "Of which girl are you speaking?"

Henrietta made a coquettish moue so exactly Julia Halliday that Anne felt a bubble of laughter well up but stifled it. The young lady was indeed talented at theatrics and had a gift for mimicry. "What about the other girls, though?"

"Some are all right, while others think they're better than anyone else because their family is of a certain status." She stared directly at Anne.

What an unpleasant child. She evinced a level of hostility toward her schoolmates that was puzzling, and given her superior attitude, perhaps she felt that fooling Faithful into thinking she saw and conversed with a ghost was funny. Anne would keep it in mind and ask Sophia Lee what she thought. "You say one of the girls gives herself airs?"

"*Some* think being the daughter of the daughter of a viscount makes one better than others," Miss Greerson snapped.

Daughter of the daughter of . . . oh, that *was* Faithful! Her late mother had, indeed, been the daughter of a viscount, according to Alethea, but Faithful had not seemed at all full of herself. "I have heard a rumor that someone here is hoaxing one of the girls, playing a mean trick. You wouldn't happen to know anything about that, would you?"

Henrietta bounced to her feet, her cheeks breaking out in patches of crimson, the color marking her neck, too, in blotches. "Is that all, my lady? I'm supposed to be going to lunch with my grandmother and grandfather. He's a magistrate, you know, and very rich."

"You may go now," Anne said to the student, unnerved by the girl's scorn. If she had to guess, she would imagine it was Henrietta Greerson behind the haunting.

Miss Alys Edisbury, Faithful's true friend, was last among the girls. She was a plump girl, rescued from plainness by a sweet expression and huge blue eyes below a broad forehead. Her cap was snowy, with blond curls escaping from it. Her white dress had pink silk ribbon bows marching down the tight-fitting sleeves and the bodice and her long braid was fastened by another pink silk ribbon. She watched Anne carefully and mimicked her movements, perhaps trying to emulate her elders.

Anne asked her about the school, and her classes, and finally, after polite answers, about the other girls. What were they like? The girl's expression sobered.

"They are all very nice girls from good families," she said, and would be drawn no further. Even direct questions about Miss Henrietta Greerson elicited nothing but a wide-eyed unblinking stare and shrug.

Next, she interviewed the two female teachers.

Miss India Hopewell, instructress of etiquette among other things, was rigidly polite. And yet there was something about her mien that shouted to Anne that she resented this intrusion into her day.

"Where are you from, Miss Hopewell?"

"Winterbourne, my lady."

"Near Bristol, correct?"

She nodded.

"You have family there?"

"An aunt, my lady. My parents died. I was an only child."

"How long have you been an instructress here?"

"Since Lent term, my lady."

Anne asked, "I understand the female teachers share a room with boarding students. How does that work?"

"I consider it a privilege to help the girls navigate this period in their lives both in the classroom and out of it. It is a duty, yes, but a responsibility too."

"Are they all friends with each other? I remember girlhood being a particularly emotional and fraught period, myself, I don't know if you agree?"

"Not at all, my lady. I disagree wholly. There is a serenity in childhood that is particularly appealing."

"Childhood, perhaps. However, these girls are in their teen years, no longer a child, and yet, not a woman."

She stiffened. "These girls are exceptional children—young ladies, as you say—from good homes, good families. Moral and instructed in religion. Are you suggesting they are cruel to each other, or play tricks?"

"It's interesting you would say that, Miss Hopewell. Has that happened?"

The teacher eyed her closely, her expression wavering among doubt, nervousness and . . . was it fear shadowing her eyes? A nerve jumped under her left eye, and she touched it with one finger. "No, of course not."

"I heard about someone being hoaxed. A trick involving a ghost?"

"If you're referring to Miss Collier at the attic window, there *was* an incident a couple of nights ago. It had nothing to do with the girls. Faithful was sleepwalking."

"Sleepwalking? But she had just gone up to her room—"

"*Sleepwalking*. I object most severely to any implication otherwise. These girls are all polite, sweet, even." She rose, curtseyed, and turned away.

"I'm surprised my questions offend you, Miss Hopewell," Anne said.

The teacher turned back with an uncertain expression. "I'm not offended, my lady, but I'm not sure . . ." She shook her head, turned away and headed toward the door.

Interesting. The best-raised girl could be vindictive or jealous or pull a prank and it had nothing to do with class or upbringing. Perhaps Miss Hopewell worried she would be blamed, as the book that incited the hoax was hers. But it could equally be blamed on the play the Lees had the girls rehearsing. It was odd.

Miss Carlotta Dankworth was next. She was an anxious sort and could not be still, even her gaze darting when her body could not shift. She hailed from Dorchester, north of Weymouth. She had been a teacher at the Lee school for four years. When asked about her employers, she said Miss Lee was an angel. Which Miss Lee? Both of them. Miss Sophia and Miss Harriet. Quite angels, both of them. Miss Sophia Lee in particular. What about Miss Anne Lee, Anne asked. She had little to do with Miss Anne except to receive teaching materials from her, she replied. The young ladies were fortunate indeed to have ladies dedicated to education for girls. "I wish I had been as fortunate. My schooling was in no way as good as this."

"How, then, did you become worthy of teaching here?"

Miss Dankworth colored, plum infusing her cheeks. "I applied myself, my lady. I read widely French literature, studied almanacks with maps. Msr. Guillaume Delisle's map of the new world, particularly of the spectacular lakes in the middle of the North American continent, is simply breathtaking!"

Anne watched the young woman, how her eyes shone, how her hands finally stopped, how she peered into an indefinite distance, discoveries yet unseen shining in her expression. "You like maps and geography?"

"Oh, I do, my lady. I want to know it all. I wonder, how much is still to be discovered? And yet, have we discovered anything, truly? For even in places poor ill-fated Captain Cook explored, in the southern seas, there were people, living lives beyond our ken. They were natives of the lands, as we are natives of these isles, do you not think?" She leaned forward, eyes shining, ink-stained hands clasped in her lap. "They lived their days, raising children, hunting, fishing, harmonious with the land, like the peoples of the Americas, you know, before European colonization. How can we have been said to *discover* places where people already live?"

Anne stared at her in wonder. Rarely was she introduced to a new thought, and yet this young lady had made her rethink what it meant to "discover" a place. She'd discuss this with Osei Boatin, Tony's secretary and a native-born African, though she was sure the notion would not be new to him. "What a wonderful teacher you are, with such original thoughts!"

She flushed pink. "Thank you, my lady. It is a privilege to teach these children. If I cannot be an explorer at least I can travel in my mind and in books and with maps." Her voice had a yearning tone.

What a remarkably pliable mind she appeared to have. How unfortunate for such an enthusiast that she had been born female and poor, for never would she have a physical outlet for this love of travel. She would have been a cartographer, perhaps, if she had been a man. Anne asked, "What is your opinion of your employers?"

Startled by the question, Miss Dankworth stammered, then said, her chin rising, "They are exceptional. They have given me the opportunity to teach even those subjects they, themselves, hold dear, such as composition, to the littler girls, anyway. They check the girls' work most assiduously and have said I may advance in my instruction, if I hold to such quality." Her admiration for the Lees was evident, and not merely flattery.

"You say you don't have much to do with Miss Anne Lee?"

"She does not teach except to tutor the duller children, but she does provide us with materials for our teaching." She bit her lip. "I wish she would let me help her, for I do not think her knowledge of the globe is adequate for her to prepare lessons. There are errors, things I could correct if—" Her eyes widened and she sat back, knowing she had overstepped her authority.

Anne let it pass. She had known the frustration of abilities not valued. "What about Miss Hopewell? As the two teachers living in, you must be close."

Her expression softened. "India is like a sister to me. I never had a sister, you see; in fact, I don't have any family. I was a foundling. We share everything and I even went to visit her home on the school holiday in the summer."

"You went to Winterbourne with her?"

"Bristol, my lady. She had . . . has a . . . an aunt there, you see." A shadow passed over her expression and she looked away.

"Did you enjoy Bristol?"

"Oh, yes, my lady!" she cried, her gaze whipping back to Anne. "It is an exciting place, being a port city. Dorchester is near Weymouth, but I haven't spent any time by the sea. The stories one hears in a port city! The people you meet, even sea captains' wives, who have been all over the globe. I can never repay India's kindness to me. I felt very low and alone until she befriended me. To have a friend is the best thing in the world. Don't you think, my lady?"

Anne agreed that friendship was important. "What is her family like?"

"My lady?"

"Miss Hopewell's family; did you like them?"

Her formerly open expression shuttered and she simply nodded.

"Do you like the students here, Miss Dankworth? Do you find them to be kind girls, pleasant?"

"The littler children are sweet. They miss their homes, and mostly need me to listen to them." She stared out the window. When she turned back, it was with a look of concentration, brows furrowed, eyes squinted. "But the older ones . . . my lady, I have thought of this a lot over the last while. I have noticed that we cheer boys on for being boisterous and hardy and tough. Boys and young men box and roughhouse and are praised for the healthy expression of their animal spirits. But girls? We expect them to be sweet and compliant and demure. And yet if you ask me, the female of any species learns to be tougher than the male to protect its young. Why do we expect different from our human girls? By forcing them into a mold of sweet compliance we deny their very humanity, the toughness that will help them survive this world."

Anne stared at her, again astonished, and the young woman colored, pink ebbing and flowing in her cheeks and neck.

"What I mean to say, my lady, is that by denying girls a physical outlet for those animal spirits, we force them to submerge them. Whatever you submerge is likely to come out in quite unpleasant ways, do you not agree?"

"I *do* agree with you, Miss Dankworth," Anne said with wonder. "And I think the girls are fortunate to have you as an instructress. What unpleasant ways does this submersion of animal spirits come out?"

"Oh, nothing tragic, I assure you; tricks and taunts and disagreements. Hoaxes that hurt feelings."

"Nothing serious, you say?"

She nodded, understanding Anne's implication. "Nothing is *meant* to be serious, my lady, but every girl is different, and will take things differently."

"What about a trick played on Miss Faithful Collier? A ghostly visitation?"

"I think the less said about it the better. It was an unfortunate event." She would not be drawn further. She did say, in what seemed an incongruous aside, "Boys are expected to express leadership and given opportunities to do so. That is not, in my experience, done here. However, we manage as best we can. Faithful, given the chance, could prove to be a leader among the girls. Though she did not have formal instruction before she came here a year and a half ago, she reads all the time, even her father's law books. She is a very intelligent young lady, very noticing, very . . . perspicacious."

It seemed like there was a kinship there, between them. "You like her?"

"I do. Very much."

She had nothing to add. Anne was left with a vivid picture of tensions among the students. The comment about leadership was an interesting one, for there were leaders toward good ends, and there were leaders in mischief. Perhaps there was a ringleader who had gathered confederates to hoax poor Faithful. Interesting thought.

Anne wasn't sure what good it would do, but she interviewed the gentlemen anyway. True, they did not stay overnight and would not have had a chance to set up the trickery that haunted Faithful, but they may know of it.

Mr. O'Brien, the choleric piano teacher, happened to be between students. A dark Irishman, he was, contrary to Anne's expectation, good-natured and intelligent, with a calm demeanor. He was a pianist with the spa orchestra, he revealed. Tutoring was a sideline, profitable in such a town as Bath. He gave private instruction in addition to teaching at the Lee school. When asked about his students, he was trying to be polite when he replied, "Not a one of them will ever be proficient. They will be accomplished enough to catch a husband, I wager." He was forthright, anyway, if not as tactful as he may have thought.

"You find the lack of ability frustrating?"

"I may have expressed it, my lady, but I'm trying to be patient. Some of the girls have better than passable voices."

"Have any of your students expressed any anxiety about the other girls?"

He shook his head, a puzzled look on his face. "They would hardly confide in me about such things."

Anne suspected that Msr. Durrand would be the usual Englishman posing as a Frenchman, but he was, indeed, French. They conducted their interview in his native tongue and spoke of his hometown, Bordeaux, where he was engaged to be married to a Mademoiselle Anctil. He feared tensions between the two nations but was relieved by the recently signed Eden Agreement on tariffs. He had a hopeful heart and foresaw a long and prosperous relationship between the two perennial enemies.

He was not in the slightest flirtatious, a refreshing absence. He sighed over the young ladies' lack of ability, but one, he said, showed promise. Anne expected him to mention Miss Halliday, for she was graceful, if a little stiff and self-conscious. Instead he named Faithful. "She has natural rhythm, and her movement is poetic. She sings while she dances. Delightful. I enjoy teaching her." When prompted, he became serious and said she had seemed sad, lately—no singing for the last couple of weeks—and he was concerned.

"What do you think has made her sad?"

"The other girls, they tease her."

"What do you think has prompted it?"

"There has been gossip, she once said. Her mother, she implied, suffered an unfortunate end and she was teased about it, very sadly. Then one of the girls learned she will be an heiress one day and it made for some jealousy. Also, she is talented and intelligent, making her a target. I fear she is sensitive. I know from experience that being sensitive to life can invite torment from others. I was such a lad as that child." He shook his head and made a noise between his teeth. *"Pauvre enfant,"* he finished.

"She is not a child, Msr. Durrand. She is fully seventeen years old, almost ready to leave school and marry."

He shrugged. "To me, she is a child still. If others would take my advice, I would say, do not rush her into marriage. Let her grow, let her toughen. She has a heart, that one, too tender for the world, I fear. Alas, she is bothered. I wish she will reveal what it is that frets her."

"I think all the things you have mentioned were enough, even without the teasing she suffers."

Lastly, she interviewed Mr. Marcus Russell, the object of Miss Halliday's affection. He was good-looking, with a sweep of dark locks that fell over his eyes. She asked the usual questions. He hailed from Dover. He was an artist, but art was a difficult profession paying little, unless one could secure a patron. He eyed her hopefully.

She eyed him severely. "Tell me, Mr. Russell, do you often meet your students outside of lessons?"

"No, of course not."

"Not even accidentally, say in the market?"

"I can't help it if girls follow me or find me out. Young ladies are often silly, you know."

"Are they indeed? Miss Julia Halliday, you mean?"

Alert and uneasy, he said, "What has she said?"

Aha. "What do you think she'd say?"

"Nothing important. She is the type to misconstrue the most innocent of compliments."

"On what did you compliment her?"

"Now see here, my lady, I have never encouraged her. In fact, I did my best to discourage . . . I . . ." He stopped and shook his head, mute until she asked him about his art. He rambled for a bit about his desire to set up a studio to sell his art, and hoped for a day when he would no longer have to teach.

"Or you could find a benefactress, yes?"

He didn't answer.

"Or you could marry wealthy?"

He changed the subject, offering to paint her, which she declined. She turned the conversation back to the girls, asking, "What about Miss Faithful Collier? Is she one of the girls who follow you about Bath?"

He pulled a pocket watch out of his waistcoat and stood, suddenly. "I am about to be late, my lady, for a lesson. I cannot miss this lad, for he shows real promise." He bowed and exited.

He was hiding something, but she did not think it had anything to do with Faithful's problem. It was interesting, though, and might be worth mentioning, so the Lees could keep an eye on the art master.

Chapter Four

Miss Lee and Alethea joined her in the drawing room. Alethea was stifling a laugh. "You, my dear friend, have every single girl, teacher and master in the school in an uproar."

Anne would not be drawn. "May we have Faithful back to speak with?"

The girl was fetched from a dance lesson. She stood before the three ladies, hands clasped in front of her.

"Mr. Durrand tells me you are an exceptional dance student," Anne said. "Do you enjoy dance?"

"I do, my lady."

"We should all have something that matters to us." Anne examined the girl. "He is concerned that something is bothering you. He does not know, of course, about the haunting, though he knows you have been teased and gossiped about." Miss Sophia Lee's gaze snapped toward Anne. "Is there anything else we should know about?" Anne continued.

"N-n-no, my lady. I . . ." She paled and firmed her lips together, looking away.

There *was* something. Anne said, "Please, Faithful, you can tell us. We are here to listen."

Tears glistened in her eyes, but she shook her head, remaining silent. Anne determined to let her think about it and revisit the problem with her. "Faithful, I need you to believe me when I tell you the apparition you saw and the voices you have heard are real, yes, but not supernatural. You're being tricked. There are unkind people in this world. To triumph over them is to live well, to follow our passions, to find purpose in every day. Will you promise to do that?"

She blinked and nodded.

"You won't alarm the Miss Lees by going up to the roof again, will you? It's not right to repay their kindness in such a way. You don't want to die, do you? Especially not because a cruel girl wishes to torment you."

She nodded, curtseyed, and departed to her music lesson.

Anne turned to the instructress. "I would like to meet with her again, once we know the ghostly hoaxing is done. Perhaps a warning should be given to any girls we think may be involved. I would watch a few of the girls carefully, especially Miss Henrietta Greerson."

"Henrietta? It surprises me that you think she would tease Faithful. They were great friends once," Miss Lee said.

"They were?"

"The best of friends."

"But not now."

"I don't know why they fell out," the teacher said. "There is no one more secretive than a girl of a certain age."

"This morning it was pointed out to me that girls have no outlet for their vigor and turn on each other," Anne said.

Alethea's brows rose on her forehead. "Who said that?"

"Miss Carlotta Dankworth. She could perhaps take on more responsibility in lesson preparation, especially when it comes to geography and perhaps other topics. She has an original mind. I found her interesting and intelligent."

Miss Sophia Lee looked doubtful. "Pardon me, my lady, but the conversation of a few minutes is not sufficient to plumb the depths of any mind. Miss Dankworth has proven to be a good instructress, but is easily overwhelmed by those vigorous spirits you were concerned about."

"You may be right," Anne said. "I bow to your superior knowledge of these girls. However, I wonder if what Miss Dankworth lacks is confidence in her position here? She has nowhere else to go, and so may worry about keeping her position beyond anything else. You know, I, too, have been guilty of not recognizing that I can be the very littlest bit intimidating toward underlings." Alethea smothered a choked laugh and Anne gave her a severe look. "I have on occasion been high-handed, but now realize that if a servant or employee is afraid of me, they cannot properly fill their position. They must be able to come to me with a problem, rather than try to cope with it on their own, or worse, ignore it completely. Perhaps Miss Dankworth, if she were secure in her position, would be better able to handle high-spirited students."

"I will consider your words," Miss Lee said with a majestic nod.

"I do not believe you will have any more difficulties with Faithful's ghost. I hope she will eventually speak of whatever is bothering her. Give her time."

Miss Lee was appropriately grateful, but Alethea was quiet on their way back to Anne's grandmother's townhome.

• • •

"When can we be alone?" Tony growled in her ear.

Anne's heart pounded and she evaded his hands. "Not until we are married," she hissed at him. "Tony, behave yourself." She said all the right things, but desperately wished she could throw herself into his arms.

He had been in Bath for a few weeks now, kissing her helpless whenever they chanced to be alone, seeking her out in her dishabille, sneaking a lascivious caress and pressing himself to her. They had agreed for the sake of her family and their reputation in Bath to wait until marriage to resume their joyful physical union. He was entirely too handsome—dark of mien, thick dark brows over brown eyes, broad shoulders shown to advantage even in fussy evening attire—and overtly self-assured. He said if he could not have her, he could at least torture himself with desire, an elegant torment.

He was not the only one so plagued. His beautifully tailored evening attire outlined his most *excellent* musculature. He was delicious to her, with thighs like tree trunks. Let other ladies admire a shapely calf, she was an appreciator of those bulky thighs. She mustn't think of them, nor remember those times when she had seen them—and him—naked. He released her but she eyed him mistrustfully as he sauntered away. Think of cool things, she urged herself: breezes, streams, rain. It didn't help. She employed her fan while Tony watched, a salacious smirk on his too-handsome face.

"Anne, you look frightfully red in the face," her mother said as she swept into the dining room on Lord John's arm. "What is wrong with you? Are you sickening? Don't tell me you are coming down with some plague." She drew back and glanced at her mother, the Dowager Viscountess Everingham, who snickered wickedly as she tottered with difficulty on her favorite footman's arm to her chair.

"Leave the girl alone, Barbara. If you can't tell a randy maiden when you see one, I despair of you. It's been too long since you had a rod to handle."

"Mother!" The dowager viscountess's scandalous talk, remnant of a bawdier time, horrified Anne's mother, who aspired to give credit to her position and the position her daughter would soon grace, Marchioness of Darkefell.

Tony bowed to his future grandmother-in-law and dropped a wink. "My lady, Grandmama-to-be, you are most perspicacious. Perhaps my intended *is* falling ill and should be confined to her chamber, where I will, of course, visit and read to her. Something biblical. The Song of Solomon, perhaps."

"You wicked *wicked* man!" she howled in glee. "If I was sixty years younger I'd steal you away for myself." She turned serious in a second, her wrinkled face lined into stern crevices. She waved her walking stick at him and said, "You will on *no* account make yourself free with my granddaughter, though I suspect my admonition is too late. However, from this day forward, no intimacy between you, no matter how tempting. No seven- or eight-month babies for her, sir."

Tony bowed. "I promise to follow your advice, my lady."

"Let us change the subject, if you please," Anne said. "Tony, do tell me how your recent visit with your former ward went?"

He had returned from a visit in Gloucester, where his mother's niece—his cousin, orphaned at the age of fourteen—lived with her husband and new baby, for whom he was to be named godfather. She had been his ward and he had the duty of managing her inheritance, approving her marriage, and negotiating her marriage settlements, everything financial in other words. He had been scrupulous, of course, and had managed her inheritance with solid investments that had increased her fortune, of which her husband now had the management. "Miriam is settled and happy," he said. "I'm satisfied with her husband. He is considerate, kind, and with enough money of his own that I don't doubt his affection for my cousin."

There had been a moment, he had once told her, when he feared she was lost forever, for she was on the road to Gretna Green, an infamous destination for fortune hunters. He had followed the absconding pair and beaten the young man, who had learned a lesson about eloping with heiresses with huge angry guardians. The fellow limped away with nothing but a few guineas to repay his carriage hire. By then the young lady had been frightened enough by events that she was glad of the rescue, and all had been satisfactorily hushed. "She very much wants to meet you, Anne. I told her we would stop at her home on our way north after the wedding."

"I'll be delighted. I shall send her a note."

Lord John and Lydia Bestwick, Tony's brother and sister-in-law, attended them at this family dinner, meant to plan the last details of the wedding of the decade, according to many in Bath society. It was not every day a marquess wed at St. Swithin's. The wedding plans were spiraling out of Anne's control, becoming more elaborate and costly every hour, it seemed. The guests the countess wished to invite would not fit comfortably in her grandmother's townhome. There had been talk of renting the Assembly Rooms.

Anne was resolute. The simple ceremony would take place at St. Swithin's in the morning, there would be a wedding breakfast at her grandmother's townhome, then the happy couple would retire to the marquess's rented townhouse in Bath. They would all celebrate the Christmas season together, and shortly after the newly minted Marchioness of Darkefell would accompany her husband north to their seat, Darkefell Castle in Yorkshire.

She had the dress she would wear for the ceremony, the breakfast would be here, at her grandmother's home, and that was enough planning for Anne.

With John and Lydia was Lolly—Miss Louisa Broomhall—that most necessary of things to everyone's comfort, the poor relation. As maligned as a poor relation was in literature, as little considered, as much spoken down to in real life, Lolly, cousin to the Countess Harecross and no relation to Lydia at all, had become more important to her than her actual relations. Lydia would do nothing without considering "dear Lolly," would go nowhere, would consider no move.

Anne was happy for Lolly, her erstwhile chaperone, a suitable companion, being old and gray and spinsterish, dutiful, virtuous, but with more intelligence than anyone gave her credit for. She was also lively and funny and sweet. With Lydia she had found, in her older age, a home among those who valued her as much as she deserved.

The Countess Harecross, now that she had no access to Lolly—whom she had scorned and thought little of before that—had decided Lolly was as vital to her as air. She ladled guilt-inducing heavy implications in every sentence, saying if Lydia cared about Anne at all, she would release Lolly to move in to the Paragon townhouse to help plan the wedding.

Lolly did love a wedding almost as much as she loved Anne, so she had been helping as much as she was able. Fortunately for Lolly, Lydia would not hear of the woman moving out, though she gave her the use of their carriage to travel back and forth to music publishers, drapers and the Everingham townhome on the Paragon any time of day. It seemed exhausting to Anne, who had removed herself from the plans as much as possible, but Lolly was bright-eyed and enthusiastic.

Anne allowed general discussion of the wedding during dinner. Once they retired to the drawing room after the meal she turned the topic to her day at the Lee school, and what precipitated it.

"Boys are tolerable, but girl children are dreadful," Anne's grandmother grumbled.

Lady Harecross bridled. As the dowager viscountess's only daughter it certainly seemed a reflection on her. "Mother, all children are a delight and a comfort."

As she clearly did not consider her difficult son Jamey a delight and comfort, nor even Anne, with whom she bickered constantly, her hypocrisy left Anne breathless. "I have to agree with Grandmama that children *can* be a torment," Anne said. "One of those schoolgirls is intimidating Faithful. I think I know which one, a horribly superior and irritating child, Henrietta Greerson, who was once her friend but has turned on her." She explained the ghost trick and its denouement, on a ledge out the attic window. "I don't for one second believe Faithful wished to die. I'm grateful I was able to talk sense into her."

Tony eyed her, dark brows raised as he lifted a glass of port to his lips.

"What?" she said crossly.

"Nothing, my lady, nothing at all. Except when I have thought I had argued sense into someone, you accused me, on occasion, of bullying them into agreeing with me. What is it you said? That their sudden silence did not necessarily indicate they had come to agree with me, merely that they were too cowed to argue further."

"I don't remember ever saying that to you," she retorted crossly.

"Speak now or forever hold your peace, eh, Darkefell?" said the dowager viscountess, and burst into a coughing fit mingled with laughter. Her favorite handsome footman poured her madeira. She gestured and he proceeded to pat her back until the fit had passed.

Conversation resumed. Anne was left uncertain that she had

handled the girl correctly. To defeat the other girls' efforts to upset her, Faithful must let them see she was stronger than they thought.

The evening seemed endless. Her mother was in a fretful mood, nervous about Anne's father's and brother's arrival on the morrow. Though they had exchanged letters to discuss a rapprochement, she had not seen her husband face-to-face for years and she was afraid. She had not seen her son, Jamey, for an equally long time. Jamey's erratic behavior was what had caused her to flee the marital home, Anne believed, but perhaps leaving was symptomatic of a deeper divide between the Earl of Harecross and his countess. He confessed to Anne once that the two had never understood each other. In that they were similar to other couples of their status. He had never thought it a problem until forced to see how unhappy his wife was.

Which was why he supported her move to live in Bath with her mother. Living apart was not unusual in their sphere. She glanced over at Darkefell, who bent his dark head to her grandmother, listening to a scandal from bygone years. He was more patient with the old lady than she had ever expected he would be, and when he cast her a smile, she warmed inside. How would she ever live apart from him now, when she knew what being together meant to her? The irritable, secretive, harsh marquess she had first met months ago was now her seductive and compelling fiancé. Finding each other had made both of their lives better. She loved him deeply, desperately, and all she wanted was for them to be married and alone.

Though they'd never be alone, would they? After the wedding they would travel north and live together in the castle. The dowager, who lived in the dower house, would require her son's company, and his twin, Julius, would be there. He belonged to others, first, and was his family's pillar, its strength and support. They all needed him even more than she did.

So she'd share him. On their wedding journey north they would have each other for as long as she could draw it out.

He held her gaze and his sweetened. She had once determined never to marry. She hadn't seen the point of giving up the freedom afforded her by a lax and tolerant father. And yet compromises were inevitable. His love was worth it.

Before he departed the house, he pulled her aside into a dark corner of the hall. By candlelight his rugged features were in sharp relief. He bent her back and kissed her breathless. She molded her body to him and felt his react. Tasting his mouth, drops of port still clinging, feeling his tongue dip into her, clutching his bulky shoulders was a delight. Nonetheless they must part. She pushed him away as the others entered the hall.

"Good night, my love," she whispered. "*A demain.*"

Chapter Five

Mary MacDougall, Anne's maid, set a tray on the table in Anne's bedchamber and swept open the drapes. Weak December light filtered in. A normal morning would begin with a tale of Wee Robbie, Mary's delightful son, and his escapades. Lately he had befriended Anne's grandmother, who, when he had been useful to her, plied him with cakes and sweets until he was becoming quite spoiled, his cheeks filled out like a red squirrel with a bounty of nuts.

But this morning Mary was solemn when she turned back Anne's bedclothes, straightened and held out a letter. "Milady, a note came by footman from Mrs. Birkenhead."

"Wha . . . ?" Anne squinted and sat up, casting aside the warmth of dreams of Tony after a fitful night worrying about the arrival of her father and brother today. She swung her feet over the edge of the bed and scrubbed her eyes, letting the cobwebs clear from her mind.

"It's urgent, it says on the ootside," Mary said, her voice threaded with worry. She again pushed the note toward Anne. "I wouldne wake you airly if it wasn't."

Anne yawned and stretched, flexing her shoulders, then took the note. What in heaven's name was so urgent? "What time is it?"

"Seven thairty, milady."

Alethea was not an early riser, so this was exceptionally odd. Anne took a gulp of tea, broke the wax seal and unfolded the paper. She read it, squinted, then read it again. She staggered to her feet, spilling tea over the bedclothes. "No, this cannot be! It's impossible!"

"What is it, milady?" Mary asked, wringing her hands.

Tears welled in Anne's eyes. Choking on a sob, she shoved the paper toward her maid and said, "That young girl I told you about, Faithful Collier, has fallen — or jumped — to her death."

• • •

An hour later, attired in her sober blue *robe à la piémontaise*, she walked toward the school in the company of Osei Boatin, Tony's inestimable secretary, a man whose discretion, intelligence and compassion she rated far above anyone's she knew. She had summoned him knowing he would come with alacrity. Tony was not available to her, as he had ridden out early for a last gallop in the countryside before guests kept him home. That was fortunate, for she preferred Osei's calm companionship in this case.

They walked swiftly, the brisk air stropping Anne's mind to razor sharpness. "This is unthinkable," she exclaimed, and told him what had happened the day before. "When I left Faithful I know in my heart she had no notion of ending her life. She never did. It was a misunderstanding."

"Do you believe she told the truth?"

"About the haunting? As much as she could. As much as she understood about the tricks played on her." Anne stilled her mind, pushing away the horror of the girl's death, and thought. "There was more bothering her. She would not, or could not, tell me what it was. My impression is, she thought she could handle it on her own."

"So not the supernatural events, such as they were?"

"No, something else she was worried about."

The maid who answered their knock was subdued and quivering. She showed them into the sitting room, where Miss Lee sat rigid, pale and frozen in horror, Alethea by her side. Anne made swift introductions. "I may have overstepped boundaries, but I have had Mr. Boatin send for his friend, Dr. Fothergill."

Sophia, her expression bleak, said harshly, "Did you not understand Alethea's note? Faithful is *dead*. What use is a doctor now?"

Anne disregarded her shortness. It was natural, and perhaps naturally directed toward her. The woman could not abuse her more than she abused herself for thinking she had solved the girl's problems. "How did Faithful die?"

Sophia blinked, shrugged, and looked down at her hands, clasped in her lap, where she was wringing a handkerchief. "The scullery maid, Ginny, found Faithful this morning."

"Where?"

"Behind the house. There are paving stones along the back wall, where there is a garden and a laundry yard. She had jumped from the very spot where my sister Anne found her the other night, like an awful force drew her there." She shuddered. "Oh, her poor broken body! How can this have happened?" She covered her face with her hands, long inky fingers pressed to her forehead, sending her cap askew.

"Where is Faithful's body? Did you move her?"

"She is in what was the butler's pantry downstairs. We needed to bring her in, to find a place for her to lay where she would be . . . where it was warm and safe." She wrinkled her brow. "How silly that sounds," she sobbed. "Not at all rational."

Gently, Anne said, "It is human and shows your kindness and care for these girls that even in death, you wish to protect them. You were right to do it. The students could not see her like that, on the pavement."

Sophia dropped her hands, nodded and took in a deep breath, letting it out as her shoulders sagged. Alethea patted her back and sent a beseeching look to Anne, but what it meant, she wasn't sure.

"Who moved her body?"

"Jonty, our man-of-all-work. Our housekeeper, Mrs. Thompson's husband, you know."

"When Dr. Fothergill arrives, may he see Faithful?"

"Whyever would . . . she is *dead*. Can you not understand it?" Her tone was crisp and annoyed.

Annoyance was better than gloominess. "Nonetheless. Alethea, help me, please," she said, turning to her friend. "The doctor must view the poor girl's body. I insist."

Her friend nodded. "Sophia, you have to allow it."

"Why?" Miss Lee said.

"When I left here yesterday I was convinced Faithful had no desire nor intention of taking her own life," Anne said.

"What do you . . ." The teacher's eyes widened, and she gasped as the implication of what Anne was saying sank in. There were three possibilities: suicide, accident, murder. If they ruled out suicide, and if accident seemed unlikely, was it murder? She shook her head, looked back down at her hands and tugged at the cloth she held. Her voice choked with tears, she muttered, "When the doctor arrives, he may see F-Faithful."

"Osei will accompany him, if you please."

Miss Lee nodded.

"I'll await the doctor outside," Osei said and bowed. "My condolences, Miss Lee, for your loss." He exited.

"Sophia, may I see the back of the school? In particular the paving where poor Faithful was found."

The woman stared at her, eyes wide. "You cannot be serious."

"I am, I assure you."

"That is morbid."

Anne gave Alethea a beseeching look. "Alethea, tell her, please; am I ever morbidly curious?"

"Sophia, let her help you," Alethea said, her voice low, her tone urgent. "If she says she wants to see the spot, she has a reason. She is no careless gossip."

"Right now, if you please," Anne said, unwilling to waste time on niceties. She needed to see the location before it was altered.

The schoolmistress nodded and rose.

"Why not have Ginny, the servant, show me? It will save you, Miss Lee, and I wish to speak with the child anyway, as she is the one who found Faithful." And could tell Anne things about the position and state of the body, she hoped.

The teacher nodded, but her expression was full of disgust. Anne wondered if she would be forever sunk in the woman's estimation as lacking pity, or for having coarse notions. "Summon her now, if you please."

Sophia rang a bell, murmured to the trembling maid who answered, and turned back to Anne as the maid scurried away. "You will find the door to the back terrace down the hallway beyond this room. Ginny will meet you there."

Anne left Alethea comforting her friend and followed the hall toward the back of the house. She found the back door, where a girl stood at the top of stairs that led down, no doubt, to the kitchen and other necessary offices. "You are Ginny?" she said, examining the child, who curtseyed clumsily and nodded, shivering. She was twelve, or maybe as much as fourteen if she was small for her age. Pale and with pinched features, her small eyes were red and swollen. "Let us go out. Do you need a shawl? Are you cold?" Ginny mutely shook her head. "Ridiculous. Of course you're cold. Get a shawl, right now, if you please." The girl obeyed, then returned and led the way to the back door.

Anne stood in the doorway and glanced around, taking the yard in. "Did you know the young lady who died, Ginny?"

"Yes, miss . . . er, milady."

"How did you know her? Your work took you upstairs, no doubt?"

"I clean an' lay the fireplaces, milady, an' tend to th'slops."

"You would not meet the young ladies?"

"Miss Collier were sometimes late upstairs or run up to get sumthin'."

"Was she kind?"

Ginny nodded and snuffled. "She allus had a kind word, milady, and give me sweets. Her auntie would send her treats and she'd share 'em with *me*. Said as how all the young ladies had families and could have whatever they wanted, so she wanted *me* to have a treat. I never et anythin' so good, milady."

With the kitchen maid trailing behind, Anne descended the few steps to the paving stones lining the back wall of the structure to a depth of about ten feet. Beyond was a lawn, divided into sections. A low wall sectioned off one part of the garden. At the very back, along another low stone wall, was a kind of hut, a rough structure with gaps between boards. She saw a flash of movement in one of the window openings as a sacking curtain was twitched into place. *Who was that and what did he – or she – see?* Anne wondered.

"Where was she, Ginny? Faithful, I mean, her body?"

Ginny pointed with one trembling finger about ten feet away, at the far edge of the paving stone. Anne advanced toward it while the girl watched. She examined the paving stones and noted a dried pool of blood about five feet from the spot Ginny indicated, and a smear along the paving, stopping in a spot where another smaller pool dripped off the paving into the dirt. Anne looked up to the windows above and noted the attic windows. It did appear Faithful had fallen from above onto the paving stones. Her body must have been moved not long after she died, or maybe while she was alive.

Why?

She scanned the yard again, noting the shed, the stone wall, and the thicket of woods beyond the wall. The school backed on a park, below the stone wall, making it accessible to anyone with a will to clamber over it. That didn't explain how or why Faithful had fallen. Or jumped. Or . . . been pushed? She didn't like questions without answers. "Ginny, what are the habits of the household?"

"Milady?"

"I mean, who locks up at night, who unlocks, and who has keys? What time does this all happen? Is anyone around at night?"

The girl stuttered through a recital of the household habits as Anne examined the blood. The household was locked by Miss Sophia Lee at night, but the housekeeper, Mrs. Thompson, did have a key. Miss Lee locked the door at about eleven or so. The household was expected to be abed before then. Mrs. Thompson unlocked the doors early, before dawn, to allow deliveries to be received.

"What is the butler's pantry used for here?" Where there was no butler.

"T'store things, milady."

"Things? Like foodstuffs?"

"Nah. Dishes, pans, fruit press, the like."

"Will you lead me there?"

The girl stood staring, her eyes bulging out, but she could not deny Anne, despite her fearfulness. She led the way back inside. Anne followed Ginny down the stairs and past the open door of the kitchen, smelling the damp odor of soup boiling and the sharp tang of vinegar used to scrub.

"'Ere 'tis, milady," Ginny said, standing back, not willing to enter.

Anne entered the cool dark room, faintly lit by a window near the ceiling. She could see the white-sheet-covered body. The light would not be good enough for what she needed to see. She said, "Ginny, fetch me a candle." A few moments passed, and Anne stuck her head out the door. There was the kitchen maid in the hall with a lit candle, tears streaming down her cheek. "I'll take that now," Anne said, careful to keep her tone kind and not impatient.

The doctor and Osei would be there any moment, no doubt, but Anne wanted to examine the body first. She closed her eyes, took a deep breath, and moved to where the body lay, on the butler's counter. She set the candle nearby and pulled the white cloth away, gazing down at Faithful Collier. Her breath caught in her throat. The girl's skull was dented above the hairline where it ought to be smooth. Her dark hair, coming loose from a braid that would have been tied with ribbon at bedtime, was matted with drying blood. Blood had run down toward the back of the head too, in crusting rivulets. Faithful had been turned over—maybe while she was dying?—

and the blood ran from her wound toward the back of her head.

She had tumbled from that great height, hit the paving stone facedown, then someone turned her over and dragged her. Anne picked up the candle and forced herself to be objective, refusing to let herself mourn, yet, the sweet and intelligent young lady she had left so very much alive the previous day. Her tongue, a deep red, was stuck out. Surely that wasn't natural, unless it happened while she was on her face, as she was dying? She shook her head. It didn't make sense.

"Whot you doin' there, Ginny? Why ain't you workin'?" a loud female voice bellowed in the hallway.

"I-I-I . . ." Ginny could not answer, of course.

Hastily, Anne pulled the cloth back up over Faithful and emerged into the hallway, where a woman with sleeves rolled up over meaty forearms stood glaring at Ginny. "I am Lady Anne Addison. Ginny is here at my command. Who are you?"

"Cook, milady."

"Surely you have a name?"

"Just Cook. Beggin' yer pardon, milady." She dipped her head and scuttled back along the hall, disappearing into the kitchen.

"You may go back to your tasks. Thank you for your guidance." She put her hand on the girl's shoulder. "Cry if you need to, Ginny. Miss Faithful didn't deserve what happened to her. Remember her kindness, and she will live on." She watched the child for a moment, wondering how much consideration she had experienced in her short life. "You can do one more thing; if you remember or think of anything that may help, let me know."

Chapter Six

Anne returned to the sitting room. Alethea and Sophia had been whispering together, but looked up as she entered. "Where have you been?" Alethea said sharply. "You've been gone so long."

"What do you think?" Sophia asked, her anxiety revealed by her hands twisted in the folds of her skirts. "Tell us!"

Anne ignored the questions. If she was to tell them outright what she thought and felt, she'd have to say that Faithful's death was no accident, nor had she died by her own hand. She had been foully and cravenly murdered. Why would anyone attempt to move her body as she lay dying if that were not the case? Though she had steeled herself to see the girl's wrecked body, she was shattered that such a sweet girl, whose life was ahead of her, had been taken from the world.

She perched on a chair and took a deep breath. Even as nothing could bring back that life there was work to be done, a killer to uncover, if she was right. "Miss Sophia, I would appreciate your account of events last night."

The schoolmistress, having regained her composure, regarded her. Cold reality was setting in. "It was an evening. We ate. We set the girls to some individual stitchery work. We retired for the night. I can remember no single instance that makes it stand out from a hundred others."

"Let us go through it. Perhaps you will recall something in particular."

"Think, Sophia . . . did anyone say anything or look a certain way, or was there any argument, or did any girl look uncomfortable?" Alethea urged.

The schoolmistress shook her head. "There was nothing, nothing at all. I can tell you this much, I am convinced — "

A bustle at the door beyond the sitting room interrupted her. Sophia stood as Kate showed in Dr. Fothergill, a gentleman of medium height and middle age, brown-haired, with no peruke on his head. He carried a leather satchel, which he would not allow the maid to take from him. Osei moved to his side and introduced Dr. Fothergill to the instructress.

He bowed over her offered hand. "I have heard of your school with much curiosity, Miss Lee. The education of women is one of my wife's great interests. I wish we had met under different circumstances. It is unfortunate that Mr. Boatin's message calling me here contained such shocking news."

Warmed by his gentlemanly demeanor and calm attentiveness, she asked him to be seated, as she took her seat again. She briefly explained the circumstances of the discovery of Faithful's body by Ginny, the scullery maid. Anne joined the conversation, describing her visit the day before. "I was certain when I left that Faithful had no intention nor desire to take her own life. I could have been mistaken, but I don't think so. I hope your examination of the body will tell us if she died from the . . . the fall, or if there were other . . ." — she glanced over at the school owner — ". . . contributing factors."

He nodded, understanding what she could not yet say in front of Miss Lee. They had experienced such doubts about a death not long ago and had been proven correct. He stood. "I would like to see the girl, if you don't mind, Miss Lee. I'm sure you wish to be able to assure her parents that you took every measure in your ability once the sad truth had been discovered."

"Her mother died in an asylum years ago. She has a brother and her father."

"How sad. What was her madness? Why was she committed to an asylum?"

"I beg your pardon?"

"Did she rave? Hurt people? Weep inconsolably?" He paused. "Try to do away with herself?"

Miss Lee said, "I don't believe it is a question I ever asked Mr. Collier. Faithful once confided what her father told her; her mother tried to hurt her when she was a baby and had to be confined."

"What age is the brother?"

"He is twenty-four, I believe."

"Does he live in the home?"

"He does not and has not for years," Miss Lee said crisply. "He took training as a solicitor," she said, confirming what Anne had learned originally from Alethea. "But he is, for the present, a clerk at a shipping office in Bristol, where he was apprenticed when the law failed him. I understand from Faithful that he lives in rooms with another of the clerks in his office and has for some time. Mr. Collier has a housekeeper, and until Faithful came to us a widowed aunt lived with them and taught the child." The teacher and the doctor exchanged nods. Faithful had been carefully guarded through her childhood. The teacher turned her face away, though, and said, "I'm afraid word of how and where Faithful's mother died has become common knowledge, I know not how. There was teasing about Bedlam and the like. I put a stop to it the moment I learned of it."

"I would like to see her now, if you please," Dr. Fothergill said, rising. "Will you accompany me, Mr. Boatin?"

"I will." Osei nodded to Anne, his spectacles gleaming golden against his dark face. He gave her a look of reassurance.

Miss Lee watched the door through which they had exited. "What an extraordinarily unusual man."

"Dr. Fothergill is, I found lately, an exceptional gentleman, as well as a skilled physician."

"I was speaking of Mr. Boatin, and how as remarkable as he is, he managed to melt into the background. I quite forgot he was here until the doctor spoke to him." She regarded Anne. "He is the marquess's secretary, you say?"

"And a friend. I count Osei as one with whom I trust my life. My fiancé has employed him for years and there is no one closer, not even family." She did not elaborate. Osei's escape from a slave ship, Tony's rescue of him, and his ongoing search for his sister, lost on the same voyage, was inspiring, and fascinating, and his own to tell or not. His connection with Dr. Fothergill, whose wife was involved in the abolition movement and an African aid society, was also his own business. "Have you sent word to the poor girl's family?"

"I have, by first mail coach. Bristol is at most a three hours' journey. I expect the family will arrive late this afternoon, or this evening."

"Let us go back to what we were speaking of before the doctor's arrival. Can you tell me of the intervening hours between me being here yesterday, and this morning's dreadful discovery? In more detail. Please, I know this is difficult, but it may prove vital."

"I hardly know what to say, where to begin."

Alethea touched her arm. "Start yesterday afternoon," she said. "What happened after Anne left? Did Faithful return to her class?"

Faithful returned to her lessons without incident, the students gathered for supper, with a few of the older girls tasked with music practice in the early evening, Miss Lee said. The little girls retired first, accompanied by Miss Dankworth. The older girls retired at ten, after evening instruction in stitchery. "That was all anyone knew until Ginny found Faithful on the paving stones at about six in the morning. I was notified immediately and went to her, but she was dead."

Sophia Lee had seen the body too. "What did you think when you saw her?"

"Think?"

"Of how she came to be there."

"Why, she jumped, of course."

Anne shook her head. "Does anyone know what time it occurred?"

"Not to my knowledge."

"Did any of the girls awaken and notice her out of her bed?"

Sophia stared and said, "I . . . don't know."

"Did anyone get up in the night to use the convenience in the garden?"

"Of course not. There is a close stool for the young ladies' use and chamber pots, of course." She flushed pink and frowned. "Someone may have gotten up for another reason. There seems a world of things I do not know."

"You cannot be expected, at this early hour, to have interrogated the poor girls," Alethea said with a glance at Anne.

"Alethea is wholly correct. But now is the time to commence. I would like to know from the girls what went on after you and your sisters retired."

"We don't even know what the doctor has to say yet. Surely curiosity took Faithful back up to the roof, or . . ." Sophia trailed off and looked away, sniffing back a tear. "What *was* she doing up on the roof again after promising she would not go there?"

"Was the window out of which she escaped not locked after the last event?"

The school owner's eyes widened. "It was, of course. I had made certain of it."

"Who has a key?"

"I do. And the housekeeper does."

"Mrs. Thompson. How long has she been with you?"

"Since September, and she has proven to be a steadfast boon."

"Reliable housekeepers are a dying breed. How did you find her?" Alethea asked.

Sophia smiled. "Where else? I advertised and she responded. She ran a boardinghouse near Bristol, I think, but found it too much for her and her husband."

"You *think*? Did she not come with references?" Anne asked.

Miss Lee stuck her chin up, a combative expression on her face. "You have no idea how difficult a thing it is, running a school at the best of times, and in the worst of times, it's almost impossible. I had a housekeeper leave, the school year was starting, there were girls to feed and a house to maintain, servants to manage, food to order and store, a thousand other things. She came at the right time, demonstrated her proficiency, and I hired her. I have had no reason to regret it."

No background check of previous employers, then. However, the woman was right; she had never thought of the difficulties attendant on running such an institution, and in this case any quibbles about how it had been handled were immaterial. "I would like to speak with Mrs. Thompson."

"Please don't upset her. If she were to leave I cannot imagine running this place. With this terrible event occurring, I will never find another, I'm sure, especially with her qualifications. She is intelligent and dutiful and comes with the added benefit of a husband. I required a man-of-all-work to maintain the house, for it was falling to bits, and Jonty, her husband, has the necessary skills. He is lazy, but Mrs. Thompson can make him work."

"Jonty?" Anne said.

"He lives in the shed in the back garden and is locked out after hours."

Anne thought of Faithful's body, dragged along the paving stone. "He is your housekeeper's husband and yet he is locked out of the house and lives in the shed?"

Miss Lee's cheeks shaded a pale rose. She turned her face away. "He is not completely . . . that is to say, he is not as presentable as I would wish to live with young girls. In the normal course of things, I would have hired a separate man-of-all-works who would live in the garden shed, but when I posed the condition when hiring them, Mrs.

53

Thompson made no demur."

"That he live in the shed in the garden."

"And that he have no key to the house," Miss Lee confirmed.

It seemed an odd arrangement for a man and his wife. However, good positions did not fall ripe from trees as plums in autumn, and the woman may not care much that her husband should not have access to her at night. Maybe she even preferred it. "I see."

Dr. Fothergill, with a grave expression, returned, accompanied by Osei, who was likewise somber. The physician shook his head when asked about a fall causing the girl's death. "I am sorry to tell you, Miss Lee, but Miss Collier was strangled to death."

Sophia gasped and slumped.

"Doctor, please! How could you be so coarse with a lady," Alethea cried and rushed to her friend's aid, patting her cheek gently.

"My most sincere apologies!" the doctor exclaimed as he knelt at the schoolmistress's side and fanned her face. "The shock I experienced I unfeelingly conveyed." He caught up her hand and felt her pulse. "Racing; no surprise. Call a maid!"

Sophia was already rousing from her faint and stayed their summons, one hand to her forehead, the other out in a gesture of calm. "Stop! I shall recover apace. Alethea, please have Mrs. Thompson fetch the sherry." Alethea immediately crossed to the door and called for the housekeeper and the sherry. Her color was coming back. Anne had watched all with sympathy and respect for how quickly the lady recovered and how little she liked the fuss she had occasioned.

The housekeeper entered with the sherry and a tray of glasses.

"Explain, please, Doctor?" Miss Lee said. "You shock me by saying poor Faithful was *strangled*?"

The housekeeper set down the tray with a crash, and the glasses jingled like bells. She murmured an apology and began to tidy a side table until Miss Lee sharply bid her leave. The doctor did not speak until she left. He indicated that the door should be closed, which Osei did.

"Again, my apologies. I should not have given such news without preparation. First, Miss Collier did indeed fall onto the paving stones from a great height. Her skull is cracked, resulting in copious blood loss. However, either before or after the fall, she was strangled. She was alive when it happened, or there would not be such bruising about the neck."

"Which killed her though, Doctor, the fall or the strangulation?" Anne asked.

"Strangulation caused death, not the fall."

"You mean she may have lived if she had not been strangled?" Miss Lee said, her voice faint with horror, her face bleached of color. Alethea held her hand, one arm about her shoulders, gazing in tender concern at her friend.

"I cannot be sure. She may have lived, but I cannot say she would have recovered. With the amount of blood I saw on the pavement outside, I would say she would likely have died anyway. The body goes into shock, you see, and combined with the blood loss . . ." He shook his head.

"I must accept that it was murder. Who . . . why . . . ?" Miss Lee shook her head and broke down, weeping. The doctor took her hand and felt her pulse, urging her to sip the restorative sherry.

Osei beckoned Anne and she escaped with him to the hall. "There was a man loitering about the garden. His name is Jonty. I did not like the look of him."

Anne glanced down the hall, noting a door ajar that, as she did not answer, was pulled gently closed. She murmured, "He is the man-of-all-work, I understand, husband of the new housekeeper, a Mrs. Thompson, both hired in September and with no references. I assume his full name will be Jonty Thompson, though you can never be sure." "Marriage" could be a loose term between men and women of that class. Maybe he heard or saw something, or maybe it was he who tried to move the body. She explained what she knew to Osei and revealed to him that she had seen the body. "How did the doctor know she was strangled?"

"'Twas not until he called for better light. His first clue was the poor girl's tongue protruding." Anne nodded; she had seen that. "He took a lantern and held it close, checking her neck for signs of violence."

"And found them?"

Osei nodded but did not elaborate.

"Can you find anything out about Jonty Thompson?" Anne asked. "Will you engage him in conversation?"

"He is not inclined to speak to me," Osei said with a half-smile. "He winked one eye and spat on the ground, then clamped his clay pipe between his lips when I asked if he saw or heard anything." He gave a significant look. "The pipe bowl is one I have noted before, carved crudely in the shape of the head of an African, but with grossly exaggerated features."

"Good heavens, why?"

"Pipe bowls are commonly tied to primary business in localities. I assume he has lived close to a port that conducts business in the slave trade."

"Sophia did say the couple was from the Bristol area."

"Center of the slaving and shipping trade. His winking and spitting may be a ritual to ward off misfortune. He seems consumed by superstition. He admitted to the doctor that he had seen a magpie yesterday—only one, not two—and knew something unfortunate would befall the household. He averred that if Miss Collier was a suicide, he was *certain* he saw her ghost after, floating along the lane, but when I asked how that was possible, when no one knew when it happened, he made a mysterious sign and slipped away to a shed at the bottom of the garden."

The shed. She recalled the hand twitching the shed curtain back in place. The back of her neck tingled. Jonty bore more questioning because it was possible that he had seen more than he admitted, or even was in some way responsible, though she could not imagine a motive. "I did not foresee this terrible outcome when I left here yesterday. How awful." Every time she remembered Faithful Collier alive—intelligent, kind, sweet—it made her ill, and then angry. "Osei, we must find out what has happened. Who would kill her? And why?"

"I don't know, my lady. The marks of strangulation are becoming more obvious with each passing hour. The doctor said that is how it goes. The girl is slight. In my opinion it would not have taken a man to do such a deed. If I may say it, a lady could perform such a deed easily, if we can allow it possible for a female to be so callous."

"I can allow it," Anne said. "Because we are mothers and caretakers we are expected to be delicate, but a female will defend herself vigorously against perceived threats."

"Are you saying Miss Faithful threatened someone?"

"Not in a physical sense." She recalled her perception that there were tensions roiling in the household. Enough to prompt murder? "Threats can be other than physical."

He nodded, his glasses glinting in the light from a candle in a sconce. "I understand what you mean. A threat can be to one's status, or position."

"As in a maid or teacher — or housekeeper — whose position was in peril."

"Or even another girl about whom Miss Faithful had information that would have sullied her in the eyes of her schoolmates."

"And it seems to me that the assailant has to be within this household, or closely allied to it."

"Or with access. The field is wider than one would think."

Anne sighed. "You're right. We cannot, at this juncture, eliminate anyone from suspicion in this terrible deed. We are looking to expose secrets, perhaps." She met his intelligent gaze. "Do you think you *can* try again to speak with this Jonty fellow?"

"He seems almost afraid of me. He had emerged from his shed after our first meeting but when he saw me again, he backed away and muttered *"god save me,"* hitched up his breeches and retired again to his shed."

"Would anyone that superstitious and cowardly be responsible for Faithful's death? I can't think he'd take such a chance as to court disaster."

"Fearful people, I have observed, my lady, are very dangerous, for everywhere they see threats."

"You may have the right of it. What do you suggest? I don't think I will be able to speak with him."

"I'll do my best, but I cannot promise I will be successful." He checked his watch, then tucked it back in his waistcoat.

"My father and brother and their retinue will be arriving at the marquess's today. We must be there to greet them," she said, knowing his punctilious nature.

He nodded. "I would never leave them to his lordship's tender mercies. I am a useful shield between the marquess and the world. To you I shall be handing over that duty in future, but for now we shall do the task together."

"The world does not need to be shielded from Tony. I find his brusqueness entertaining, and whomever doesn't can leave him alone. My sole care is for my father and Jamey. Father respects Tony a great deal, and Jamey adores my odd fiancé, so I am content."

"His lordship is kinder to your brother than I have ever seen him with another soul."

"You're right," she said, her voice breaking. "And Jamey loves him for it. Tony has a way with him like no one else but my brother's servants, firm but kind. Even Father cannot manage him the same." There would come a time when Jamey's care would come to her. Where once she feared that moment — her brother could be difficult when things didn't go his way and upset him — she now knew she would have a partner in that duty.

"I have time, though, my lady, before their expected arrival, and will fetch you there to greet them. And I *will* discover what I can from Jonty, if it's possible. Even if he had no hand in this tragedy, given his shed's proximity to where the body was discovered, he may have seen something."

"We need to discover who did this deed, Osei, for everyone's sake. Faithful was despicably murdered."

There was a noise above them. Anne looked up the stairwell. Alys, tears streaming down her face, had been listening. She whirled and ran down a hall, her footsteps clattering and echoing.

Chapter Seven

"Oh, Lord, what have I done?" Anne muttered. "I should know in a place like this the walls have ears. I'll talk to her. Find out if Jonty saw or heard anything. If you see Alethea, please explain what I'm doing."

"I will, my lady, but after that I may need to go for a short time to take care of arrangements for your father and brother's stay."

She nodded and they parted. She ascended, hearing the murmur of voices from above. Perhaps the girls were being kept to their rooms until it was decided what was to be said about Faithful's death. Anne followed the sound of weeping and found Alys alone in a schoolroom where tables lined a wall. She sat in a chair, her head cradled on the table in front of her. Anne knelt by her. "I'm sorry you overheard me."

The girl looked up from her arms, but remained mute, her round face twisted in unspeakable sorrow as she glared at Anne.

"And I'm sorry you've lost your friend. I want to know what happened, and I suspect you do too." She wondered if her appeal would strike the mark. Softly she said, "Will you speak with me, Alys? Please? I wish to help."

She nodded.

"Come, sit with me." She stood and took up the girl's limp hand, raising her and leading her to a low settee by the window. Alys was unresisting, but a wary gleam in the depths of her gray eyes hinted that she was still making up her mind how far she would trust Anne. "I am going to treat you as a rational young lady, Alys. I know you are sorrowing and likely confused. I also know you wish to understand what happened to your friend."

The girl nodded, still mute.

"Alys, all we can do for Faithful is discover what happened and how. Do you want to do that?"

Alys nodded, as Anne knew she would. What girl could resist such an appeal, to do a final kindness for her friend?

"You knew Faithful believed she was being haunted?"

Alys again nodded. Repetitive, but at least it shortened the questioning.

"What did she tell you?"

Alys reiterated all Faithful had told Anne the day before, but nothing beyond it.

"Did she speak with you yesterday after our conversation? I told her I believed she heard voices, but I did not think them supernatural."

The girl looked doubtful. "We didn't have a chance to speak. Do you mean someone was playing a trick on her?"

It was Anne's turn to nod.

"I wondered, you know. Some of the girls whispered together and had a secret, but they wouldn't tell me what it was. But how? And why?"

"The why I cannot yet say, but the how is simple enough, if one has confederates. Which girls would work together? Is there one who would lead and have others follow?"

She nodded. "Some girls are not malicious, but they will go along to be safe, or to have friends."

"It's hard to resist when others threaten to withdraw friendship." She watched Alys. What was she not saying? "Who here would do that?"

"I don't think I understand the face in the mirror, and the light Faithful followed upstairs. How could that be done?"

"Trickery, easily accomplished by a clever person. I will need to look at the place carefully before I know the answer positively."

"Why would anyone do such a cruel thing?" Alys burst out. "*Why?*"

"Some glory in tricking others. They wear it like a badge of honor, certain in their superiority. Alys, will you help me find out who did this to poor Faithful?"

"How can I help?"

"Answer me truthfully." As focused as she was on Alys, still, Anne had part of her attention elsewhere and heard a bustle downstairs. It occurred to her that the moment Sophia had learned that Faithful's death was not by misadventure or her own hand, she would have had to call in the magistrate. Perhaps it was his arrival she heard. "Did Faithful speak to you yesterday, after I talked to all of you?"

She shook her head. "She said she didn't feel well. She begged to be allowed to go to bed early, but Miss Hopewell would not allow it.

Faithful was being weak. Ladies must not be weak, she said, or they will never survive."

"How did Miss Hopewell look as she was saying this?" Anne interjected, curious. Such a statement seemed pointed.

"Fierce. Not like herself. She said she must make us all tough. She would make a strong young lady out of Faithful even if it—"

"Even if it killed her?"

Aly's lip trembled, but she nodded. "Miss Hopewell is excessive in her phrasing. My brother says it is a sign of weakness to exaggerate."

"Your brother has an interesting way of looking at the world. It is a dramatic turn of phrase, certainly." Anne very much feared that in her certainty that she had solved Faithful's troubles, she had a hand in the girl's silence. As much as she wanted to quiz Alys on which of the girls may have set out to trick Faithful, she had to go gently, for the girl may be loath to name names. "I would like to go back, Alys, to the night Faithful went up to the roof. She said she was being directed by a spirit. Did she confess that to you?"

"She thought that . . . she thought . . ." Alys hesitated.

Anne suppressed the urge to hurry things along, to fill in, to conjecture, perhaps wrongly. Silence, in this case, must be her method.

"She thought perhaps her mother was beckoning her from beyond the grave."

Her mother who had died in an asylum. Whatever Anne had expected, it was not that. "Why?"

"It was the ghost story Miss Hopewell told one night."

"Ghost story?"

Alys smiled. "Miss Hopewell is pleasant. Not like Miss Dankworth, who can be abrupt and cold with us. I'm glad Miss Hopewell is in our room. She doesn't let the older girls bother the younger." Her smiled died. "When she's around, anyway."

"What about the ghost story you mentioned? How long ago was that?"

"Two weeks ago, I suppose."

"Why did she tell it?"

"When the lights are out Miss Hopewell tells stories. At first it was about her life. Did you know she comes from a very good family? A baron and even a viscount!" The girl flushed and slid a glance at Anne. "I . . . I forgot, my lady, that I shouldn't be—"

"Please don't worry, Alys," Anne reassured her. "You can say anything to me, anything at all. Carry on. Tell me about the stories she tells."

The teacher had a vivid and rich imaginary world. She started with stories about her fiancé's adventures on the high seas. He was a ship's captain, Alys said, and wrote her long letters about his adventures. He had fought pirates and been to exotic locales like the Carib Sea.

Anne doubted there was any fiancé, or surely Miss Hopewell would not be teaching. Nor did she believe the young woman was related to a baron and a viscount. Alys went on; when the girls tired with her romance stories, she told them haunting tales. One in particular the girls liked was the Ghost of Lamb's Inn. The landlord had two daughters who experienced such torments! Such pricking of skin, such biting, and pulling of hair, and knocking on the door, with no one there. Finally it was decided a witch, enlisted to torment the father by a business rival, was to blame and they must call in a "cunning woman" to put a stop to it, at which point all were safe.

Anne could imagine the teacher telling such a tale with knocking on the floor beside her, and bigger girls pinching the littler girls to make them squeal. Harmless enough when made plain that it was a tale to while away the dark hours, but to a susceptible girl like Faithful perhaps, and with the tale suggesting to one of the girls that such occurrences could easily be repeated for a hoax, it had an effect. "Alys, do you think perhaps Miss Hopewell's tales inspired a hoax on Faithful?"

There was a sound at the open door and Anne turned. Miss Dankworth glared at them both. "Alys, Miss Hopewell sent me to find you," the teacher said. "She says you will not slack off today."

"Her closest friend died," Anne said. "I think she should be allowed—"

"Pardon me, my lady," she said, dropping a curtsey. "Not to be rude, but if we allow the girls to wallow it will encourage excess sensibility. You are doing Alys no kindness by listening to her wild imaginings."

"But—"

"Come along, Alys," she said, reaching out and beckoning. "Do not take up any more of her ladyship's time with your silly tales."

Alys obediently followed the teacher, who grasped her elbow to guide her. The girl was barely allowed to pause at the door to drop a curtsey before being tugged away. How odd. Until that moment Miss Dankworth had not figured in Anne's suspicions.

• • •

Curious about the serving staff in the school, Anne descended the servant stairs. The basement was a warren of hallways. She was familiar now with the one passing by the large kitchen at the back of the house and the butler's pantry, but there was more to explore. Again the food odors strengthened, of soup and fish and cabbage. She slid past the kitchen and butler's pantry to an airless, windowless office off the hall. The door stood open, and a middle-aged woman sat at a table writing out a receipt from a book.

"Mrs. Thompson, how are you?"

The woman jolted, almost spilling the ink. She leapt to her feet.

"Why are you sneakin' up on a body?" she yelped.

Anne smiled and said, "I am speaking to everyone about that poor girl's death. Faithful Collier. You knew her, of course."

"As well as I knew any of the girls," she said, her accent careful and stilted. "To pass by, but not to speak with."

"I understand you and your husband came here from Bristol, where you had a boardinghouse."

The woman nodded.

"What happened to it?"

"Wished for a change of scene. Th'sea air did not agree with my 'usband's breathing. Too damp."

"I understand you sleep in the servants' quarters in the attic, but your husband stays in the shed outside." One inside, one outside; how ideal that would be as a murdering pair. The woman nodded. "Last night you would have been upstairs abed, as were all the staff. How many in all?"

"We have Cook who sleeps in, and Ginny who does pots and fireplaces and scullery, and there are the maids, Kate and Elly."

She had thought there would be more. "You have others who come in? A laundress?"

"Aye. And the laundress brings her daughter with her for heavy cleaning."

"I see. Did you hear anything last night?"

"Not a thing. Fast asleep, I was, as were Cook, Kate, Ginny and Elly. Not a one of us heard a mouse, I'll swear on the Lord's word. Now, pardon me, miss, while I take this receipt to Cook." She bustled past Anne and escaped to the safety of the kitchen.

Escaped. What was she hiding? Anne headed back up the stairs and found that the magistrate had arrived and was in the middle of a heated discussion with Dr. Fothergill. It was not the kindly magistrate she had dealt with last time. This was a narrow-faced, thin, acerbic gentleman, gaunt of face and choleric of disposition.

"Doctor, I find it incomprehensible why you were summoned, and how you determined foul play."

"By the expedient method of looking at the girl's body, sir. If you would look yourself—"

"Outrageous that you would suggest such a thing to a magistrate and a gentleman, sir," he huffed. "Abominable. *Sickening*, what you leeches are willing to say and do for a farthing."

Anne cleared her throat and stood, chin up, awaiting notice. Dr. Fothergill, his face flushed unusually, for him, whirled. He took hold of his temper and bowed. He turned and said, "Lady Anne Addison, may I introduce to you Mr. Thomas Brereton, magistrate of Bath? Mr. Brereton, Lady Anne is affianced to your tenant, the Marquess of Darkefell. Her father, the Earl of Harecross, will temporarily reside with the marquess until the gentleman and lady's wedding next month."

Fothergill's words had an electric effect, transforming the magistrate's angry expression to calm. He bowed low, sweeping back the skirt of his frock coat and thrusting one pointed shoe forward. "My lady, how enchanting to meet you. Er, despite the circumstances."

"Those tragic circumstances being the murder of a young lady. Mr. Brereton, if I may state my opinion, accepting Dr. Fothergill's medical finding is surely the correct thing to do. He's an esteemed physician and has made a sad discovery. I trust we can *all* agree that we must make haste to discover who is responsible."

He eyed her, his head tilted to one side. "I seem to have heard your name lately." He thought a moment, then his eyes lit with knowledge. "You are the young lady who was involved in that disgraceful fake mystic trouble." His lip curled, nostrils flaring as if he had smelled a foul odor. "My colleague told me you were instrumental in catching her," he said of his fellow magistrate. "Surely your fiancé does not approve of such notoriety?" She remained silent. He nodded as if he had made a valuable point. "Does his lordship enjoy his rented property? I hope all is satisfactory?"

"This is hardly the time or place for such a discussion, sir," she said. Dr. Fothergill gave her a look of warning, and she realized that this man before her could either help or hinder their investigation into Faithful's tragic end. With a milder tone and a slight smile, she continued: "My father, the Earl of Harecross, arrives in Bath today and will be staying with my betrothed. When I go to the marquess's to greet my father and brother this afternoon, I will ask Lord Darkefell how he enjoys his temporary home. It will be mine, too, after our wedding and until we leave Bath."

He smiled, bowing again. Alethea came into the entry that moment and froze in place. When Brereton straightened, he saw her and his expression chilled as hers had.

"Your servant, Mrs. Birkenhead."

She nodded in stiff recognition of his greeting. Anne glanced from one to the other. There was a story there, one she would need to discover later. Alethea approached and murmured in Anne's ear, "Sophia, who does not trust the magistrate—nor many people—has asked you to take this on and find out what happened to Faithful. You are to have free reign in the household, though she would prefer that you not upset the staff."

"I'll do my best," Anne murmured in return. She would have done so anyway even without the teacher's permission, but it was good to have the official backing.

"Let us speak before you proceed about . . ." She cut her eyes significantly to the magistrate.

"Certainly."

Alethea turned to the magistrate. "Mr. Brereton. How are you, and how is your wife? I have not seen her for a while."

"No, I don't imagine you have," he said. "I have had a discussion with her about the friendships she makes in Bath, and she quite agrees with me that we must be careful of our position here."

Anne linked her arm in Alethea's, beginning to understand the problem between the two. Perhaps Alethea's friendship with the magistrate's wife had been too warm, too fervid, for his liking.

"Mrs. Brereton was in my literary society for a time," Alethea said to Anne. "However, the magistrate does not approve of literature for ladies. Or *any* entertainment for ladies."

"How sad . . . for his wife," Anne replied.

"And his granddaughter. You met her: Miss Henrietta Greerson."

Ah, yes, the spiteful girl who seemed to dislike Faithful and who may even have been her bully. She could see where the girl got her unpleasant personality. It ran in the family.

Alethea nodded to the two, doctor and magistrate, unlinked her arm from Anne's and swiftly departed, turning her fashionable skirt to sweep gracefully through the door to the sitting room. "She is a delight, is she not?" Anne said. "We have renewed an old acquaintance. Mr. Brereton, I understand your granddaughter lives here. Where are her parents?"

"They are in India. Mr. Greerson has business with the East India Company."

"But you and your wife live in Bath. Why does Henrietta not stay with you?"

He glared at her. "I hardly think it your business, my lady, but the child is happier here with her friends."

Not from what Anne could see.

"We have her come to us on school holidays." His expression clouded. "In fact, I know Miss Faithful Collier came with our Henrietta to stay with us during the last school break. Poor child."

Hardly a child. She was seventeen, though she had looked much younger. "She stayed with you? Why did she not go home to her father?"

He was silent for a long moment, his mouth primmed. He eyed her. "It is none of our concern, my lady, I hope you don't take that amiss." It appeared he was trying to find a way to frame what he wanted to say, to phrase it delicately. He burst back into speech: "Mr. Collier is a widowed gentleman with no wife. When the child lived in his home, it was with his widowed sister's accompaniment, but she has gone to Scotland to live with her daughter. A man alone, with a daughter . . . not an ideal situation for either."

What was he not saying? What had Faithful told him that she had, perhaps, told no one else?

Chapter Eight

Dr. Fothergill, impatient, tapped his toe, eyeing the magistrate with aversion. Anne wondered what the doctor had against the magistrate, and hoped she'd have the opportunity to ask him. Osei entered at that moment, returning from his tasks, and bowed to the magistrate. The doctor made the introduction, with the same emphasis on the marquess as with Anne, making sure the gentleman knew Osei was his trusted secretary.

Dawning knowledge spread over the magistrate's face. "It is you who negotiated his lordship's tenancy."

"I had the privilege, yes, sir. When I arrived to take possession of the keys, I met your agent."

"He manages such details for me. But he never said . . . I never suspected . . . your hand is gentlemanly, your words . . . perhaps you have aid?"

"Brereton, never say you think the marquess's secretary has a secretary," Dr. Fothergill thundered in disbelief.

"I did not know he was . . . was an African."

Anne bit her lip to keep from laughing at the magistrate's befuddlement, but sobered as she realized that such prejudices as he was exhibiting likely explained Dr. Fothergill's dislike of the man.

"How does that relate to your correspondence?" the doctor said, despite Osei giving him significant looks to let the topic drop.

"I thought by his name he was perhaps Welsh, or Irish."

"A perfectly understandable mistake," Osei said through gritted teeth.

"That's not the point, Osei. Whether you are Welsh, Irish or African matters not at all." He turned back to the magistrate, whose hostile gaze was now fixed on the physician, even as Osei had stiffened in irritation at his friend's admonishment. "You're not answering the question, Brereton," the doctor said, unwilling to let the subject go. "What does that have to do with your correspondence with him? His *gentlemanly hand*, I think you called it?"

She understood and suspected the doctor did too. "Did you wish to speak to me?" she asked Osei, who appeared put out by the confrontation between his friend, the doctor, and the magistrate.

He took her elbow and drew her away from the squabble, which was more about the two men's dislike for one another than anything. "I spoke with the driver of the post-chaise. He passed your father's coach on the highway. Your father's driver is holding to his word on the time and will tarry until the exact moment to approach. We should be at his lordship's townhouse to greet them when they arrive."

Jamey must be handled with composure, no hurry or bustle, or he would become obstreperous. Anne being there would distract him, give him a focus. The Carters, who looked after his needs, would have made sure he was comfortable, but upon arrival they would be occupied. Besides which, she longed to see them both. "Shall we go?"

"Your conveyance awaits, my lady. I have the hired curricle I have been using to travel about Bath. I pray you will not be too cold."

"Good thinking, Osei. We mustn't shock the upright Bath gentlefolk by using a closed carriage." She turned and curtseyed to the two men, who had suspended their quarrel for the moment. "I'll speak to Miss Sophia Lee before I depart."

"I will await you outside." Osei bowed to the two men. "Gentlemen."

Dr. Fothergill said, "Hold one moment, Osei, if I may accompany you outside and speak with you?"

"As you wish." Osei waited for his company.

The doctor turned to the magistrate. "If our conversation is done, sir, I will depart. To return to the true matter at hand, I cannot change my judgment of what befell Miss Collier and I will not lie to spare anyone's feelings, even her family's. Even if I would, there is no concealing those marks on her neck. If I were you, sir, I would not attempt to hide the truth, but neither would I broadcast it. For the nonce, let the gossips tattle, while we give them no fodder. That is my advice, take it or leave it, as you will." He glanced about. "I will be advising the Misses Lee to keep a sharp watch and never let their girls — or themselves — be alone."

Anne felt a chill down her back and met Osei's steady gaze. There was, in all likelihood, a killer in this place. Osei held the door for him and followed as Dr. Fothergill departed.

The magistrate said, as the door closed behind the physician, "That man speaks above his station."

"The doctor speaks plainly, but truthfully. I don't think murder has a station," Anne said.

"These young ladies, the Lee sisters, are in over their heads and drowning." He paused, deep in thought. "Perhaps it would be best if they step aside. I shall take over this problem for the moment."

"This *problem*? You mean the murder of one of their students?"

"I have the requisite experience to take care of these matters. They may go about their business and attend to their students. I will look into it and discover what has happened to that poor child. She was a guest in my home for a time, and it is my duty, as if she was my own." He frowned and looked down at the carpet. "Perhaps it would be safer to close the school and send these children home."

Anne stiffened but calculated her words to give as little offense as possible. The magistrate was in a position of power and must be convinced rather than castigated. "I beg your pardon, sir, but this is the *Lee* school. As magistrate it is, of course, in your purview to investigate, but close them down? That would be death to their business."

"Better than to lose another child!" he thundered, raising one finger in the air.

"Surely there is a middle path." Dr. Fothergill had suggested one, but she would not remind the magistrate that it was the physician's proposal. "The Lee sisters know these girls better than you. Shutting them down and sending the girls home would put them out of Bath and away from being able to answer questions that might reveal the truth."

He looked doubtful.

"Don't you think the Lees and their girls may remain safe by all staying together as much as possible? To close the school down would, I firmly believe, be a mistake."

"I don't make mistakes, my lady." He frowned. "However, I will not be hasty. I'll consult with my wife on this matter."

"You mean consult with her about the murder? Or whether to close the school and send the girls home?"

"Good lord, of course not about the most unfortunate matter of poor Faithful Collier's death. I hesitate to even break it to her. She liked the child very much. Her death will break her heart. No delicate female could be expected to understand the evil men will do." He gave her a questioning glance, one brow raised, and she understood the implication, given that he had already sneered at her involvement in the mystic affair. "My dear wife is delicately bred. Nor could she hope to have an opinion on whether to close the school and send the girls home. I shall consult with her whether we should take Henrietta out of here and put her elsewhere for the time being."

"As her grandfather you will decide your own course of action. I would recommend against such hasty action."

"Your advice will be considered as of course, your past . . . *experience* in murder must give you insight." His tone was full of wounded sensibility and shaded insinuation. The magistrate thrust one foot out, bowed, then departed in a huff. Who knew whether he would take the doctor's counsel on how to report this death? Or whether he would leave the school open, take his granddaughter out, or *what* he would do. In her experience those who brayed the loudest about what they would do rarely did much at all, preferring to dither, foisting blame on those more decisive.

Alethea would remain with Sophia to give succor. After explaining that she would return, but given her duties perhaps not until the next day, Anne departed to the open carriage. Osei handed her up, despite the staring looks of passersby, and jumped up beside her. Pulling a shawl about her shoulders and huddling into it, Anne said, "Onward to Upper Church Street, I suppose."

Osei took up the reins and set the horses in motion.

She muttered, "Why do folks stare?"

"I suspect they are startled by my complexion, my lady. I do stand out here."

"I hadn't thought of that." She glanced over at him. She hesitated sometimes, unwilling to offend such a private man, but said, "How difficult it must be for you, Osei, to be stared at, and yet you handle it with grace and composure."

He said nothing for a moment, but then, his hands tightening on the reins, remarked, "Because you see me composed, don't mistake my calm for indifference. Have you ever watched swans on the river? So graceful, so serene, and yet under the water is a tumult of movement. My quietude at times masks an inner fury."

"I'm sorry, Osei, for what you must endure in our country."

"It is not always. It is not everywhere. I recall in my youth what a stir erupted in my home village when someone different arrived.

People are the same everywhere. Here, it is I who cause the stir. In London I am not remarked on at all." He cast her a glance. "I will be going there, you know, while you and his lordship travel north on your wedding trip."

"To London? Whatever for?"

"Mrs. Fothergill is to accompany me and introduce to me people she knows who may have information on those who were transported on the same ship as my sister." She had been on a different ship than he, and he did not know her fate.

"Do you think she survived the voyage?" They had canvassed the delicate subject before, but Anne wondered if he had confided his true thoughts and fears.

"I'm afraid to hope." He clicked to the horses and turned the carriage expertly onto Julian Road.

Osei was a closed book most of the time, with such stories contained within him as dazzled her when he did speak, of his life as a young prince of his people, a warrior, slave owner, the presumed heir to his father's position. When a rival tribe invaded their territory, slaughtered their family and captured him and his sister, they took them directly to the slave markets along the western coast of Africa. They were sold and boarded on ships that were to take them in bondage to the Caribbean islands to be sold again individually as laborers to work on the sugar plantations. He, weakened by the illness that ravaged the human shipment, was one the sailors were throwing overboard to be claimed on insurance as lost cargo. His sister, on a different ship in the same convoy, had traveled on, as far as he knew.

"I hope you find her. What will you do if you discover where she was taken?"

"I will go and get her."

"Even to America?"

"Even to America."

"That would be perilous, Osei." He could be captured, enslaved, brutalized. He could be lost forever, no papers provided by the marquess enough for determined slavers.

"There are anti-slavery advocates even there, my lady, in the new nation, and channels through which families can be reunited. The struggle against slavery is led by Quakers and other abolitionists who provide a chain of safe houses." Unspoken was the fact that he was a warrior, and would take it on as a battle he must win. "Even as those white men fought for their own freedom, there were those among them who fought for freedom for *all*. The Society of Friends is first among those toiling toward universal emancipation, the battle I have joined, having seen it from all aspects: warrior, slave owner, captive, enslaved, and free."

"I pray they prevail one day, and support those in our own nation who are trying to do the same. We cannot, as the Bible says, look for a mote in our enemy's eye ignoring the beam in our own."

"Slavery in the Americas is hardly a mote, my lady."

"You're right, of course. And our nation's benefiting from the slave trade is bigger than a beam." She shivered and huddled into her cape, burying her hands in the folds. As complex and philosophical as such matters could seem, there was only one right side, and that was the abolition of slavery, everywhere and for all time.

Her thoughts returned to the problems at the school. "What did the doctor wish to say, when he left with you?"

"First, he apologized for speaking for me."

She smiled over at him. "I saw your irritation. He meant well."

"Do not apologize for him, my lady. He of all people should know better than to speak for me. I am perfectly capable of speaking for myself, and will, if the situation occasions it. In this case the magistrate's ignorance had a banality I have encountered far too often. I could have sparred with him, if I had chosen, but I did not choose."

"I thought the contretemps had more to do with the two men's dislike of one another than anything else."

"You may be right, but Dr. Fothergill should have let the topic drop. We have pressing matters to focus on. He knew it, therefore he apologized, and the matter is closed." He was silent for a moment. "He's worried about the school. He consulted with me on what I thought the best way to protect the Misses Lee and their charges."

"What did you say to him?"

"That there was no way of knowing how to keep them all safe except, as he suggested, to make sure nobody was alone with anyone else at any time."

"The ladies must trust no one."

He agreed.

"The magistrate suggested he'd like to shut the school down and send the girls home. I told him that was a bad idea and would end in the school closing forever."

Osei was silent for a moment.

"Do you agree with him?" Anne asked. She trusted Osei's judgment and wondered if she had been hasty in her own reasoning.

"No, my lady, I agree with you. But it's a balance, is it not? The girls, if they are sent home, will indubitably be safer, but could, as you worry, destroy the Lee school."

"Such a course—sending the girls home—would delay or forever abandon any hope of identifying and capturing the killer. Could the school ever reopen safely if the murderer was not caught?" She thought of the roiling tensions she had felt among students and staff. Was the murderer one of the girls, even? Her heart recoiled from the possibility, but her mind and logic admitted it. "If we are to solve the crime, we cannot decide on a culprit and make the crime fit him. Or her."

Chapter Nine

Lined with pilastered townhomes, Upper Church Street connected, ultimately, with the Royal Crescent and Brock Street. The marquess's Bath residence was a gracious, unspectacular townhome that suited Tony in every way. Anne regarded it as they approached; Brereton owned this lovely building? He had money, for these were not inexpensive properties.

It was tall, four floors above ground, and a lower level for kitchens. In the weeks since the marquess had arrived she had not had occasion to examine the place. Darkefell dined with Anne and her family often, though he had threatened to hold a dinner party. With the earl arriving, it was now likely.

Anne entered, looking around with interest. The house was elegant, with the stairs directly to the right, as one entered. To the left was a reception room. She longed to look about but there was a clatter on the street. "He's here!" Anne cried. "Papa is here." She swept out the door to the street, bouncing up and down excitedly. She adored her father and had missed him. The carriage was large, with trunks strapped to the roof. The vehicle door burst open and Jamey, red-faced and weeping, tumbled out, followed by the couple, now married, who lived with him and looked after his needs.

"Lord Jamey, mind your footing," Alf Carter said. His wife, Dorcas, stepped down, helped by Osei, who had followed.

And finally, the Earl of Harecross, wig askew, waistcoat rumpled, cravat stained, book in hand, monocle dangling from a chain attached to said rumpled waistcoat, stepped down, blinking blearily. While Alf organized the trunks and Dorcas took care of Jamey, settling him as only she knew how to do, Anne enveloped her father in a hug so tight he was laughing and puffing by the time she was done. "Anne, dearest daughter, let a fellow breathe!"

She released him and stepped back, staring at him through eyes swimming with tears. "I've missed you so, Papa."

"And dear Jamey, too, of course?"

Anne turned. Her brother, calmer now that Dorcas had managed him, gazed at her longingly. She embraced him and he lifted her off the ground with his enthusiasm. "And of course my dearest brother Jamey!" she gasped, relishing the novel sensation of her feet being off the ground.

"Annie, Annie! I didn't think you'd be here, Annie."

She kissed him on his soft, plump cheek and said, "Jamey, darling, let me down!"

Inside the townhome, as Jamey was settled into his suite with his caretakers, she visited with her father in the grand salon, made comfortable with an upholstered grouping near a roaring fire. A footman brought a tray with Madeira and glasses and poured for them both. They chatted for a moment, her father lauding the young Quaker woman, Miss Clara Simmons, who Osei had recommended and who was now his secretary. She was intelligent, organized, tactful, and happy to work on her own while he was gone.

"Papa, what upset Jamey? He was weeping when you arrived."

"He believed we were hoaxing him. He could not believe we were to see you on arrival. You have been away lately, most of the spring and summer, and now in Bath."

"I was in Kent for a good while in the summer. And Papa, he *must* learn to go on without me. I will be in York most of the year."

"We'll manage, my dear. I shall miss you too, but it is the way of the world." The earl sighed heavily and sipped the sherry. "I am beginning to understand that I cannot keep him always content. The Carters are marvelous good at keeping him as happy as can be."

Voices in the entry announced the marquess before he entered. Anne felt a tremor of happiness to see him again, though it had only been twelve hours. He crossed to her first and took up her hand, searching her expression. He had heard about the murder, she knew in an instant. Of course Osei would have apprised him of it.

"How are you?" he murmured, cupping his hands over her shoulders and squeezing, putting into that simple gesture all he could not do, which was to sweep her up and kiss her.

"I'll do, Tony. I'll do. We can talk of it later."

He turned to Anne's father, who had stood. "Sir, it is gratifying to see you again, and looking in good health. Did you and Jamey have a good journey?"

"Tolerable, Darkefell, tolerable. Jamey had his tears at times, but all is sorted now. I cannot say how I appreciate you taking us in like this. If we are any trouble, you must cast us out on the street. We can take rooms at a hotel."

"Nonsense. You're welcome."

"Papa, he would be insulted if you stayed elsewhere." She took her fiancé's arm and squeezed. "Please do not think it."

Politeness out of the way, Osei entered and greeted the earl, who was his great friend and consultant on a scholarly work they were planning on African dialects. Knowing her father, Anne told him he could not set straight to work again until they had done the rounds in Bath and made themselves known. "Mother is fretting, you know."

Her father nodded. "I understand all you cannot say, my dear daughter." What she could not say was that her mother's position in Bath was of great importance to her. Some of the fretting was how Jamey was to be presented. Company could be overwhelming to him and on occasion he reacted poorly. "I thought a promenade in the Pump Room tomorrow to take the waters would suffice for Jamey, at least at first. What think you?"

Anne nodded. "You judge right, Papa. We can leave if things are too much for him."

"I will, of course, accompany you," the marquess said, gripping her arm close to his side. "Let them stare, if they dare."

Anne bit her lip, thinking of her fiancé's basilisk stare, which could quell the most fearful of social demons. But even he could not stop the gossips. "I'll see if Quin will meet us there," Anne said, about Alethea's brother-in-law Quin Birkenhead, newly married. She explained Quin to her father, and why she thought him a good companion. "He saved my life, risking his own in the process. Quin has a unique gift of sweetness allied with intellectual curiosity. Not many men can match his intelligence. I think he and Jamey will get along."

"Are you saying I do not have the gift of sweetness?" Tony thundered. "First Quin is your hero and now you laud his sweetness of temperament and brilliance of mind."

Anne laughed out loud. "And let us not forget Dr. Fothergill," she teased. "He is a gentleman for whom there is no praise high enough. He and Osei have become fast friends, and you know the esteem in which I hold Osei and his judgment in friends."

She sobered as the thought of the doctor brought her back to the problem at hand of the Misses Lee's school and the tragic death of Faithful Collier. She wanted to go back to the school and speak with the students and teachers in the wake of the tragedy. Her father appeared weary. Could she slip away?

Osei entered with two packages. He exchanged a look with his employer and crossed to the earl. "My lord, the marquess wishes to give you and your son welcome gifts." He placed them on the low table in front of Anne's father.

The earl's eyes lit up when he saw one package that was clearly books. He eyed the other parcel, a long tube wrapped in brown paper. "This is for Jamey? What is it? He is not fond of surprises."

"It is a telescope," Tony said. "There is a hatch that opens to the roof. I thought Jamey and I could go up there at night to look at the moon."

Anne turned and stared up at him, her heart thumping. She might praise Quin's sweetness, and Osei's consideration, but if all the good and fine men in the world got together to create their perfect amalgam, they could not have found one more flawless in her eyes than the Marquess of Darkefell. He had that indefinable something more that made her love him. "Oh, Tony, you have found the ideal way to keep my brother occupied while in Bath!"

A rare smile curved his lips, and he held her gaze for a minute. "I'm happy you approve, my lady," he said, his voice husky.

Jamey adored discovery and spent his time at home documenting the flora and fauna of their estate. Collecting and cataloguing it all was his joy, suiting his precise, orderly mind. This gift to Jamey from Tony was a gesture of his love for *her* so profound, she knew she could never find its equal. How could she tell him, show him, *teach* him how much she loved him?

He gazed down into her eyes and, unbelievably, his own misted. "I know how important he is to you, Anne," he murmured, a quaver in his rough-timbred voice. "How could I fail to do my best to think of ways to make him happy in his temporary home? One day he will be my ward. I will forge a connection with him now, so we can be happy all together." He cleared his throat. "I have had the servants set up a spot on the roof with two chairs and a table." He paused, and when he spoke again, his tone was lower, his voice held a dangerously soft tone, and he murmured, "Jamey and I can sit there and gaze at the stars while I long for your company."

The earl cleared his throat. "I may join you, Darkefell, I hope?"

It was agreed. The marquess's servant prepared a late luncheon for them all. As much as she longed to return to the problem at hand, Anne must leave it for the morrow, as it was already getting late in the day. Over luncheon she chatted with her father as Jamey, the marquess and Osei perused the books he had brought. Osei and the two future brothers-in-law conversed about the books and plans to watch the skies.

"The coming days will be difficult," the earl murmured, watching his son with worried affection. "First the Pump Room with a multitude of distractions and noise and then your mother."

"We'll manage it together," Anne said, covering his hand with her own and squeezing.

"What books have you found me, sir?" the earl said to his future son-in-law.

The marquess passed the earl a string-wrapped stack of books suited to his particular interest, dialects and language. "Osei found you a tome on the Hebrew language, and some on German dialects."

"You spoil him, Tony," Anne laughed. "We shall not see him again this month."

"I did the very best thing I could think to do, and sent Osei to find the books for you, sir."

"For the earl there are the books you mentioned on dialects, my lord," Osei said. "I chose a travelogue of the Arabian Peninsula, with references to nomadic languages in that part of the world, by an Orientalist. I found a newly published book, William and Caroline Herschel's *Catalogue of Nebulae and Clusters of Stars*." He looked over at Anne. "I thought you would approve, my lady, of my inclusion of the sister of the astronomer, as she is a scientist in her own right, with many discoveries to her credit. Until a few years ago she lived right here in Bath."

Anne looked around fondly. "I am surrounded by good men, it seems, all conspiring to make my life more pleasant. I trust Miss Herschel is as fortunate. Papa, I hope you mean to rest today, before we assault the Pump Room on the morrow? We shall take the Carters with us, of course, and perambulate. Jamey can see the Roman Baths. He'll be fascinated."

"Today Jamey and I shall occupy ourselves with settling in and exploring the marquess's munificence. Tomorrow we will mount our campaign to the Pump Room. The next day we dine with your mother and grandmother."

"I'll see you tomorrow, Papa." She left him at the dining table looking through the books that Osei had unwrapped, exclaiming with glee over each new title of philosophy, science and language.

"Yes, yes, of course." He flapped a hand in farewell and hunched over the stack of books, saying, "Osei, now that I have you, I brought my work on the book of African dialect and hoped we could fit in a few hours here and there?"

The secretary smiled and bowed. "I will do my best, sir, whenever his lordship or your daughter do not need me. If you will excuse me, I must go see to the carriage again. Lady Anne has need of it, I believe."

Tony followed Anne to the entry as a maid brought her shawl. There she would wait until Osei fetched the carriage. "I could not raise the topic earlier, but Osei told me what you have been through today," he said. "What is this about a student dying at a school?"

She waited until the maid disappeared back down the hall, led him to a private alcove and sat with him on a mahogany settee. She told him all, including the arrival of the magistrate and his antagonism toward Dr. Fothergill. "Oh, Tony, that poor girl, strangled and tossed from the roof as if she was naught but a rag doll to discard," she said, grasping his arm. "I should never have belittled her fears of a ghost and haunting."

"*Did* you belittle her?"

Anne thought for a moment. "I hope not."

"I'm sorry I teased you about it yesterday." He pulled her closer to him. "Do you now believe she was being haunted and there is a ghost in the school?"

"No, of course not."

"Then you did nothing wrong by telling her the truth." He lifted her hand, peeled back the glove and kissed her wrist. "What else could you do but what you did?"

Warmth coursed through her body. He felt her tremble and gazed at her in the dim light of the shadowy hallway, a questioning look in his dark eyes. What he saw impelled him to take her in his arms and kiss her until finally he groaned and pushed her away. "I shall be unfit for company unless I leave off now. You have me bewitched."

"There are those who believe to capture you I have used a potion or cast a dark spell," she said, tucking her fichu back into her bodice. It had been disrupted by his questing hands, leaving her flushed with desire.

"Maybe they're right," he said with a throaty chuckle. "I'll charge you with witchcraft."

"Scoundrel! What shall I do with you?"

"You'll kiss me more thoroughly if you know what is good for you."

They did, which left her breathless yet again. "We will have to spend a good month in the bedchamber to wear out our appetites," she whispered, resting her forehead against his as he bent to her.

"'Twill never happen," he whispered. "For my appetite is bottomless, which I cannot say about you," he said as she stood. "Damned flouncy dresses," he growled, making a wild grab for her skirts, though she swished out of reach. "I cannot tell where you end and the dress starts. I know your bottom is in there, but it is too adequately concealed."

"I suggest we both keep our minds on other things for the next weeks, my lord," she rejoined tartly, as a maid passed through the entry and into the reception room with a tray for the earl. "Shall I expect you to accompany my brother and father to the Pump Room tomorrow?"

He stood and bowed as the maid returned without the tray. "I shall be at your service, my lady. Sleep, Anne," he said, watching her. "You look exhausted."

"Thank you for that critique, exactly what every lady wants to hear from her groom weeks before her wedding, that she appears haggard," she retorted. "I can't swear I'll sleep, not while worrying about those girls and the Lees."

Chapter Ten

"I'll speak with the teachers and students this morning," Anne said the next day, as Osei capably handled the horses, weaving through the busy streets of Bath toward the school. Wishing to be of service, he had picked her up at the Paragon townhome of her grandmother rather than let her walk alone. "This afternoon will be very busy. I would decline going to the Pump Room any other day, but Papa and Jamey must be seen about town to make it plain that the entire family will be attending my wedding."

"Except for the marquess's mother and brother."

"John and Lydia will be there. Lord Julius may still surprise us." Lord Julius Bestwick, Tony's long-lost younger twin, had returned from the colonies after escaping a fraudulent murder charge. For the time being he appeared to be enjoying his freedom, traveling about the country with his wolf dog Atim. "As for the dowager marchioness, I do not expect her," she said of her future mother-in-law. This time of year especially, Lady Darkefell was prone to black moods that left her incapable of effort. Rather than risk such an eventuality, she chose to remain north, where she had her gardens to plan at Ivy Lodge, the dower house of Darkefell Castle.

"No, I do not expect she will come." He directed the carriage around a cart in the road that had upset its load of wine barrels before a townhome. "But she will greet you when you reach the castle. I hope you give her my best wishes at that time, as I shall not return for at least a month or more."

"I hope you find news in London of your sister, Osei. How old would she be now?"

He thought a moment. "She would be about nineteen."

"So young when she was lost to you!" Anne exclaimed, her voice clogging, thinking of what she endured. "I would like to meet her someday. I don't believe I've ever asked, what is her name?"

"Spelled in your language it is A-b-e-n-a, Abena."

"I hope Abena is returned to you."

They arrived at the school. Osei leaped down and helped Anne to descend, while a boy held the reins, staring at the secretary with wide-eyed fascination. "I will leave you here, my lady, if you do not mind. I have tasks to perform for his lordship. He has expressed an interest in the Royal Agricultural Society. I will see about an invitation to join, or attend lectures, at the very least."

She smiled and shook her head. "Shall I be married to Farmer Tony, Osei?"

"He does wish to broaden his understanding of farming so he can speak more easily to his farm manager about new methods."

"Perhaps it will be something for my father and him to talk about," she said with hope. Though the two men were well-disposed toward each other they were vastly different, the earl interested in academic quests, the marquess in physical pursuits. However, Lord Harecross understood his own farming concerns, the growing of hops for local beer brewing in their county, despite the prevailing opinion that he was a head-in-the-clouds scholar. If Tony was becoming interested in his farms, it was all to the good.

Osei tossed a penny to the boy, mounted the carriage and drove away. Anne entered the school and asked to speak with Miss Sophia Lee. She was shown to the drawing room by the red-eyed maid. The teacher entered, hands ink-stained and expression solemn.

"You see before you, my lady, a wretch finding solace in writing." She displayed her inky hands. "I have sought refuge there, but alas these current troubles consume me, regardless. I make no progress."

"I hope I can help you to find peace. I am taken up this afternoon with familial obligations, but I wonder if I might interview the teachers and students again, since this tragedy has occurred?"

With a brooding expression, her face lined with anxiety, she turned to the window and stared unseeingly. "Who would do this? I find myself pushing it away, denying it, saying to myself, there has been a mistake. Faithful cannot have been murdered. It is impossible. And yet . . . the doctor is right. I have looked at F-faithful and . . . there is no mistaking it. She was murdered."

"I'm sorry you had to see her like that."

"I had to, to accept it, for the brief view I had of her body the first day did not show me all her wounds. I am so *angry* at it all! I pray for that poor girl's soul and can do aught but castigate myself that I did not foresee the disaster looming. It seems we are doomed in life to be plagued by misfortune, and to race to defeat it."

"You could not know. I could say the same, Miss Lee," Anne said gently. "I wish I had asked more questions, paid more attention, but instead my damnable self-assurance told me we had solved the problem of Faithful's flights of fancy, never knowing what that very night would bring." She stopped. *That very night!* Had the mere fact of them all looking into it hastened Faithful's death? The girl had been holding back. Would she have lived if she had confessed all that was troubling her? "We must put all our effort into discovering the murderer and giving the family peace and a measure of justice. Have they arrived yet, Faithful's family members?"

"I received a message that they arrived in Bath last evening, but they have not yet come here. I expect them anon. We'll take care of all the tedious bookkeeping required by death and pack her belongings, then arrange for the poor child to be taken hence to Bristol."

Slowly, Anne said, "Perhaps it is best not to hasten her removal."

"Why?"

Instead of answering, Anne asked, "May I speak again with the girls in Faithful's room, and the teacher, Miss Hopewell. Are any of the male teachers here today?"

"Yes, we have Mr. Russell, art master, and Mr. O'Brien, music. He is presently in the music room with Alys. I considered canceling classes but Miss Dankworth quoted Watts's *Divine Songs* and made the pithy comment that Satan finds mischief for idle hands. I stay away from Watts as much as possible, for he is cloyingly sweet, but she made a good point. Keeping the girls occupied will be, I believe, a kindness. Miss Dankworth is out walking with her class."

"May I start with Mr. Russell?"

Mr. Russell would be followed by the others as she summoned them by way of the maidservant.

The good-looking art teacher strolled in with a frown of puzzlement to find Anne there, again. She had felt he was hiding something. Perhaps it was merely that he was going along with Miss Halliday's ardent love for him, flirting and exchanging inappropriate notes. "Mr. Russell, did you have Miss Collier as a student?"

He eyed her in puzzled alarm. Her question was almost rude, it was so direct, and yet his image of himself as a gentleman gave him few ways of avoiding answering. "First, may I say how shocked I am at the news of her death. Miss Lee did not tell me much. How did she die?"

"If Miss Lee didn't tell you, I shall certainly not. Did you have her as a student?"

"At first, yes, but her father recently stopped paying for my tutelage. He pointedly said he saw no benefit in art."

Julia had told her something along those lines but was that belief in general, or specifically for his daughter, Anne wondered. "Art promotes and encourages the inner workings of the imagination. Was Faithful an imaginative girl?"

"I would not say so. She had a pedestrian understanding of art. I did not find her to be stirred or moved by the artistic process, nor to have the imagination to accomplish much beyond stitchery patterns."

If she could believe him—and she saw no reason not to—it confirmed her belief that if Faithful said she saw a ghost it would not be the result of her imagination. She saw something made to look ghost-like. If it had been young Fanny, she may have thought differently. "I take it that it was no loss when her father discontinued her lessons?"

"No loss? To her or the art world in general?"

"Is there a difference?"

"Of course. Even inferior art gives pleasure to those who create it. *Good* art offers that pleasure to the world."

An interesting thought. She examined him with renewed interest. "Would you say it was a loss to *her* when the art lessons were halted?"

"It gave her a way of expressing herself. Perhaps instead she commenced writing poetry or netting purses."

A disappointing answer. "Mr. Russell, do *any* of your students display artistic talent?"

"Why, yes, my lady. Some show great promise."

"Which of the girls is promising?"

"Oh, you mean among the girls of this school?"

"That is of whom we speak, is it not?"

"I teach in other schools, my lady, and give private lessons," he said in his most pompous of tones. "I have a couple of students with the making of fine artists."

"Am I to understand you mean among the boys or young men you teach?"

He nodded. "No slight to the girls, my lady. Women are not formed for great artistic achievement. Otherwise, would we not have already seen a female da Vinci, Michelangelo, or Tintoretto?"

"Perhaps if the Leonoras of the period had been, at fourteen, apprenticed to painters and sculptors as Leonardo was, we would have female painters of note. Instead, young ladies of the Renaissance were not given lessons and were instead bartered off to marry and have babies, or tend to other people's babies, or work in the kitchen or still room or in every other way never given the same opportunities as males." Her tone had become strident.

Startled, Russell stared. Finally he said, "These young ladies *are* given lessons, by me, and not a one of them shows much talent at all."

"Do you say your tutelage is the equivalent of Verrocchio's?"

"Ver . . . who is that, my lady?"

She closed her eyes and counted to five. "Andrea del Verrocchio, the painter sculptor in whose workshop Da Vinci was reputed to have apprenticed." She opened her eyes and stared at him. He looked blank. Her heart hardened. He was the fool she had thought him from the start. "Not a single girl in this school shows promise, not even Miss Halliday? Do you not find her very . . . artistic?"

He flushed and narrowed his eyes. "Whatever your ladyship has heard, I am most careful when giving these young ladies their lessons."

"I have heard nothing beyond extravagant praise I find puzzling, given your attitude toward women as artists."

"I don't think you understand." He hesitated, seeing warning in her expression. Her position in society was elevated. It could be a good connection, he must have been thinking. However, he was sure of himself and his beliefs. "Let me explain myself, my lady," he said in his kindest, most ingratiating tone. "It is said that teaching ladies art is dangerous, as it encourages the imaginative process that leads a young lady into dissatisfaction with her future realm, as wives and mothers. I disagree."

A good beginning, Anne thought.

"Teaching sketching and art appreciation is important. Beyond the pleasure it gives gentlemen to see their ladies engaged in a genteel art such as sketching and painting watercolors, it teaches those women how to tutor their children before they, too, venture off to school and more talented masters."

She took in a long breath and let it out. "Mr. Russell, you do not reside in the school. Are you ever here after school hours?"

"Never, my lady."

"Not even to meet a lady who might slip out?"

"Never!" he said adamantly.

"What if you were seen lurking about late at night?"

Red-faced, he leapt to his feet. "A lie, my lady. See here, who has been spreading such foul rumors?"

She smothered a smile of satisfaction at getting to him. He was conceited beyond his years and station. "I was merely posing a question, which you have answered, adequately. You may go back to your students."

He hastened away. She prepared her thoughts for the questions she would pose to the students, and asked for them in order: Miss Fanny Patterson, Miss Henrietta Greerson, Miss Julia Halliday, and Miss Alys Edisbury.

Fanny had been crying. She didn't appear the fey creature from before, but rather a scared little girl. Anne regarded her and said softly, "Fanny, would you like to talk to me?" The girl nodded. "Come, sit by me." She patted the settee upon which she sat. "Would you like anyone in here with you?"

The girl sat down on the settee beside Anne and moved closer, shaking her head. She took Anne's hand in hers and clung to it. "I *want* to talk to you. They are all saying Faithful was bad, that she jumped off the roof, but she didn't."

"How do you know?"

"I heard her talking to Alys about being on the roof that other night. Alys said *what were you thinking, Fay?* That's what she called Faithful . . . Fay. And Faithful said, *don't worry Aly*—that's what she called Alys—*I'd never do anything thoughtless, you must trust me.* She would never do anything so awful unless God told her to, she said, and God would never ask her to jump."

"Fanny, what do *you* think happened?"

"The ghost pushed her."

"Ghost?"

"The one she talked to." She had heard about the ghost, she explained, when Faithful and Alys whispered together. They didn't mind her sitting with them when the other girls were cruel, sometimes, and shooed her away.

"When the other girls were cruel to you? You told me all of the girls got along."

Blinking and sniffing into her sleeve, Fanny bit her lip.

"Fanny, you can tell me the truth. I'm on your side. I'm on Faithful's side. I *will* find out what happened to her, truly, and without blame."

"Some of the girls are not as kind as the others."

"Which ones in particular?"

Fanny shook her head.

Anne waited, but the girl remined silent. "Fanny, I promise I want to make everything right."

"Henrietta," she blurted, then covered her mouth with one hand, eyes wide.

"Henrietta Greerson? Was she cruel?"

The girl nodded, relaxing now that she had said it. "To Faithful, yes. I don't understand why, my lady. They were friends, once. Faithful went to stay there when we were on vacation."

"Here in Bath, you mean, to Miss Greerson's grandfather's home?"

She nodded.

"They weren't friends after that?" Did something happen on the vacation to set them against each other? Two girls forced together for an extended time; perhaps they argued. "They came back from vacation and were at odds?"

Fanny shook her head. "It wasn't directly after, my lady. They were still good friends. Faithful sat with Henrietta and talked to her for hours. Alys felt left out. It was . . . oh, *weeks* before they started bickering. Months, even."

Something happened between them at school. "What other young ladies are cruel, Fanny?"

She bit her lip. "Julia is short with me. She called me a little fool once. And she and Henrietta were laughing together about Faithful."

"When was that?"

"It was in the music room, you know, the night Faithful first saw the ghostly apparition."

Aha! Perhaps that was who conspired with Henrietta to construct the ghastly image in the mirror. "Fanny, we are certain the ghostly happenings were a hoax, a trick played on Faithful. Do you think

Henrietta could have been involved in any way, from planning it to taking part?"

She nodded miserably. "Henrietta has been unhappy lately, and I think . . . I think she's frightened."

Maybe frightened of her part in the haunting being discovered. "Two nights ago, did you see or hear Faithful get up out of bed?"

She frowned down at her hands clasped around Anne's. She played with Anne's ring. She seemed very much a little girl at that moment, instead of a young lady on the brink of her teen years. "I heard *someone* get up. I thought they were using the chamber pot, so I turned over and tried to go back to sleep."

"What time would that have been?"

"I don't know. Later I heard a cry. It startled me awake."

"What did you do when you heard the cry?"

"I was afraid. I put my head under the covers." She knew nothing else, she claimed.

Anne dismissed her with kind words.

Henrietta Greerson was next. From being an unpleasant and superior girl the day of their first meeting, she had undergone a transformation into a timid and frightened one. Death will do that to you, Anne thought, eyeing her. Or was there more to her change in demeanor? That was what she would try to find out.

Henrietta stood near the door. Anne asked her to come over, and she perched on the edge of the settee as if it was a cliff she was frightened to fall from, her hands gripping the seat edge until her knuckles were white. Anne asked about the night of the murder and she answered in monosyllables, only expanding when forced. According to her, she heard nothing, saw nothing, and slept the night away.

Anne regarded her with skepticism. "Henrietta, I hope you know you are safe telling me anything."

She shook her head. "I didn't see a-anything, my lady. Truly."

Anne seized on the statement. "You did *hear* something." Henrietta stared down at her white knuckles and would not say another word. "If you know anything at all about Faithful, please share it with me."

"I . . . I'm frightened," she gasped, her voice clogged.

"Of what? Or of whom?"

"My lady, I've been dreadful. I was the one who did the voice, you know, that told her to follow . . ." She sobbed into her hands. "It was meant to be a hoax."

"But she ended up dead." Anne watched Henrietta, wondering if the emotion was real. "Miss Greerson, what are you not telling me?"

She shook her head, the tears streaming down her cheeks as she dropped her hands and bunched her skirt in her fists. She was plain and blotchy, her thin lips twisted downward, her face marked with blemishes becoming deeper red with her extreme emotion. "I cannot say."

"Tell me, please. Did Miss Halliday help you with the illusion?"

She started to nod, then blurted out, "It's not her I'm worried about, though. It's—"

"Excuse me, milady?" Elly, the younger of the two maids, curtseyed in the door. "Would you be takin' tea, milady?"

"No, thank you." As she turned to speak, Henrietta rose and tripped out of the room, squeezing past Elly.

"Henrietta! *Henrietta!*" Anne bolted to the door, but the girl was gone. Anne decided to let her calm down and speak to her later, if she could.

Julia was next. She, too, had been weeping, judging by her red-rimmed eyes, but she was composed and solemn, her ebullient manner flown. "I was awake. Miss Hopewell snores and was particularly loud. I was thinking of what I said to you earlier that day, about poor Faithful. I was . . . I was feeling bad about . . . about what I said about her. About Mr. Russell and her, I mean."

"Ah, yes, what you said about her. You weren't too fond of Faithful, were you?"

"I'm sure I don't know what you mean."

"You helped Henrietta with the trick played on her, the ghastly illusion in the mirror, using the skeleton hand from the theatrical props."

Her eyes filled. "We didn't mean anything by it. We were just having fun."

"Was it fun to tell her to kill herself?"

"I didn't . . ." She broke down and sobbed, wringing her hands. "That was Henrietta who said that, not me. I don't know why she said it. It was cruel, especially since we know what happened to her

mother. I was shocked. I didn't do anything else after that first time."
She was adamant; after what Henrietta had said to Faithful, she had
refused to have any part of future hoaxing. "I don't know why she
didn't like Faithful. She was angry at her about something. She
wouldn't tell me what."

"All right, back to the night of Faithful's death. Did you hear or
see anything that night?"

"I heard a pebble clattering against the window."

"Did you get up to investigate?"

"I did. I thought it might be . . ." She blushed and turned away.

She thought it might be the art master, Mr. Russell. "You looked
out the window. Did you see anyone?"

She hesitated, then shook her head. "No. I returned to bed."

The hesitation worried Anne. "Are you *sure* you didn't see
anything?"

She frowned, her brow wrinkling as she concentrated. "I thought I
saw movement, but it could have been that . . . that *man* who lives in
the shed."

"Jonty? Does he roam the grounds at night?"

"He is supposed to be a night watchman, but he is often drunk,
from what I have overheard Mrs. Thompson say to Cook when she
thinks no one can hear her. He goes to a tavern nearby, I have heard. I
thought maybe it was him coming home." She wrinkled her nose.
"He's a disgrace."

"What time was it?"

"It was after midnight. I heard the midnight chime of the clock in
the hall, you see, as I rose to look out the window. I had returned to
bed and was falling asleep when I heard the clatter again, but this
time I stayed abed. After a moment I heard one of the girls get up and
creep out of the room. I thought perhaps they were going to the close
stool in the hallway closet. Henrietta has been . . ." She blushed and
turned away. "Poor Henrietta has been troubled by her courses, and I
thought she needed to attend to private matters. There is little enough
privacy here. We try to give each other as much as we can."

Anne considered the string of occurrences. The first pebble had
brought Julia to the window, but maybe she was not the person the
stone thrower had been summoning, so they hid in the shadows.
When they again tossed a pebble, perhaps it elicited the intended

response. "Could the person who left the room have been Faithful?"

"I suppose."

"Is that all you heard?"

"No, my lady. There was another."

"Another who left the room? Who?"

"I was almost asleep. I don't know who either person was."

"And you didn't see an empty bed, or notice from where in the room either person moved?"

She shook her head.

Was she telling the truth? Anne rather thought she was. "How much time had passed between the first pebble and the next?"

"I don't know."

"How long after the second pebble did the first person creep from the room?"

"I don't know, my lady. A few minutes."

"And how long after did the second person leave the room?"

"Another five minutes." She was an astute and intelligent girl when not in the throes of infatuation, or trying to make an impression.

"Thank you, Miss Halliday. You've been very helpful. Tell me, do you remember if Miss Hopewell was still snoring?"

"She was not."

Perhaps, then, *she* was gone from the room. "Did you not open your eyes at all? Did you see who was still in your room after the two crept out?"

"'Twas dark, my lady. I'm sorry."

"No impression at all, not even a guess, who left the room?"

"No."

"Miss Halliday, are you sure it was pebbles thrown against the window?" Anne asked.

"I . . . no, I'm not sure. I suppose it could have been another noise that sounded like it. But I don't know what." That was all she had to say.

Chapter Eleven

Alys Edisbury was last among the girls with whom Faithful shared a room. Of them all, she was most distraught, to be expected as they were particular friends. When asked about the pebbles against the window, she said she heard them and knew Julia had gone to the window to look out. She added additional information. "She has crept out before to meet . . ." She caught her breath and looked frightened.

"Please tell me, Alys. This is important. No duty of friendship can supersede the one to Faithful, I hope you believe that. I want the truth, and nothing extraneous that does not have to do with her death will be passed on to the magistrate."

"I have seen Julia with Mr. Russell before, at the market and walking in the park."

"And has he been here before, at night?"

"Once," she whispered. "I know Julia crept from the room once to meet him, but that was a long time ago, when the weather was warm. Early October, my lady."

"And you're sure it was to meet Mr. Russell?"

"I think so."

"When you saw them together in the park, were they talking, laughing, perhaps?"

The girl nodded.

"Flirting?"

Alys appeared at sea, not sure how to respond. Anne explained what she meant, and the girl nodded. "But I don't think he meant anything by it, my lady. Some gentlemen behave so, my mother told me, because that is all they know to do."

"I understand there were more pebbles thrown, and two people left the room. Do you know who?"

"I'm not sure." She paused. "Will she get in trouble, my lady?"

"Will *who* get in trouble?"

"Miss Hopewell . . . oh! I didn't mean to say her name!" She colored pink.

"Miss Hopewell left the room?"

Alys nodded. "And Faithful. I don't know which left the room first."

Anne asked a few more questions, but the girl had nothing to say. "Thank you, Alys. This was important, and I appreciate you telling me. Faithful seemed like a dear girl. In the coming days you will miss her. Can you go home to family for a time?"

She shook her head and took in a deep breath. Her gaze became trusting, Anne's kindness like sunshine on a closed bloom, opening it in the warmth. "There was a second time later in October when Julia crept out to meet Mr. Russell in the garden," she whispered confidingly.

"A second time?"

"When she came back in she cried. He was not there despite having pledged he would be, and she said it hurt, for she loved him, but he could not love her and treat her so cruelly."

"She went to the window that night when she heard pebbles. Why would she if she had no more hope of Mr. Russell?"

Alys frowned. "I don't know, my lady. Perhaps she thought he regretted the other time when he disappointed her."

"You've told me who left the room, as far as you know. Could Miss Halliday have also left the room? After the other two?"

"I don't think so, but I was tired, my lady, and slept."

Anne nodded, understanding. "Is that all you can think of, Alys?"

She shrugged helplessly, scrubbing her red-rimmed eyes with nail-bitten fingers. "It's all I remember, my lady. I wish . . . I wish this would not have happened. I miss Faithful." She cried even as she curtseyed and departed, the sounds of her sobs fading as she retreated down the hall.

Anne felt her heart constrict. The poor child. There was a bustle in the hallway, and male voices. Sophia Lee's voice was clear and controlled as she offered a hello to guests. The parlor door opened and she preceded two gentlemen, both somber of mien, though not appearing overwhelmed with sadness.

The teacher made introductions. "Lady Anne, may I present to you Mr. William Collier and his son—Faithful's brother—Mr. Augustus Collier. They arrived in Bath last evening and sent a note that they would attend me today. Gentlemen, this is Lady Anne Addison, daughter of the Earl of Harecross and soon to be the Marchioness of Darkefell." She gave no explanation for Anne's presence.

Both men bowed and she nodded to them, examining them with interest. Mr. William Collier, a gentleman in his fifties, tall, lean, prosperous, with a red bulbous nose and tidy clothing, was the very image of a self-satisfied self-made man. He appeared to have a fondness for brandy, she guessed from his red nose. He held his left arm close to his body, but whether it was withered or otherwise damaged she could not guess.

The Colliers were not impressed by her eminence, and she was not offended by their lack of obeisance. The older gentleman appeared grave and saddened, though not as burdened by his sorrow as she would have hoped.

But the younger . . . ah, there was an enigma. Mr. Augustus Collier's gaze darted about the parlor, anywhere but to his hostesses' eyes, or Anne's. He could have been mourning his sister's death, or he was simply uneasy. When he finally gazed toward Anne, his nostrils flared, and he looked down his nose, aloof and haughty. She observed him in puzzlement. Augustus was Faithful's *brother*. Sadness would be expected; uneasiness was surprising given they did not yet, presumably, know how she died, and hauteur was even more astonishing. About what did an office clerk have to be so conceited?

It would be politic to leave, but if she was to solve this tragedy, she needed to stay and dig for answers. She'd lean on the audacity her position in society allowed her and remain unless her hostess asked her to go. Miss Sophia Lee explained the circumstances of Faithful's demise to the two men, and asked if either gentleman had any questions.

"I want to know what outrageous place this is that such an event could occur?" Mr. Collier said, his cheeks reddening.

Ah, there was the righteous anger Anne would expect.

Miss Lee soothed him as best she could, as Anne engaged the younger Collier in conversation. "Mr. Collier, you are from Bristol. Are you employed there?"

"I am, my lady," he said. "I am a clerk in the offices of Hawkins Africa Shipping."

Slave traders. "And yet you were trained in the law, I understand?"

He started and stared. "My lady?"

"A friend mentioned it."

"I am honored to have been the object of your curiosity," he said, his lip curled.

"You won't pursue a career in law?"

"Shipping seems more amenable to my talents," he murmured, casting a quick glance at his father, who was railing at length about his daughter's death to Miss Lee.

"You traveled here with your father?"

"Why do you ask?"

Mr. Collier the elder rose and bowed. His son jumped to his feet as well. "We are off now to engage suitable transport. I will have her conveyed to Bristol in a suitably decent manner," the elder Collier said, his tone frigid. "It is a sad thing to bring your daughter to school in a carriage and take her away in a hearse."

"I wish we could do more for you." The schoolmistress accompanied them to the door as Osei was stopping his carriage there.

Anne followed them out the door. "Mr. Boatin, have you come to fetch me?"

"The weather is become inclement, my lady. I thought to hasten your excursion to the Pump Room," the secretary said as he hopped down from the open carriage. He turned and bowed to the two men, saying, "I apologize, gentlemen, for interrupting if you were conversing with her ladyship."

"Not at all," the elder Mr. Collier said. His polite answer was abrupt. "Our conversation was not with Lady Anne, but with Miss Sophia Lee. Nonetheless, good day, my lady," he said, doffing his hat to Anne. "And to you, Miss Lee. We will speak again later when we have completed arrangements." He and his son strode off down the road at a brisk pace.

"Will you wait a moment, Osei?" Anne said. He nodded, and she turned to Miss Lee. "How well do you know Faithful's family?"

The woman, standing with her arms folded over her bosom, watched the two men, heads close together in conversation as they walked away. A cold wind blew down the street, lifting tendrils of her hair. She swept them away with impatience. "I cannot say I know many of my students' parents and siblings well unless their children have been here a while. Faithful has been with me for a year and a half." She turned to Anne. "I met Mr. Collier when he brought

Faithful for her first term. They were accompanied by Mr. Collier's sister, who had lived with them while Faithful was a child. Mr. Augustus Collier I met briefly at the same time but I have never spoken to him. I understand he is Faithful's half brother, from Mr. Collier's first wife. However, I may have heard gossip about his habits; I know ladies from Bristol, and he is said to be a gambler and wastrel. Of Mr. Collier the elder I have heard nothing bad. Why do you ask?"

Anne turned and watched the diminishing figures of the men. "I'm not sure." She took in a deep breath, distressed by all she had learned, and all she still did not know. She turned back to the schoolmistress. "I am expected to attend my father and brother at the Pump Room. I'm sorely troubled by all of this and wish to help. I have experience in discovering the truth behind tragic mysteries such as this, which is why Alethea brought me to you."

"I shall be taken up with the Colliers again later today. There are arrangements to be made."

Anne looked around, to be sure they were not overheard. "I would like your thoughts on this tragedy. What do you believe happened?"

"I don't know what to think right now. I am perplexed."

Anne regarded her, head cocked to one side. The woman was unhappy and worried but unwilling to share her fears. A foggy rain dewed her pale lashes and misted her skin. "Miss Lee, you have no reason to confide in me, I know that, but you must face facts. Faithful Collier was pushed and strangled, or strangled and pushed. When the assailant tried to drag her away, they were either interrupted or found it too difficult. Regardless, *someone* had access to that poor girl inside this institution."

The schoolmistress, mouth primmed into a hard line, looked either unconvinced or undecided.

"Let me help," Anne urged. "Let me discover who did this, and why."

The woman nodded slowly. "I keep trying to convince myself this nightmare is a tragedy, but not a crime. Logic dictates I accept the simple facts. It is as you say, murder." She shuddered. "The magistrate has given me no confidence that he will try to solve this terrible crime. I'm not saying yes to you — I will consult the others —

but what do you want, if I agree to proceed with an investigation of the occurrence?"

"I have been creeping around and asking questions. I'd like to not hide what I am doing. I'd like to speak with all I did not see today. The music and dance masters, the other teacher, and the other girls. The housekeeper and maids. I need to question them *all*, with no interference."

Her voice breaking, she said, "This has been so terrible. The only way past it is through it, I suppose."

It was a tacit yes. "I will wait upon you tomorrow, Miss Lee, and Harriet too. I would also like to speak with your sister Anne."

"What do my sisters have to do with this?"

"They live and work here and are intelligent women. Perhaps they've noticed things you did not. Until then, if I may offer advice, gather the girls around you, be kind, but be vigilant. Keep your eyes and ears open for anything troubling, any sign of guilty knowledge or fearful awareness."

The teacher's intelligent gaze sharpened. "And you are convinced the evil came from within?"

"Not convinced—I make no hasty judgments—but afraid it may be so."

"I'm deeply troubled, my lady. Such things as this occur in the flightiest of novels and nowhere else."

"I'm sure you're distressed." Anne reached out and touched her cold, damp hand. "You and your sisters must look after yourselves." She turned and took Osei's hand, gathering her voluminous skirts with her other as with his help she climbed into the carriage. "Tell me your view of this tragedy," she asked him, as he expertly handled the horses.

He was silent for a moment, his spectacles dotted with misty rain. "We know the poor girl did not kill herself. My second conversation with Jonty was illuminating, to say the least."

"You've spoken to him again?"

"I found him at the livery stable, where he was talking to a friend."

"The stable? You followed him!"

Osei smiled over at her. "You would do the same, my lady."

"I would."

"He *is* married to the new housekeeper, legally he claims. They came as a pair."

"What does he do?"

"He is a caretaker, tidying the outdoors, sweeping, repairing things, though he is hampered by an injury to his arm. This job suits him, as he makes his own hours. Already his fear of me is wearing off as he sees I am a man like any other. I believe he is hiding something."

"Something?"

"Knowledge, secrets, I don't know. That is not to say it is about this death. A man like him? There is a multitude of other possibilities."

"His past, perhaps? Jail?"

"Or desertion from the navy or army. Unsavory details he would not want Miss Lee to know about."

"Can you learn more?"

"Perhaps."

"Wait, Osei, stop the carriage!"

"What is it, my lady?"

She had spotted Mr. Russell walking ahead of them along the street. She called out to him and he turned, saw her, and approached the carriage.

"My lady," he said, bowing low.

"Mr. Russell, earlier, when you spoke to me, you did not tell the truth. I have it on good authority that you did indeed return to the school in the evening on at least one occasion. I know, in fact, you met a young lady in the back garden."

He colored and clapped his hat back on his head. "I have no comment to make on such scurrilous rumors."

"Rumors? You have been making love to your students, sir. What say you to that?"

"I say it's a damnable lie. Excuse me, my lady. I'm late for my next lessons." He scurried away down the street, scuttling to a side street and disappearing from view.

Anne watched him go. Was it innocence or guilt that made him color so highly?

Chapter Twelve

It was a dreary day, the sky dark and wind blowing newspapers and debris along the street, a day to draw your cloak close and mutter imprecations at the weather. Even so, the Pump Room was in a constant tumult, with people going in and coming out, meeting and chatting on the steps, hurrying to drink their daily quaff of the odiferous mineral waters, then departing to allow access to the healing waters for the less fortunate being wheeled in Bath chairs. Inside, as Anne escorted her brother and father about, stopping to introduce them to acquaintances, hurrying past those judgmental sorts who would put Jamey out of countenance, she spotted genuine joy. Her friends had answered her plea.

"Papa, there are people I would like you to meet." She tugged Jamey, who was openly staring at a lady with a very elaborate bonnet with watered silk ribbons. It also sported gleaming silver fishes caught in netting, which he admired. "Come, my brother, to meet the Birkenheads," she said cheerily, demanding Jamey's attention, physically pulling him away as the woman began to mutter to her companion, casting glares in her brother's direction. Anne had spotted Alethea, who accompanied her brother-in-law Quin and his new bride, the former Susanna Hadley, now Susanna Birkenhead.

Quin, who tired easily, walked with the two ladies on either side of him, appearing to escort them while in truth they supported him in his necessary perambulation. He looked good, better than he once had, stronger and certainly happier. Marriage—a quick affair Anne had attended with great pleasure—agreed with him. The Birkenhead brothers and their wives were in the process of moving together into a much larger townhome residence on the Crescent overlooking the lovely green park and haha in front of it. The move was imminent.

Susanna glowed. Perhaps society pitied her; she had married a man with physical limitations, true, but with a heart and mind so expansive it encompassed a world beyond what most saw or felt or experienced. Anne was happy for Quin. Susanna was the perfect helpmeet, her past pain and trouble making her a sensitive and tender companion.

The only shadow in her newly sunny life, Susanna had confided to Anne, was that a small inheritance that was supposed to come to her upon marriage was tangled in paperwork. Inheritance laws were archaic, in Anne's opinion, for though girls and women could inherit, the money was generally controlled by a man, in this case Susanna's father, nominally her guardian before her marriage. Once she married the money was supposed to come to her, but her remarried father was delaying, tying things up in a suspicious manner. Had he misused or misappropriated the money? Anne wondered. The Birkenheads were rich enough to pursue the matter. Lawyers were involved, but it could take time to sort out.

Not that Susanna needed to worry about it, for Quin was wealthy in his own right. She would never need to worry about money again. Still, there was a principle involved, for the money was hers.

Introductions were performed. Anne's father was immediately engaged in an involved conversation with Quin on abstruse scientific points concerning the Bath springs, the geothermal origins specifically. From there they spoke of the new science of geology, and theories on rock formation. This was not what Anne had intended. Once her father got on a topic of interest to him he could be single-minded and so focused he could not be swayed. This outing was to help Jamey adapt to Bath, and to show Bathonians that Lord Jamey was to be accepted as a temporary resident of their city.

She beckoned to Susanna, who helped steer the gentlemen to an out-of-the-way spot with comfortable chairs. Susanna guided her husband to a seat, while Anne ensured that her father and Jamey were seated on either side of Quin. Anne then asked the right questions to channel the conversation toward the ancient history of the Roman occupation of Bath. Portions of the Roman Baths had been unearthed in the earl's youth, and he was easily redirected, while Quin—who winked knowingly up at Anne—was knowledgeable on the subject. Jamey, whose darting gaze from spot to spot in the new surroundings warned of trouble if he was free to wander, became interested in Quin's informative conversation. Soon he was wholly taken up in esoteric information about the chemical makeup of the water and why it was thought to be beneficial, according to Dr. Fothergill.

Anne sighed with relief. Jamey needed a focus to help keep him happy in such a public forum, where the tumult could make him distracted and peevish.

Alethea, seeing Anne's family occupied, drew her aside. After greetings, and speaking briefly about the day before, she said, "Did you speak with Miss Collier's family?"

"I did," Anne murmured, looking about and smiling, nodding at those she recognized. She described the father and son, and how neither seemed distraught that Faithful was dead. "I was appalled by the two of them." Given her own warm association with her father, that aspect of the girl's life disturbed her more than any other. "Her stepbrother is a self-satisfied and smug fellow, but the father is a codfish with no warmth or genuine feeling."

"You judge him harshly," Alethea murmured.

"I judge him as I find him."

"I'm sure she had a perfectly fine home," Alethea responded with asperity. "Was the topic of her murder broached?"

"We could hardly come right out and say it, Alethea. I'm determined to discover who did it and will be going back there tomorrow morning. In fact, I will—" She broke off and stared. "How odd."

Alethea turned and gazed in the direction Anne was looking and murmured under her breath, "Who is that with Miss Dankworth?"

"Mr. Augustus Collier, Faithful's older half brother."

"Should we slink away and hide?" Alethea said, staring.

"On the contrary, we will make ourselves known to the pair and see what explanation is offered for two people meeting and speaking so urgently, when neither *should* know the other as well as this meeting implies."

"Won't that halt this interesting exchange?"

"Perhaps, but in this instance catching them out is important to discovering their business. Allowing them unfettered communication helps us not at all." She sailed across the Pump Room floor to the colonnade, by which the two were in urgent conversation. "Hello, Miss Dankworth, Mr. Collier. Delightful to see you here, though in such sad circumstances. How do you know each other?"

The teacher started back and gasped, but the gentleman was a cooler character.

"My lady, I noted your party's arrival," he said with a courtly bow, thrusting one buckled shoe and clock-stockinged leg in front and making his obeisance exaggeratedly deep. "Your father, perhaps? He favors you, as does . . . is it your brother, the other gentleman?"

"Yes, yes," she said impatiently. "My father and brother are here for my wedding." She eyed the teacher, who had shrunk back, her eyes wide. What a contrast these two were, one all confidence, the other all unease.

"You have met Miss Dankworth?" He smirked sideways at the woman, who colored deeply, appearing anxious. "She made herself known to me, seeing me and my father here taking the water for dyspepsia. My sister's teacher, I collect. Outré for her to be so forward, but what is a gentleman to say but *hello*, and *howdyoudo*?" He turned and stared at the lady. "What did you say you taught, Miss . . . er . . . Dankworth?"

"I t-teach c-composition, p-penmanship and introductory geography."

"There you go, it is *c-composition* and *p-penmanship*," he said, with a mocking lift to his brow.

She curtseyed to Lady Anne. Her color did not recede as, forced into the story the young man told—clearly a lie—she said hesitantly, "I thought I'd say hello to M-Mr. Collier, you see, and ask after his father. Such a tragic thing, losing a daughter so." She squinted behind her spectacles.

"You followed him here to the Pump Room and introduced yourself? Are you not needed at the school?"

Alethea, who had followed and listened in with interest, snickered. Mr. Collier gave her a sharp look before turning his attention back to Anne. "She did not need to introduce herself. We met at the school, yesterday."

Yesterday? She had understood the two men had arrived only yesterday evening. When would he have had time to meet the teachers? "And she didn't express her sympathy then?"

He narrowed his eyes. "Perhaps she wished to express a deeper sympathy."

"Mr. Collier, you are such a young man to be taking the waters. May I ask what ails you?" Anne said.

"Nothing afflicts *me*. My father is troubled by dyspepsia. He *was* here," he said, flicking a glance at Miss Dankworth, ". . . but has gone now to attend to the necessary arrangements for my sister."

"Your half sister, I believe?"

"As you say, she was the product of my father's unfortunate

second marriage."

"He was unfortunate in having two wives who died young, is that what you mean?"

"My stepmother was not young when she died."

Anne regarded him, wondering at his tone. He had not liked his stepmother and did not seem to care much for his sister.

Miss Dankworth, who had been dithering about as the others talked, sank into a curtsey and said, "I should be getting back to the s- school. I'm sure we'll meet again, Mr. Collier. My lady, Mrs. Birkenhead." She whirled, gathering her shawl about her shoulders, and fled.

The small hairs on the back of Anne's neck prickled as she watched her go. Something was up with that woman.

"You frightened her," Collier observed. "How cruel."

Alethea drew her breath in sharply. "How dare you say —"

Anne put up one hand to halt her friend. "He is entitled to make an observation, Alethea. But why *should* she be frightened, I wonder? And what makes you think it was cruel to ask questions? I'm sure she faces worse every day of her life, or she is not a woman. We are constantly being asked where we are going, what we are doing, and with whom, though we are rarely asked what we are thinking."

"You are perhaps the only woman I've ever met who would have an interesting answer for that, a question of what you are thinking."

"And you call *me* cruel?" She smiled to soften her quick remark. "You casually dismiss my entire sex with one pithy critique."

He smiled and bowed. "As they say in fencing, my lady, *touché*. You cut me to the quick."

"You are a fencer?"

"Merely a gambler who will bet even on fencing matches, and so I pick up the jargon. I will bid you adieu, my lady. It has been fascinating." He too hurried away.

"What are you hiding, young sir?" she muttered.

Alethea watched with her. "Do you truly think he could have anything to do with his sister's death?"

Reluctantly, Anne shook her head. "He was not even in Bath, and so cannot have been directly involved. But perhaps in some peripheral way?"

"The heart shrinks from such a thought, Anne. A brother to

murder his sister? And for what?"

"Perhaps my recent experiences have made me see danger and disillusionment everywhere. My imagination fails me for once. I cannot think of a single reason why he would want his sister dead." She looked back toward the happy group that conversed still in their absence. "How good your brother-in-law is to Jamey; look at how he keeps him engaged, including him in the conversation every moment. Quin is the best man I know."

"Do you include your husband-to-be in that?"

Anne smiled and glanced at her witty friend. "I do, you know. Tony is many things, but he is not so good as Quin, which suits me, you know, for I am not as good as Quin either."

"Be careful, Anne. You make Quin into a plaster saint," Alethea said.

"I think not. I don't know what you mean."

"A plaster saint is a modeled image of sainthood that would be shattered in an instant if it fell."

"And . . . ?" Anne stared at her quizzically.

"It is an image that will not stand up to rigorous testing," Alethea said. "Our image of others should be able to take a beating, withstanding stormy seas and gale winds."

Anne cocked her head to one side and examined her friend. "Would you say Quin is *not* good? Or not as good as I think him?"

"He is every bit as good as you think him." She smiled lovingly at her brother-in-law. "I cannot argue the case, I suppose, not with Quin being who he is."

"Then you have no argument. Let me think him a saint, to love and praise in a pious manner. What does it matter if he has faults I cannot see? I can never marry him now he is married, anyway."

"Now I *know* you jest," Alethea said. "You would not give up your Tony for anything, despite there being something of the devil about him."

"How right you are," Anne murmured with a shiver. There was a vast difference in her love for Quin, she acknowledged, an idealized love for a man beyond her understanding, and her love for Tony, earthy, carnal and impatient. Alethea had never seen the private face of Darkefell, the kindly, patient, gentle side of him.

It struck her how the image we have of anyone is a very personal image, made up of impressions, interactions, conversations, merely the public face of an individual. What did it have to do with reality? She had decided, from her conversation with Augustus Collier, that the man was intelligent to a degree, not overly fond of his half sister, sly, devious and satirical, a mocking fellow who thought himself far cleverer than he was, as those for whom mockery is a hollow talent so often do.

But what did she really know of any of the Colliers? She would have to correct her lack of insight if she was to discover the truth of Faithful's murder.

• • •

The next morning Anne took her tea at the desk in her room, reading letters as Mary bustled about tidying. Irusan wailed and clawed at her lap. Anne heaved him up to her shoulder. "What a big boy you are, my clever cat!" He clung to her, digging his claws in. "Ow, Irusan!" He was not usually clingy.

"He's bin unhappy, milady, all day yesterday, pacing and whining at the door," Mary said, pausing in her work and eyeing them both. "I let him into the garden, but he scratched the puir little scullery maid when she was sweeping the paving stones. He made prey of the broom and wouldne let her past him. Wee Robbie got him tamed, finally."

Wee Robbie, her son, was a clever lad of nine, small for his age but fierce and a fast friend of the beastie, as Mary called the cat. Irusan, named after a Celtic cat of myth and legend, was not small, weighing in at almost a stone and a half.

"What ails him, do you think?" Anne asked, carefully untangling his claws from her brocade gown.

"He's missing the country, milady, and missing you. For so long it was just you and him and me and Robbie, traveling and visiting, then back to home. In Bath you have much on your mind. You were gone all day yesterday, late into the evening."

Anne had gone back to the marquess's townhome with her father and brother, had dinner there, and examined the new celestial viewing platform on the townhome rooftop, despite the inclement weather. After, she had time alone with her fiancé, enjoying kisses that left them both irritated with the wait until they could be together as man and wife.

"Have you discovered what happened to the puir dead gairl, milady?"

"Not yet, but I will. She did *not* do away with herself, and I'll let no one say it. She was strangled, Mary. Who could do such a thing? I can't help but think it must be a man," she said, thinking of Jonty, or the dance, music and art masters.

"You've never seen Cook strangle a chicken? Her hands are great meaty paws, big as a man's and twice as strong. Dinna put yerself into that mind, milady. Was she a big strong lass?"

"No, not at all. She was tall but slim, not frail, but not robust, either."

"Then dinna say 'tis a man's doin' until ye know for sure."

Anne descended to breakfast, read the newspapers—in which there was no mention of the murder—with Irusan at his chair, paws on the table, eating a plate of creamed mackerel from the cook, who loved him dearly, and sent in his food in a Wedgwood saucer she kept for him.

She returned upstairs to dress. "The cream wool dress today, Mary, with the redingote. This evening, the *robe à la Anglaise*." The gown she'd wear that evening was new, a lovely sage green brocade with a sprinkling of embroidered ferns over the skirt, jacket and stomacher. It had an edge of embroidered roses along the open front, showing the exquisite lace petticoat underneath.

"Aye, milady," Mary said. "And the silk ferns for yer hair this evening, milady?"

"Yes, perfect."

Irusan stretched out on her bed, sated by creamed mackerel and a visit to the kitchen. "I'm nervous about dinner tonight, Mary," Anne said as her maid tied the waist of the cream gown. "My mother and my father in the same room for hours? It may be a disaster."

"His lordship the marquess will be there too, milady, and you know how your mother is around him."

"You have a point." Her mother was in awe of the marquess. "Mother will be on her best behavior. Grandmama may not be, though."

"Your grandmother likes his lordship verra much, though, milady.

Don't borrow trouble. It'll all be for the best. And whate'er happens, it'll soon enough be over."

• • •

Anne's plans to return to the school were destroyed by her mother, who would not hear of her leaving. If she was going to be upset and nervous and distracted about the dinner party, Anne would suffer alongside her. The countess made numerous descents to the kitchen to shriek at the cook, then rampaged elegantly to the housekeeper's office to have stern discussions about fish forks, marrow scoops and oyster forks. Why could they not get the caviar she wanted? For royal palates only? Balderdash, she raged.

Anne followed, soothing hurt feelings and calming frayed nerves, only to find that her mother had gone on to frighten the maids and harry the footmen. The countess then returned to the housekeeper, changing course removes that had already been discussed and causing commotion in the kitchen again. Anne's grandmother railed at her daughter for being a pudding head and the countess, in tears, needed to be soothed. It was exhausting.

Anne sent a note to the Lees giving her excuses, that her mother and grandmother required her. She put it into a footman's hand and sent him off. She would much rather have been investigating, but this hubbub concerned her wedding. In fairness, she must help her mother.

The afternoon was spent much the same way. Irusan crept away to sleep in Anne's room, aware that the countess, not fond of him at the best of times, was in a rare taking, flinging things about and insisting loudly that no one in the house was cooperating with her.

Anne and her mother had a testy relationship but this one time she understood that the countess was terrified. She had not seen her husband in years, nor her son. Jamey had frightened his mother years before by accidentally hurling Anne out of a second-floor window. Anne was badly hurt and suffered even now from a lung ailment, but she knew that her brother did not mean her harm. She had never blamed him, for they had been playing too boisterously and he was stronger than she. However, the countess insisted he be sent away. It took years to right that wrong and find a solution, but the countess had never recovered from the shock. Her habitual manner of handling distress was to retreat, and so she had, with her husband's agreement, moved to Bath.

Remembering that awful time while Jamey was away made Anne determined to help her mother and brother rediscover a relationship. The countess was not hard-hearted, but she was emotionally fragile and needed time and coaxing to see a way through it all.

Finally, it was time to get ready. Anne held Irusan on her lap as Mary did her rich chestnut hair. Her mind returned to the thorny problem of who killed Faithful Collier. "What an unnatural pair that father and brother are! Neither one of them terribly upset she was dead."

"P'raps it's their way, milady. Not everyone's the same."

"True."

"You said yerself you dinna think the brother had whate'er to do with it."

She watched Mary's skillful hands in the mirror, silk ferns woven into her dressed hair, with golden pearls to contrast the sage green of her gown. "Perhaps the seed pearl parure tonight?" she murmured.

"Aye, milady," she said, and fetched a velvet box. She set it on the dressing table.

Anne opened it and stared at the set, an intricately woven collar of seed pearls surrounding baroque cabochon pearls, with a bracelet, earrings and hair decorations to match. It had been left to her by her paternal grandmother, and she treasured it as a reminder of that great lady. What had Faithful had to remind her of her mother, she wondered, or her grandmother? And to whom would it go now? "Faithful was hiding something, I don't know what. Why would she fear a ghost cursing her family?"

"P'raps it were those tales she heard, you know, all that nonsense in books: castles, ghosts, curses!" Mary's *r*s rolled over her tongue in her most dramatic brogue. Anne smiled. Clasping the necklace about Anne's neck, Mary regarded her in the mirror. "What do the gentlemen do for work? Could it nae be aboot that?"

"The father is a barrister. The son studied the law but was not successful in making it a career and is now a clerk in a shipping company. A *slave* shipping company."

"How did the gairl feel about that? P'raps she felt he was cursed for workin' for such folk?"

"You may have something there. But it's entirely possible that what she feared had nothing to do with her family but was about something else." She stood and shook out her skirts, patting her hair as she turned and viewed herself in the mirror. "Mary, you're a genius. You've taken this poor partridge and turned me into a gilded swan."

She descended to the ground-floor reception room to await their guests. This expansive and gracious townhouse on the Paragon in Bath, Everingham House, belonged to Anne's grandmother, the Dowager Viscountess Everingham. The current Viscount Everingham— Anne's cousin—was a dutiful son and faithful correspondent presently studying in the Holy Land. Unmarried, with no children, his estate was cared for by the heir presumptive, another cousin. Anne's mother had been living with the dowager for a few years now, her entrenchment in Bath society complete. She had her own clique of friends and a benign beau in Lord Westmacott, who escorted her to every social engagement, from the opera to the theater to the Upper Rooms.

Anne fidgeted, her mother's anxiety like an infection, spreading to her. The countess swept in, calmer now the battle was about to be joined. She had taken great pains with her appearance, Anne noticed, pouring her anxiety into fussing with ribbons and hair and jewels. She wore the Harecross parure, an elaborate old-fashioned set comprising a diamond and emerald collar with a pear-shaped emerald drop, earrings, a wide bracelet, and a tiara that encircled her high powdered wig. It was too much for a small family dinner party, but Anne was not about to chastise the woman. "You look wonderful, Mama," she said.

Lady Harecross nodded, a tight smile on her powdered and made-up face. The dowager viscountess toddled in at that moment on the arm of the handsomest footman, who aided her to an upright chair with a seat not too low for old knees. She sank down, sighing deeply, then glanced around, nodding at her daughter's and granddaughter's appearance. "Shall we begin the festivities?" she asked dryly. "Sherry, Griffiths. And bring the bottle."

Chapter Thirteen

Lydia and John arrived first. Happy to be out after a long confinement, Lydia prattled happily to the older ladies, gossiping, laughing, gesticulating, gasping in astonishment at every tidbit of news. Lady Harecross had invited her beau, Lord Westmacott, and he was an inveterate gossip of the best kind, with a determined wit and gentle wisdom. Truffle, the butler, ushered him in and he was immediately pressed into service, relaying witty stories and keeping everyone merry.

A few minutes later Truffle announced, in his plummiest tones, "His lordship the Marquess of Darkefell, his lordship the Earl of Harecross, and Lord James Addison."

Tony caught her eye and nodded. Anne's father, appearing anxious, paused on the threshold, but Jamey rushed forward, nervous and frightened, agitated by his emotions. Anne's mother stood, took a deep breath and said, "Jamey, my son, how are you?" Her voice faltered and cracked, but it was well done.

The portly young man's eyes widened as his gaze fixed on the countess. Anne's brother had an exquisitely perfect ear for sounds. He could identify birdsong in the forest, the softest cheep to the loudest caw. This time he recognized his mother's voice. He darted to her and stared into her eyes, hands clasped in front of his protuberant stomach. He lurched forward and seized her in a strong hug, so powerful that Tony strode forward and murmured something to him. He released his mother and looked up at the marquess confidingly, nodding, then turned and made his bow to his mother.

To Anne's astonishment, Lady Barbara's lined eyes welled and one single glistening tear trailed through the powder on her cheek. "Jamey?" she said, her voice breaking.

"Mama?"

As Anne watched, tears welling in her own eyes, they hugged again. He took Lydia's place between his mother and grandmother, happily telling them about the new telescope and how he was going to watch the stars with Tony and Papa from the roof of the marquess's townhouse. Among his chattering was strewn Tony this and Tony that. The earl ambled over and took a low chair nearby, listening with a pleased expression. His wife darted glances at him, and finally put out her hand. He took it and squeezed. Something intimate passed between them. He nodded. She offered a trembling smile.

Anne sagged in relief. "Oh, thank God," she murmured, a mixture of prayer and thanksgiving. Tony took her hand and led her out to the chilly entry, folding her into his embrace. She leaned on him, inhaling his smell: good wool, port wine, leather and something else that was all him. "Oh, Tony," she murmured. "This is all your doing. You've been so good to them, and you've worked wonders with Jamey. How did you manage it?"

She could feel his lips curve into a smile against her forehead. "My darling, I was merely the conduit through which goodwill flowed. I enjoy his company, you know. He is honest with his emotions, and unafraid of me, when others find me —"

"Intimidating?" She laughed up at him.

He chuckled, a rumble in his broad chest. "Maybe that's why I love you so much. You've never been afraid of me. My only hope is that Jamey trusts me."

"He does, Tony, he trusts and relies on you." She looked up at him. "His mind works differently. With Jamey, some days are better than others, and we have learned to tell what is a good day and what will be a bad."

"I think I am beginning to learn that too."

"I don't know why, but he was never able to learn how to control his emotions when he was a child. He is much better now than he was when we were young. Then, he was unable to calm himself. Now, given the right focus, he can. That is what the Carters do for him, and what you have learned to do."

They stood together in silence for a long minute. Darkefell finally said, "Jamey has a brilliant mind and a good and kind soul. He *wants* to please. He adores you all and it overcomes him." His voice had become clogged and he cleared his throat. "I have come to love him, Anne. For a while, I thought his mind childlike, but it isn't, and I will never condescend to him again. He has taught me much." He frowned, struggling to explain his revelation. "His is a curious view of life. It is not, however, a child's view, but that of a man with a unique perspective and understanding. His skills of observation are truly impressive. He will be my brother and will be welcome in our home when the terrible day comes that your father is no longer with us,

God willing it is not for a score of years or more." He turned back, gazed down, and kissed her, his lips sweet from brandy.

Time passed and she finally murmured against his lips, "We must get back to them. They'll notice us missing."

"I don't think I can go back yet."

She chuckled. "Let us sit for a moment in this cold entry and talk." She broke away from him, took his hand, and led him to a pair of chairs along the wall. He would have continued the kissing but she smacked his hand and said, "My lord, you forget yourself." Truffle eyed them as he passed through the entry, which aided the marquess in his cooling.

Her thoughts returned to Faithful's murder. Anne had already told Tony what she had witnessed the day before in the Pump Room. "I don't know what to think," she said, returning to the puzzle. "Why would the teacher be meeting Faithful's brother in the Pump Room? Despite their claim that it was an accident or a coincidence, it felt clandestine, secretive. She was not pleased that I saw her and spoke to them. He was nonchalant about it, but he is the kind of young man who thinks he has it all in order. That he can dupe anyone with his dubious charms."

"You don't like him," he said dryly. "And I do trust your judgment. No doubt he is a loathsome pup. Do you truly suspect him of killing his sister?"

She considered it. "He was not in Bath at the correct time, arriving after the fact with his father."

"That is not an answer. Do you suspect him of killing his sister?"

"Why *would* he kill Faithful? I can't think of a single reason."

"Still not an answer, Anne," he pointed out. "Can you think of a reason for *anyone* to have murdered the poor child?"

"She was hardly a child, Tony. She was seventeen. Some girls are married at or even before seventeen."

"I cannot think of the girl you describe as anything but a child. Some girls at seventeen are quite ready to wed and many more are not. However, I asked a question."

She thought about it, drawing her shawl about her shoulders in the chill of the entryway. She should be in the sitting room making sure her mother and Jamey were getting along. She should be supporting her father. She should be making sure her grandmother was comfortable. She should . . . she sighed and felt her shoulders slump. So many *shoulds* and just one her. And yet, there had been no outcry from the next room. No loud tones, no angry words. They would get along without her at least for a while. They *must* get used to being without her, for within the month she would be married and on her way north with Tony.

"I suppose that's the problem," she said, in reply to his question. "None of it makes sense to me."

"You're missing a piece of information that would *make* it make sense."

"True. And you're right, I don't like Augustus Collier and would prefer he is the killer. That's not rational, I know, but I don't want the killer to be from within the school." She thought it through. "That's the problem: to be completely honest I *can* think of reasons why someone would kill Faithful, but it would mean someone in the school is a murderer. I pity Miss Lee, should it come to that. She has worked too hard and does too much for girls. I see the pain on her face, in her eyes."

"But the more quickly this is solved, the more quickly she and her sister can move on with restoring her school to equanimity."

"Sisters," she said automatically.

"What?"

"She has two sisters there, Harriet and Anne. All right, Tony. Let me see." She settled against his bulk, in the curve of his arm, and spoke into the chilly dimness of the entry. "With whom should I start?"

"With the Misses Lee."

"Oh, Tony, no!" she said, looking up to see if he was smiling in jest. He was not. "Neither lady would do such a heinous thing."

"Why do you say so?"

She sat, mouth open for a moment, then shook her head firmly. "No. It is out of the question. They are ladies. They would no more hurt one of their students than I would."

"Aha, because you see yourself in them, you discount the possibility that there rages in their bosoms strong emotions: love; jealousy; desire; cupidity." He paused. "Hatred."

"All right, say I give you that point, those are emotions, not motives."

"One I did not mention comes to mind: fear."

"I beg your pardon?"

"Fear. We all experience it at times. And it is a motive for murder, certainly. I have seen men driven by cowardice kill to avoid a loss."

"A loss?"

"Of a loved one, money, or even of standing."

She sat up straighter, away from his sheltering warmth, and shivered. "Oh."

"You've thought of something."

She had, the possibility of fear. "When the Lee ladies' father died five years ago, Sophia took every cent of her earnings from *The Chapter of Accidents*, a successful play at the Haymarket Theatre, and sank it into the Bath school. It supported her, her sister Harriet and their sister Anne. It is *everything* to them, Tony. It is their livelihoods and their independence, their home and . . . and their pride. If the school's reputation is ruined, it will ruin *them*."

"And . . . ?"

"And if Faithful knew something or was about to reveal something . . . purest speculation," she said. "The girl was troubled by something and I'm no closer to knowing what it was than I was the day I spoke to her." She shook her head. "Tony, it doesn't make sense to suspect the Lees. Whatever loss of standing or reputation you think would happen to them, it is far worse that a student was murdered in their school."

"Did they know it would be discovered as murder?" he insisted. "If you had not brought in Dr. Fothergill, would it not have passed as tragic misadventure by a superstitious girl?"

"They called me in themselves beforehand, to solve her ghostly troubles. Why would they if they were guilty of a nefarious deed?"

"If I was planning a heinous act that's what I would do. They brought you in before the deed, and you witnessed the odd superstitions of the girl. You would be a valuable witness to her state of mind that they could point to if she killed herself, or even if she disappeared."

Or if her body was found in the River Avon. "You're saying I was used?" Her voice echoed in the chilly hallway.

"Perhaps."

"I cannot, at this time, exclude the Misses Lee. However, I would argue that bringing me in was too much of a risk if they worried about the disclosure of some awful secret. What was to say she wouldn't confide in me, exposing them?"

"You have a point."

"Going back to the Collier son, what do I know of him? Nothing."

"You said he was not in Bath at the time, though."

"Do I know for sure? I was basing that on their story that he arrived with his father from Bristol, after a summons from Sophia."

"And so it is with the father. Whose word do you have that he was not in Bath the whole time?"

It seemed far-fetched to her he would plot to kill his own daughter. "However, we need not strain credulity. As much as I dislike it, there *are* suspects aplenty in the school itself. My father has spoken of William of Ockham, who posited that one should always prefer the simplest explanation."

"Not quite what Ockham —"

"Tony, do not argue with me," she said, one hand up. "I know that's not exactly what he said, I'm paraphrasing."

He grabbed her hand and kissed it, then moved to her neck, his teeth nipping at her flesh in a most delectable way. She gave in for a long moment, gasping with pleasure, but pushed him away. "You have to leave me alone, Tony," she whispered. "Or I shall go mad with wanting you."

He sighed and straightened. "Who else could you suspect of ill doing within the school itself?"

"The others are the students, of course, but also the two female teachers. And there are three men, the dancing, music and art masters. Though they do not live in, they may have been let in by someone. Above them all in my list of suspicious characters are the housekeeper and her husband, who though he is not allowed inside, is as untrustworthy and dubious a character as I have ever met."

"Do not judge him a killer because of it, though. Many men are of dubious character and are not killers."

Irritated, she said, "Tony, I hope you know me better than to think I will take the easy way out of this tangle. I am not naïve enough to believe that because I loathe the man he must be guilty. And I hope our life together will not be a constant barrage of telling each other obvious things."

He smiled in the dimness and touched her cheek. "I should know better. Duly noted, my future wife."

They rejoined the others, who looked knowingly at each other, nodding and smiling at the engaged couple's return. Jamey leaped up and trotted to his new favorite, put his arm through the marquess's and led him about the room, showing him all the things he remembered from his childhood visits. When the viscount came back to Bath from the Holy Land, on occasion, he brought treasures from faraway destinations, ancient pottery, statuettes, vases and goblets. Jamey remembered them all and explained them in clear, ringing tones.

The countess and earl carried on a stilted but friendly conversation, aided by Lord Westmacott. Lydia kept the elderly dowager entertained with her observations on the perfidy of nursemaids and how they would not let her touch the baby unless she sprinkled rosewater on her hands. John followed his older brother and Jamey about, earnestly offering his opinion on their sojourn in Bath, what they should do, and what Jamey should see.

Anne watched it all with delight and relief.

Dinner was announced. They trooped in together. It was lovely to see the countess on her husband's arm, though Lord Westmacott looked out of countenance to be left alone. Anne took Jamey's arm, and Tony took the dowager viscountess, to her delight. She flirted up at him, using her fan to shield her crepey, rheumy eyes in a way that would charm any human with a soul.

Lydia continued her vivacity but began to weary during supper. The gentlemen agreed not to linger at the table and to join the ladies in the drawing room, where all eschewed cards for the moment, and conversational groups formed. Lord Westmacott, in his element, retailed gossip to Lydia, as John indulgently held her hand in a most scandalously fond manner.

The elderly beau finally turned to Anne and said, "Your reputation as a fierce lady of intelligence after solving that mystic misfortune is set now, and we must call on you to solve all of our little mysteries henceforth. I hear you are tangled up with the Misses Lee and their school calamity. Shall I tell you what all I have heard?"

Tony cast her a humorous glance. To hear her solution to the mystic mystery related in such a beneficent and condescending manner would in the normal course of events drive her wild. But she had long known the gentleman and excused him, understanding his heart and his friendliness. The gentleman could not bear evil in the world, his sympathetic heart wounded deeply by tragedy, so he coped by reducing the tragedy to a mystery for his friend to untangle.

There was no better source on Bath gossip than his lordship. "Do tell, Westmacott. I shall hang on your every word."

He spoke of how the Misses Lee were regarded. "They do not move in society, of course, but as a playwright, Miss Sophia Lee is respected. One of our theatrics club members begged her to write a play for us, but alas, she claims to have no time."

And likely no inclination, for the amateur theatrics society to which his lordship alluded would never think of paying for such a service. Miss Lee was a writer, yes, but a businesswoman too. "You know them, sir?"

"I know Miss Harriet, but not the other ladies. Miss Sophia is busy with her writing and Miss Anne . . . nobody sees *her* much. Have you read *The Recess*?"

"I am awaiting it from the subscription library."

"Oh, my dear, I have all three volumes and shall loan them to you whenever you wish. Most entertaining. I do not know how she manages with so many girls in her school. And she has had trouble, between staff and parents . . . it must be a nightmare." He shuddered in an elegantly distressed manner at the tribulations of those who work for their living, and fanned himself.

"What kind of trouble have they had, sir?"

"Keeping a housekeeper has been a challenge."

"She seems happy with Mrs. Thompson."

He made a face.

"What of it? Do you know anything?"

"Oddly enough, I do." He bent toward her and murmured, "My housekeeper is sister to the cook at the school. She is a veritable gushing fountain of information!"

Anne suppressed a smile. Lord Westmacott, for all his posturing, would sit down for a cozy gossip with a highwayman, a charwoman, or coal shoveler if he thought he'd learn aught of interest. "And what has she said about the Thompsons, wife and disreputable husband, Jonty by name?"

"Their cook is concerned, my dear, for she has heard things at night. She says that the housekeeper woman creeps from her bed at night and has been seen out in the garden, speaking with a man."

"Her husband sleeps out in the shed in the garden. I had supposed she does creep out to spend time with him."

His lordship dropped a wink. "Not her husband, a runty little man, I am told, but a tall fellow." He raised his brows and waggled them.

Anne wasn't sure what she was supposed to take from that. "Westmacott, are you saying it was an assignation?"

"What else could it be?"

"I can think of a hundred things it could be other than an assignation, sir."

"Name one," he said.

"She would not be the first housekeeper—nor the last—who made extra money by selling waste from the household."

He stared at her. "I don't think I understand."

"Your housekeeper, dear sir, will sell the used tea leaves from your table," she informed him. "She will sell ragged linens that are beyond darning, she will sell anything you have expressly agreed to throw away."

He was silent.

"And that is because she is a good servant. A good one is allowed to sell candle stubs, tea leaves, scrap paper, as I said. A bad one will sell any number of things she thinks won't be missed: whole candles, tea, wine, food . . . even silver, or dishes."

"How do you know all of that, my dear? A girl like you, properly raised, genteel. How?"

She glanced over at her mother and grandmother. "I don't think gentlemen realize that the world in which women live is consumed with household drama. I was my father's housekeeper for a time, when ours left after Jamey . . . after a problem." She turned away. That bad time was over; life was now on an even keel and headed to safe harbor. She smiled and turned back toward him. "In short, the housekeeper may have been in the garden by moonlight arranging for the surreptitious sale of such items, maybe even stolen items from the household. The information will not go unheeded, for I had my suspicions about those two, and this aids my investigation. If she is meeting a tall man outside at night—"

"Oh! I've remembered that my housekeeper said the Lee cook told her the tall man was a gentleman. And she could tell even from above, out the window on a moonlit night, that he held his arm close to his body in a most peculiar manner."

A shock ran through Anne, as though she had touched metal on a thundery day. A tall man who held one arm close to his body? She could think of one fellow who answered that description admirably.

Mr. William Collier, Faithful's devoted father.

Chapter Fourteen

Though she chafed at the obligation, Anne knew her duty; church attendance was mandatory in Bath unless one was infirm. Service at St. Swithin's was as good a chance as any to catch up with others who may be able to aid her in any number of ways, domestic or investigatory, so she sent a note to invite Susanna and Quin Birkenhead to share their family box. Alethea accompanied them, while her husband begged off, as he had things to arrange at the new home they were to move into soon. It took Quin a few minutes to mount the steep stairs to the box, but Tony helped him up.

As they all settled, Tony made sure his guests were comfortable. Following the service he would be taking them for a drive in the country, after which they would explore the city. The countess had agreed to accompany her husband, their future son-in-law and their son. Though Anne was invited, she had declined, for she had investigating to do.

Anne spoke softly with Alethea, filling her in on all she learned and suspected. She related what Lord Westmacott had told her the night before, of the Lees' housekeeper's suspicious behavior, and the man in the garden with the lame arm. "That must be Faithful's father. What is he doing creeping into the school garden for an assignation with a housekeeper?"

"Are there no other men with one lame arm about Bath?" Alethea whispered. "When was this?"

"You, my friend, are supposed to go along with my every discovery and agree readily with all of my conclusions," Anne said with a smile. "Else what are friends for?"

"And here I thought being a friend meant being honest and expressing my beliefs in a forthright manner." Alethea smiled back.

"Of course, you are right. As my elder, I must listen to your wisdom." Anne giggled.

Her mother gave her a stern look. "Girls, behave yourselves in church," she hissed.

Which sent both younger ladies into fits of suppressed laughter. "I am ten years old again," Alethea said.

"Likely the last time I feel that way," Anne said, glancing at her husband-to-be. Her thoughts returned to the puzzle of the Lee school tragedy. "Poor Faithful," she said. "If it *is* her father who murdered her, I'll see him hanged. I lost all yesterday to Mother's demands. Today I will spend investigating. Look!" She indicated with a nod the gathering congregation below. The Misses Lee had entered, followed by her two teachers and the older students.

Quin, sitting on her other side next to his wife, leaned into her. "Is that who I think it is?"

Anne gave an affirmative and whispered their names. While the Misses Lee kept themselves rigidly composed, the same could not be said of the teachers, nor the students. Miss Hopewell, it was true, kept her demure gaze fastened on her gloved hands, clutching a hymnal, but Miss Dankworth's frenetic gaze traveled all about the place until it lit on one fascinating object.

Following the line of her stare, Anne discovered the Collier gentlemen, seated near the doors. The father was composed and interested, examining the architecture of the church—she noted that incriminating withered arm pressed close to his frockcoat—but the younger gentleman was gazing back at the teacher. He nodded and winked, touching one finger to the side of his nose. Miss Dankworth glanced at her colleague—to see if she was being observed?—and, noting Miss Hopewell was staring in the other direction, nodded in return.

"That is the young gentleman with whom that teacher was speaking in the Pump Room yesterday," Quin murmured, glancing at Anne. "And he indicated it was a chance meeting between two people who did not know each other."

"And yet today they communicate in a rather familiar matter. Why, I wonder?"

"An affair?"

Shaking her head, Anne frowned. There was no romance there, or she was not as astute an observer as she fancied herself. And yet, there *was* an intimacy. Perhaps the lady wished there was a romance; the intensity of her gaze behind her spectacles was fevered. When Miss Hopewell turned her attention to her colleague, Miss Dankworth averted her eyes. "How odd," Anne murmured.

"But not necessarily related to Miss Collier's murder," Quin said. When Anne swiveled to stare at him, he smiled faintly. "Fothergill tells me everything, you know."

"I disagree, Quin, that it's not necessarily related." She told him what Lord Westmacott had said, about his housekeeper's information concerning the man with the lame arm, and how the description matched the elder Collier. "And yet it is the son who is communicating secretly with a teacher. There is a secrecy I do not like." Were the father and son *both* involved in a plot to kill Faithful? She had all but dismissed them as having no motive, and yet . . . there it was. The nagging suspicion of the two had returned.

Quin turned as Susanna asked him something. The service began. Anne noted that Jamey was becoming restless, twisting and turning in his seat, chatting to strangers in nearby seats, hallooing down below, waving to everyone. Her mother was pink-cheeked in embarrassment, for these were her people. Even though she did love her son she had always found him difficult, especially when he was drawing attention to himself, unlike others his age.

This would be the test of her mother's determination to make a new start with her family, Anne thought. Would she separate herself from them, or would she take ownership of the situation? Tony saw the turmoil and was about to intercede. When Anne shook her head slightly, he frowned, but sat back.

The earl, unfazed by his son's exuberance, smiled at some gesture and nodded. He included his wife in the conversation, and the family whispered as the sonorous tones of the congregation lifted in a hymn filled the church. "All Ye Who Seek for Sure Relief " rang out, the pipe organ majestic and filling the upper pews with resonant tones. The countess took her son's hand and urged him to sing with her. His lusty but tuneless voice joined her warbling soprano, drowned by the diverse voices of the whole congregation.

The rest of the service passed. Tony, with a lingering touch of Anne's cheek with his ungloved hand to carry throughout her day, departed with the earl, the countess, and their son to his awaiting carriage, where Osei also waited to tour Bath and its environs, after which they would dine at the marquess's townhouse. He told Anne he considered it an honor to look after her family for the day.

Anne approached the Lees, who were gathering their things to follow their teachers toward the door. Both women were hollow-eyed. Harriet shared a glance with her older sister and, taking her elbow, tugged Anne aside. "May we speak, my lady?"

"Certainly, Miss Lee. Shall we go out to the lawn?" They strolled out into the chill of a December day. "How were you all yesterday? I'm sorry I was not able to come when I said I would."

Harriet nodded, distracted. She strolled to the green lawn and kicked at a clod of dirt. "Yesterday was awful. The girls are all upset. And as for me . . . I can't sleep with anxiety. I keep thinking of that poor girl, remembering Faithful. She was such a nice child, but something had been worrying her lately. I'm devastated we didn't pay attention, didn't notice."

"Does it help to know she did not kill herself?"

Harriet gave her a sharp look. "Not really, because it means there is a killer about, and we know not who it is. We've tried to keep the girls calm, but the more timid ones are fretting."

"I'm sorry for what has befallen you and your students and staff," Anne said. "And most of all for what Faithful went through in the last moments of her life."

"I don't know what to think," Harriet said, pacing and twisting her gloves in her ink-stained hands. She was a clear-eyed woman, intelligent, with solid opinions and a lively mind. "Nothing in my study or reading has prepared me for the sensations of being close to such a tragedy." She turned and stared at Anne. "How could this have happened at our lovely academy for young ladies? I am bereft."

"What did you think of Faithful?" Anne asked, curious about her friend's impressions.

Harriet took her time, ordering her thoughts as she toed a stone, rolling it over. "Faithful had wit. She had imagination. How much more did she need?" She frowned and stared at an elderly yew tree in the church garden. "Clearly the whole ghost story . . . preposterous. She was *too* imaginative, perhaps."

"And yet I have been told she was not that imaginative at all."

"I disagree with that," Harriet said.

"I found her intelligent and thoughtful."

"The untutored intelligence of a child. She was young for her age."

"You speak of her imagination. Is it her belief she was being haunted you speak of?"

"All that nonsense was in her imagination."

"Her death wasn't."

Harriet winced and looked away, shivering in the cold, waving to her sister, who had gathered the students together on the walk, awaiting her young sister. "I must get back," she said duly. "We hold to a schedule even on a Sunday."

"Harriet, please, wait. You *know* that Faithful's imagination, far from running away with her, was fed by factual evidence of her eyes and ears. She *was* being haunted, though the specter was not supernatural but very real."

"What you are saying is the haunting was a prank."

"For heaven's sake, did I not say it from the outset?" Anne said with an exasperated sigh. "Did your sister speak with you about it?"

"I can't help but think that it seems so very unlikely. I cannot believe it. Who would do such a cruel thing? And why?"

"It may have started off as a joke, then devolved from there." Anne hesitated, watching Harriet for a moment, then said, "I've come to wonder if there was a sinister motive behind it."

"What do you mean?" Harriet asked, staring at her.

"It feels more menacing than a prank. The suggestion that she kill herself was despicably cruel. Can you think of anyone who would benefit by her dying?"

Harriet shook her head. "Not a soul. How would anyone benefit by a seventeen-year-old girl's death? I'm baffled by the whole affair. How will it end?"

"I hope it ends with us finding the culprit and bringing them to justice."

"Will you come back with us today and dine?" Harriet asked with sudden decision.

"I accept," Anne said with alacrity. "Will the two teachers be at the table?"

"Of course. Do you suspect either of them?" Harriet asked with alarm.

"I'm not sure yet what I think." She would withhold what she had observed of Miss Dankworth with the younger Mr. Collier for the moment. For a female teacher's reputation was as important as her credentials. To sully the young woman's prematurely could be to ruin the woman's life.

Harriet nodded. "Walk with us?"

"Let me say goodbye to my friends, first, then I will join you."

Harriet looked toward the door where Alethea, Susanna and Quin were slowly exiting. "If you would like Mrs. Birkenhead to come we would welcome her."

"I'll extend the invitation. She may have plans with her husband and brother-in-law. Maybe she can join us later if she's busy now?"

Harriet nodded.

Anne strolled back toward the door, pausing to glance toward the schoolgirls gathering on the walk, clad alike in their pale cream dresses and blue spencers, their hair dressed almost identically except for the colors of their hair ribbons, each individual, perhaps so they did not become confused. Miss Hopewell, wearing a fetching bonnet with a white plume drooping over, stood with them, but she cast a worried glance into the distance. Anne's followed hers. There was Miss Dankworth, half hidden from view by a yew hedge. She appeared to be arguing with young Mr. Collier. The gentleman took her shoulder roughly and shook her, after which she broke away and fled across the green expanse of autumnal lawn toward the others.

Anne, alarmed, was about to go after her, but she could tell the young woman was not hurt and was returning to the security of her friends. Instead, holding her cloak about her in one fist and her hat with the other, she hastened after Mr. Collier. She followed him down the steps from the lawn to the Paragon below and caught up with him. "Stop! Mr. Collier," she gasped, out of breath. He whirled and stared at her, his face blank of recognition at first, while anger obscured his gaze. Then he sneered and bowed with little pretense at politeness, such was his fury. "What is going on between you and Miss Dankworth?" she demanded, panting.

He glared at her. "What is it to you?"

Rudeness was a wonderful tonic, freeing her from courteous restraint. Bluntly, she said, "You took Miss Dankworth's shoulder roughly. You shook her. She fled." She stared at him and smiled brightly. His cheeks were red, his brows drawn down over dark eyes clouded by anger, but he didn't answer. "You claim the merest acquaintance with Miss Dankworth. How did that give rise to such strong emotions as were evidenced by you seizing and shaking her?"

He fought his anger and appeared to win, taking in a deep breath and letting it out in a long sigh. "If you must know, she accused me of . . . never mind."

"Did she accuse you of killing your sister?"

"What? Why would I do such a damnable thing?"

"That is not an answer. Did you kill your sister?"

He stiffened. The color ebbed from his cheeks as insolence crept back into him. People strolled toward them. He swept a low bow to her. "My lady, I bid you good day." He strode away.

Troubled by his attitude and failure to answer—though he was certainly not required to answer, but why wouldn't he, after all?—she returned to the lawn above where Miss Hopewell was speaking with Miss Dankworth, who had returned to the group. It hadn't escaped her that he had seemed surprised that she surmised Miss Dankworth had accused him of murder, so what *had* she accused him of?

Miss Sophia Lee had joined her sister and looked askance at Anne. "I understand you raced after a young man?"

Anne stiffened and her chin went up. Miss Sophia Lee was a few years older and perhaps felt justified in criticizing, but Anne was not one to be chastised by anyone. "I accosted Faithful's brother, as a matter of fact, for laying hands on Miss Dankworth. I would like to speak to her, if you don't mind, and find out of what she accused him."

She turned and stared at Miss Dankworth, who shrank away in fear, tears running down her face. The young woman stumbled away and appeared to be trying to get herself under control. "I'll have a word with her."

Miss Harriet Lee glanced across the lawn at Miss Dankworth, then touched her sister's sleeve. "Perhaps it would be better if Lady Anne speaks to her first."

"Harriet, a teacher of ours should not be speaking to either of the Colliers, much less accusing one of doing anything at all," Miss Sophia Lee said. "That is not their business."

"I saw them together in the Pump Room yesterday," Anne said. "Maybe she was merely expressing condolences. I'd like to ask her about it." Silence from the schoolmistress, who appeared undecided. "You did ask me to look into this."

"I know I did, but things have . . ." She stopped and sighed, nodding. "As Harriet's friend and with Alethea's recommendation, I suppose I must trust you. Come along, everyone," she said, raising her voice for the benefit of the students, who were milling about whispering to each other.

"I have not yet spoken to Alethea Birkenhead," Anne said to the younger Miss Lee. "I was distracted by the Collier situation. I don't see her anywhere."

Harriet said, "She approached me to ask where you were. I told her, then extended the lunch invitation. She said she has a commitment but will see us later in the day."

Anne nodded. As the Lee sisters gathered their straying students, she noticed Alys standing alone and went to speak with her. "What's wrong, child?" she asked the girl.

Alys looked up at Anne, her eyes wide with fear. "I don't understand why any of this is happening, my lady."

Anne gently said, "I am going back to the school for lunch. Shall we walk together, arm in arm? Do you have a friend who will walk with us?"

With a glance, Fanny Patterson was invited. Seeming chastened and fearful, the fey child took Anne's arm on the other side. They followed the group of teachers and students as they departed the churchyard onto the Paragon, then turned to the left and walked.

Fanny was silent, and looked troubled in a way that suggested there was something on her mind. They had already discussed the possibility of Henrietta Greerson being involved in the tricks played on Faithful. Was there more? When they arrived at the school and were about to enter the front door, Anne took Fanny's arm. "Fanny, would you walk with me?"

The girl nodded and allowed Anne to draw her away as the door closed behind Alys.

"What do you want, my lady?" the girl said.

Anne regarded her kindly and said, "Let's just walk." The child acquiesced and they strolled. Anne glanced back and saw a flash of blue in an upstairs window, and a curtain drawn hastily. One of the girls was watching them. They strolled a ways down the Belvedere to a quiet green lane between buildings. Anne drew her to a bench and sat with her for a moment in silence. Gently she said, "Pardon me if I am mistaken, Fanny, but I had a sense, as we chatted, that there was something you wished to say but you hesitated. Perhaps something you did not want Alys to hear?" She searched her companion's face.

The girl, her cheeks pale and her expression frozen, stared at a shrub and worked her lip between her pearly teeth. Clasping her gloved hands together, she said, "Oh, my lady, it is nothing, except . . . except I cannot think what she said to Faithful, and what she gave her."

"What who said to Faithful? Fanny, I'm not sure I understand what you are saying. Which girl spoke to Faithful?"

"Henrietta."

Chapter Fifteen

Anne remembered Fanny's contention that the two girls had gone from friends to enemies only recently, and how Henrietta had seemed so evasive and afraid when last they spoke. "Henrietta spoke to her the night Faithful died?"

"When we were getting ready for bed. I saw her whispering to Faithful and giving her something, and she nodded."

"Which of them nodded?"

"Faithful."

"What did Henrietta give her?"

"I think it was a note. Faithful unfolded it and read it."

A note. Anne couldn't decide if it was relevant to Faithful's death or not.

"And there's something else, my lady. Later Miss Hopewell was gone from the room too."

"Miss Hopewell was gone from her bed that night at the same time as Faithful?"

She nodded. "I was awake, you see. Perhaps I am accustomed to the noise Miss Hopewell makes when she sleeps. When it stopped I couldn't sleep."

"So, you saw Henrietta Greerson give Faithful a note. Later, Faithful was gone from her bed, as was Miss Hopewell," Anne summarized. The child nodded, looking relieved to have told. "Why did you not say this earlier?"

"I didn't know if I *should* tell. Henrietta never left the room, so I knew she hadn't done anything but . . . you won't tell her what I said, will you, about the note?" she implored.

"Are you afraid of her?"

"She's mean sometimes. B-before, I had Faithful to look out for me, but now . . ." She sobbed, tears streaming down her face. "Poor Faithful is gone!"

Anne offered a muslin handkerchief to the distressed girl. "I will not say it is you who saw her. Tell me, when did Faithful leave the room?"

"I don't know," she whispered, dabbing at her eyes.

"What about Alys and Julia?"

"Alys was still in bed. She is next to me, by the wall. I think Julia was there, but I'm not sure."

"Is there anything else, Fanny?" The girl shook her head, looking weary but mightily relieved, her eyes drying. It had been a weight on the poor child. "We had best get you back to the school," Anne said, taking the child's gloved hand and walking with her the short distance to the school.

At the door Fanny paused and handed back the soiled handkerchief. "What shall I say if they ask me what we talked about, my lady?"

"Tell them it is none of their business," Anne said tartly. Fanny's eyes widened and she looked worried. Of course the child could not say that. "Tell them I was asking you questions about the school. Be vague. Say I wanted to know what you thought of the art master, and the dancing master. When I speak with the other girls I'll ask the same questions. What *do* you think of the male teachers? Like Mr. Russell."

"I don't like *him*. He doesn't give me lessons that help. I want to paint fairies, and he says I cannot paint fairies because they are not real. I must paint things that are real." Real to him, in other words. On the other hand, the dancing and music master were kind, she said.

Anne reached out and cupped her cheek. "Fanny, you paint whatever your imagination tells you to paint. Paint, draw, sing, write anything at all. I wish I was artistic, but I am not. To those who are, I say, do what *moves* you, what gives you pleasure, what soothes your soul."

Fanny's smile as she looked up at Anne was radiant and she grabbed Anne's hand tightly, leaning into her with all her slight weight. "Thank you," she whispered. "And thank you for caring about Faithful."

A bell was chiming as they entered. Miss Sophia Lee shepherded girls toward the dining room, a line of giggling little ones going first, followed by their more sober elders. She gave Anne a sharp look, primmed her mouth, but nodded regally. Harriet took Fanny's hand kindly and led her behind the others.

Miss Sophia said grace, with a special remembrance of Miss Faithful Collier. Luncheon, a more elaborate affair on Sundays than weekdays, Anne learned, was served. There was soup—adequate, though not perfectly cooked—and a joint of roasted mutton. Anne watched the young ladies and the teachers as she ate. Fanny had provided interesting background. What other information was being withheld? Who had seen something but was too afraid or embarrassed to say it?

After lunch the girls were to sit in the dining room around the table and engage themselves in stitchery, art, writing letters, or some other quiet task. Both teachers were to monitor their work and give help when required. Anne beckoned Harriet Lee to the front entry, the most private spot on the ground floor. "May I speak with the girls and the teachers this afternoon?"

"My sisters and I are having trouble believing any of this is real," Harriet said. The pale oval of her face was touched with gray light coming in the sidelight windows on either side of the door. "I know I'm repeating myself, but I can't quite grasp it. Was Faithful truly murdered, or is there another explanation, something we've overlooked?"

"It was not an accident, and it was not self-harm," Anne snapped. She took a deep breath, calming her temper. She took her friend's hand and led her to a bench. "I know the polite heart recoils from the thought of such evil as would take the life of an inoffensive young lady. Harriet, admit the facts and be done with it; Faithful was strangled. If you had seen the body, you would not be in doubt. One does not strangle oneself falling from the roof."

Harriet caught her breath at the harsh speech. "Poor child! Can you truly discover who did it simply by talking to the students?"

"No, I need to speak with the teachers, the masters, and Jonty Thompson." Harriet looked troubled. "I'd like to speak with Mrs. Thompson before her husband." She thought of Lord Westmacott's assertion that the housekeeper had been seen in the garden talking to a gentleman.

"That's not exactly what I meant," Harriet said. "I'm asking how can you find out who killed Faithful just by talking to people, *any* people?"

"How else do we discover truths but by talking to one another? People lie and are caught. I ask questions until someone contradicts themselves, or says something I know to be blatantly false. Now, tell me about the household. Will you show me the layout of the sleeping quarters?"

"They're on the second floor. Sophia and I have a suite of rooms, while Anne has her own small room." Harriet looked over her shoulder toward the door. "Wait here." She strode away, then came back. "The girls are occupied and Sophia is speaking with Cook about supper. I have a few minutes before I'm required again."

They mounted the stairs to the first floor. "Where do you find the time to look after school matters and your writing?" Anne asked. "Surely your real work suffers from the demands of running a school for young ladies."

"Who is to say which is my real work?" Harriet muttered. She looked over her shoulder with a faint smile. "Aren't women kept dependent on others to tell us our place? Ladies I am acquainted with discover their true vocation when their gentlemen tell them what it is. Usually, their life's work turns out to be whatever pleases them. The gentlemen, that is, not the ladies." She shook her head. "Ignore me. I am full of pique for the moment. I don't mean to slight Faithful — she was a sweet girl — but I will be irritable and annoyed until I can return to my routine and see progress on my writing."

Anne was silent, not sure how to answer.

Harriet looked down at Anne's face in the shadowy half-light of the staircase. "I've shocked you." She shrugged. "I'm selfish, and I know it. I have managed to build for myself a routine that allows me to devote the better part of my emotion and time to my writing. I react badly when my schedule is upset, even by something so tragic as murder."

"I sympathize with your plight most keenly," Anne said, looking up at her friend. "It does answer my question; your writing is your real work."

"I suppose that's true, but other tasks must be done first, unfortunately."

They continued upward.

"Obligations. Can we ever escape them?" Harriet muttered. "After our father died Sophia felt responsible for me, our sister Anne, and our other sister. She took the entire proceedings of her successful play, *The Chapter of Accidents*, and established this school." Harriet's voice held tension. It seemed she had no choice in the matter, to live and work here, in Bath. "I can do aught but work my hardest to make this a success, and now this . . . this horrible event threatens it all."

"You have been here in Bath five years, though. It is a goodly amount of time."

"We are women; reputation, that fragile social shade of our real selves, is all to us," she said as she reached the top of the stairs and turned. "And besides, the safety of our girls is paramount. We spoke of what my real work is. I carve out time for my writing, but most of the day's daylight hours and most of my effort and thought and ambition *must* go to making this school a success, to pay for our living. It is like dancing on a razor's edge at times."

"You have a brother, though," Anne said, of George Lee. "Should he not be contributing to your living?" It was his responsibility in law, as their closest male relative, to financially provide for his sisters.

"Our younger brother pursues his own prosperity," she said shortly. "He learned from our choleric father that the theater is a beguiling but treacherous mistress and considers himself better off working as a clerk at Mr. Drinkwater's cotton mill in Cheshire." She said dully, as she swept one hand along the hall, "This floor holds the schoolrooms." She led the way. "There's not much to see. We have a music room with a pianoforte and harp."

Anne looked in and crossed the floor to a trunk. She opened it and saw, in the faint light, that there was a tumble of gray diaphanous fabric—like that of the image Faithful saw in the mirror—and a skeleton hand and skull. Everything needed to create the phantom image, as she had suspected.

Harriet didn't comment on Anne's incursion into the music room. She led on to two other sizable chambers, where the girls took their lessons on history and literature, mathematics, geography and other useful topics. "We balance our own thoughts on the education of women with the inevitable wants and needs of parents," Harriet said. "We do our best to turn out thoughtful young women."

She opened one door onto a room where stood a circle of small tables with a slate tablet on each, chairs lined up behind. Beyond that, lining the walls, were spacious low shelves with books on England and the world. On top of the shelves were folios of maps and globes. Anne strolled into the room and picked up a pocket globe, opening the case and taking out the earth, a smooth painted representation of what was known of the world upon which they lived. Inside the case was a representation of the heavens, a celestial map of the stars and constellations.

"How amazing," she murmured, turning it over and over. "What a lovely place we live upon," she said, tapping the globe, "and yet we sully it with pain and hate and murder."

An exclamation behind her made her whirl. Harriet was sobbing, tears wetting her cheeks, as she leaned on a table, wiping her eyes with the back of her hand. "How *awful* this is!"

"I'm sorry. I didn't mean to raise unpleasant associations."

Harriet shook her head and said, "It's not you. I've been trying to suppress my feelings, but they *will* be acknowledged, or I shall run mad. Poor Faithful! What did she suffer in her last moments? To know she was choked and tossed like a rag doll —"

"Harriet, did you have any inkling she was afraid of anything. Or anyone?"

"Not at all." Harriet took in a deep breath and let it go, her shoulders slumping. "And yet she stared out her window and seemed sad. Having met her father and brother, perhaps that's not surprising."

Pleased to hear the natural acerbity back in Harriet's tone, Anne said, "You don't like them. Why?"

"Mr. Collier is a man I have met many times . . . or let me clarify. Though I have met him only once or twice, I have met his *type* many times. He has little or no use for females in general, not even his own girl-child. He will do his duty but no more, as on the ledger of life she exists in the debit column. I hope she was happy here, at least. I will never be sure."

"What of the son?" Anne asked, thinking that of the two, father and son, he certainly seemed the more unreliable a character.

"Mr. August Collier, failed solicitor," Harriet sniped with a grimace. "He is another type I have met before. You know them too, I would imagine, for they proliferate in society. He is expensive and vain, vacuous, and yet smug. He is a young gentleman who is conceited beyond any quality of mind or character one could imagine him to possess. None of which he does possess, by the by, in my estimation. Faithful was his superior in heart and mind, for she was the soul of kindness, sympathy, and innate intelligence, and yet she would, in their household and beyond, be his inferior. Her treatment of little Fanny, who the older girls laugh at for her flighty ways and imaginative mind, was more than laudable, it was . . ." Her voice choked as emotion was again victorious over self-control. "Faithful's behavior was all I would wish to see, if I had a daughter."

"Faithful was experiencing bullying. Have you ever witnessed such behavior among the students?"

Harriet straightened and stared at Anne, tears drying in pucker trails on her cheeks. "Do you know the bullies?"

"I do, but both appear to regret it now. It seems it was a thoughtless hoax. It may be more than that, but I need to look into it further to be sure."

"That's what the haunting was all about, a stupid hoax to bully poor Faithful? I will say, I never thought the girl was a fabulist attempting to draw attention to herself. She wasn't the type."

"That's what I told Faithful when I met with her, that she was being tricked."

A young maid hastened down the hall, her shoes clattering on the polished hardwood floor, and stared into the schoolroom at them. "Miss Harriet, Miss Sophia needs you right away."

"Why?"

"She didn't say, miss. But she was most insistent." She appeared frightened, then looked over her shoulder and back to Harriet. "Two of the girls are quarreling, miss," she whispered. She fled back downstairs, the sound of her hasty retreat disappearing with her.

"We can come back up after I've dealt with this," Harriet said, moving toward the door.

Anne did not follow. "Let me look about for a few minutes longer, then I'll follow you downstairs. I do wish to settle that little matter of which we were speaking."

"The haunting?" she murmured.

"Yes. I'd like to examine the angles and the mirrors and the light upstairs, in the girls' rooms, if I may? To see how the hoax was performed."

"Why? Faithful is dead. She can no longer be tormented."

That was true, but she had other motives for wishing to be alone upstairs. Instead of enumerating them, she simply said, "Maybe there will be a new victim. Wouldn't you rather I explore every possibility?"

The schoolmistress stared at her for a long moment, then turned to go. "I will leave you to it." But she turned back at the door, hand rested on the jamb, her expression haunted with fear and worry. "I know there is more to your desire to look around. It isn't the haunting hoax. Go wherever you need to go, my lady, and explore whatever will help you come to a conclusion," she said. "I trust you to help us. I'll make sure you're undisturbed."

"And then I will speak with Miss Dankworth, in particular, as well as others."

Harriet nodded, then turned and swept out of the room, her booted feet tapping along the corridor.

The girls' chambers, servants' quarters and egress to the roof were Anne's immediate concern. She quietly moved from the schoolroom to the hall and listened at the head of the stairs. The sound of a dispute rose to her ears. Anne turned to the stairs to the next floor and started her ascent.

Chapter Sixteen

As she climbed, she imagined Faithful doing the same, following a specter that floated to her, urging her to self-destruction in the name of her mother. Faithful said the voice told her that her mother had been punished for being immoral, and that she was headed down the same path to destruction. Henrietta had confessed to bullying but was she the sole voice, or did someone with a motive to harm Faithful take advantage of the hoax?

Hand on the banister, she paused and listened, imagining the scene in the dark. The staircase was open, turning and turning upon itself at landings, two runs for each floor, making it economical as to the space it took within the house. Sounds echoed upward in the vertical space, voices from rooms below murmuring to her like a whispering. Even before she had seen this, while Faithful was still alive, she had imagined how the trickery was accomplished. A voice from above would float down to one like a ghost's whispering, drawing one upward seeking the source. And the stairs, turning upon each other . . . using a mirror and candle one could create spectral flashes of light in the staircase even as one remained hidden.

That was how Faithful's ghost was created, the spirit that led her to consider death. She was tricked with the aid of her own beliefs and fears and her past suffering, along with the physical aid of light and mirrors. Despicable. Anger burned in her heart that Henrietta would misuse her erstwhile friend.

And yet . . . how was Faithful lured up to the attic on her final night if Henrietta was abed, as other girls claimed?

Perhaps the hoax was used by another to trick Faithful into going upstairs on the night she died. Or did she have another reason? Anne stopped at the next floor and glanced about. Two hallways stretched out on either side. She knew from conversations with the Lee sisters that their rooms were to the left, and the girls' rooms were to the right.

She had dismissed the Lees as suspects so she turned right, familiarizing herself with the layout of the other rooms. A reading room fitted with chairs and a study table offered nothing of interest. The two girls' bedchambers were at the end of the hall, one facing the front of the house, one overlooking the back. The one overlooking the front was the little girls', overseen by Miss Dankworth. She glanced into the rooms but would explore the roof access first before the dispute below quieted down and Harriet or Sophia came looking for her.

She climbed the staircase to the attic floor, where the servants were quartered, vacant this time of day as everyone was busy downstairs. Directly in front of the staircase was a deep alcove with a double set of casement windows letting in midday light, brightening every corner of the drab hall. Did the windows open? They must, for this *had* to be Faithful's point of egress.

Anne strode across the hall and examined the sill. There were scuff marks, but she already knew Faithful had climbed up there voluntarily one night. She put her hand on the painted metal latch of the window, about halfway up the frame in the center. Could Faithful have climbed out alone? She would soon find out. She wanted to know two things: was it possible for a girl to climb out the window, and what would she find once she did? It would have certainly been simpler for Faithful than Anne, given that she would have been in night attire at the time.

Anne twisted the stiff latch but it resisted, so she put all her force into it, twisted and then pushed. The window wrenched open with a screech that echoed through the hall and down the stairs. The momentum of the sudden opening made her stagger forward, and for a moment, cold air flooded around her. She was staring at the ground below, the very paving stones where poor Faithful died. She grasped the window frame and clung to it, keeping herself from tumbling out, her heart pounding in alarm.

It would have been all too easy to fling oneself out the window.

But given that noise, how could Faithful have done that herself in the quiet of the midnight school without awakening every single person on the attic story? She couldn't. Servants would have been abed nearby and the sound would have echoed. She was a slight girl and had not appeared strong; would she have even been able to wrench that latch?

The window had to have been left ajar for her. It must have been done even before the servants retired for the night, she supposed. Anne examined the latch and noted the window could be closed without latching it.

"What are you doing up here?"

Anne yelped, whirling, her skirts belling about her. She stared at the young woman before her and didn't know how to answer. She stood on the penultimate step, hand on the newel post, her eyes fixed on Anne. She was dressed fashionably in a pretty moss green round gown with a lace tucker, so she was not a servant, and she was too old to be a student. Anne glanced down; she was shod in soft house shoes, kid-soled, no doubt. That's how she had crept up the stairs quiet as a mouse. "Who are you?" Anne asked.

"I beg your pardon, I think I have more right to ask that question. Who are *you*?"

Examining her, Anne traced a resemblance. "You are the other Lee sister," she said.

"That sounds like an accusation," the young woman said with the trace of a smile. "I suppose I'll admit it. Who are you, and what are you doing up here? I was preparing a lesson plan for Harriet and heard the most dreadful clatter. You, it appears, wrenching open the attic windows." She shivered and rubbed her shoulders. "It's too cold for open windows."

"You and I have something in common," Anne said with a faint smile. "We are both named Anne."

The other lady's expression lit with understanding. "You are the Lady Anne my sister Sophia has been speaking of."

"And you are Miss Anne Lee, sister to Miss Sophia and Miss Harriet Lee. You weren't with them in church this morning."

"I don't attend. You want to know how Faithful fell," the younger woman said with a nod toward the windows.

"I already knew how, but I wished to see it for myself. Not idle curiosity, I promise. I am trying to learn what happened. How she died. It's so noisy that someone must have left the window unlatched and perhaps even ajar in advance of her arrival. This racket in the middle of the night, with servants who would have retired or were in the process of retiring, would have brought too much attention."

"There is a way to open it quietly," she said. "Look." She went over, closed it, then lifted it in a particular way and opened it. It made not a sound.

"You'd have to know how to do that to open it quietly."

"And she was unlikely to have that skill. I see your point. You surmise it was a plot beforehand, not a sudden urge." She crossed her arms over her chest, hugging herself and shuddering. "It's terrible to contemplate evil seeping into the very bones of this house."

Startled by the vivid imagery, Anne examined the young woman. She was pleasant-faced, of medium height and coloring, her hair simply dressed. On closer inspection it became evident that her gown, though neat, was worn, cuffs turned and stitched and turned again, ink-stained and slightly grubby, bony wrists poking out. She was not the public face of the Lee school, whether by choice or of necessity, Anne did not know.

"I thought I heard something that night, you know," she said, eyeing the window and considering.

"What did you hear?" Anne moved to the window and examined it. There were those scuff marks she had observed on the sill, of boot heels, it looked like. Faithful had been wearing kid slippers, had she not?

"Sophia and Harriet share a room, but I have one alone, a tiny closet by the stairs, off our sitting room. I do think I heard this window being opened, or perhaps the thump I heard was Faithful climbing out the window. I'm not sure now if it is my imagination running away with me, but I would *swear* I heard a cry in the night."

"What time would it have been?"

She ruminated. "I was reading a book, one we are considering for the students, and finding it impossibly boring. Not bad, boring. My attention was not overly engaged and I may have been nodding off. Everyone had gone to bed, maybe as much as two hours before. I believe I heard the chimes for midnight. The sound came, as close as I can recall, shortly after."

Anne lightly touched the scuff marks on the sill. "I am not convinced Faithful climbed out the window that night on her own."

"Was her previous foray out the window a mere coincidence?"

"I spoke to her the very day before she died. She had no intention of climbing out there again for any reason. Tell me, Miss Anne, what time does the serving staff go to bed?"

"Who knows when that old cow Mrs. Thompson goes to bed? I've seen her creeping out to her husband's shed after midnight."

Out to her husband's shed, or out to meet the mysterious withered arm gentleman? "Have you, indeed? Is it possible that her husband gains access to the house at night?"

"He's not supposed to. It would mean his job if he were discovered inside after hours and both their jobs would be forfeit if his wife let him in. Sophia is strict about the 'no men in the house at night' rule. But I don't know for sure that he doesn't. Do you suspect him in Faithful's murder?"

"Do you think he's capable of it?"

She chewed her lip, her gaze distant and unfocused. "I suppose I can imagine it, but that means little."

"You don't like the Thompsons."

"Not at all."

"Why?"

Again there was that pause as she reflected, the lip chewing a necessary part of her reflection, it seemed. "He is sly, yes, but there is malevolence in *her* gaze occasionally, when she thinks she is unobserved. It is in a flash of her eyes as she watches Sophia walk away, or a sneer as she regards Harriet. Am I being imaginative?"

"I don't know. I've not noticed anything in the woman, nothing untoward, anyway, but I have only met her on her best behavior. You have lived with them. That is a big difference, and I'll keep it in mind."

"It's quite possible she does not like me and there is nothing at all wrong with her."

"What an odd thing to say!"

"Why?" the woman asked. "Have you never had an unreasoning prejudice toward someone? Or has no one ever not liked you, and you don't know why?"

"I suppose," Anne said. "But when it happens, I am determined to understand it."

"I can't be bothered. There are already too many people in the world to deal with. When someone doesn't like me, they'll avoid me, and that works out perfectly. What were you going to do next if I hadn't interrupted you?"

"I was going to climb out there and sit on the window ledge."

Anne Lee looked horrified. "Good Lord, our school would never recover if you tumbled to the pavement below. The newspapers would scream about the elegant Lady Anne dying in a horrible accident at the notorious Lee school for young ladies."

Anne snorted in laughter. "All right. But I *must* know how easy or difficult it would be for Faithful to do so, in the middle of the night."

"Let me," Miss Lee said, striding past Anne to the window. "I'm thinner than you and my gown is less fashionable and less . . . puffy." She leaned forward and thrust the top half of her body out, looked to the right and left, and shuddered. "How high from the ground do you suppose we are?"

"Forty feet, at least," Anne replied, amused by the intense Miss Lee.

"I overheard Sophia and Harriet talking when they thought I couldn't hear. As ridiculous as it seems, they feel the need to shelter me as their younger sister." She gave a short humorless bark of laughter. "They don't, but I won't correct them. It keeps me insulated from having to listen to much of the politics of school life. Anyway, your doctor friend informed them Faithful had been strangled and tossed out the window." Anne Lee's hand crept to her throat and she shuddered. "So isn't it immaterial if she could have *climbed* out the window? And yet, would she not struggle? Would she not cry out? Why would I not have heard her, or the servants?"

Anne considered Miss Lee's comments. She moved toward the window. The woman was right. There were servants right down the hall. Faithful would have screamed and kicked if she had been strangled in this hallway. "There would have been a lot of noise if she struggled. You're right, I suppose, and neither of us need sacrifice our comfort for the sake of that experiment. So that is evidence that she was thrown out the window in a surprise attack, then strangled below." Anne eyed the window with a frown. "It does raise a question: how much strength would it take to throw the poor girl from the window?"

"How much would Faithful have weighed?" Anne Lee asked. "I'm terrible at estimating weight."

Anne considered it. "Seven stone, or close to it. On second thought, I don't think she would need to be *thrown* from the window."

"What do you mean?"

Anne stared at the window, strolled to it, looked out and down. She put her hands up as if she was strangling someone, then shook her head. As bizarre as this moment was, with Miss Anne Lee she was not self-conscious about it. "If he — or she — surprised Faithful, who was moving toward the window anyway, say, and pushed her suddenly, would she not have fallen out?"

"Practice on me," Anne Lee said.

Anne eyed her thoughtfully. She was serious. Anne Lee moved toward the window and faced it, relaxed, trusting. Anne moved toward her, put up her hands, grasped her shoulders and pushed the younger woman toward the window. The sill was low, below the hip, and as Anne pushed Miss Anne Lee she realized that if she made the motion violent enough, Anne Lee, about the same height as Faithful, would have sailed out the window with force. "It wouldn't take strength, just surprise and determination."

Anne Lee nodded and turned. "Exactly what I thought."

"It had to have happened swiftly with no time to scream or struggle." She took in a deep breath and closed her eyes as she let it out. "I hope she didn't suffer," she whispered.

"So we have established that anyone could have done it. Come with me," Miss Anne Lee said. "You will want to see the girls' rooms."

The young woman turned out to be a good collaborator. She stood near the door of each room watching in bemusement as Anne carefully strolled about, examining books left on tables by beds, bureaus against walls and one near the door to the hall, clothes hung on hooks, and finally stopped by the bed closest to the door.

"This is Miss Hopewell's bed," she said.

"You're right," Miss Lee said. "How do you know?"

"It's obvious," Anne replied, fingering the tin of face cream, a leather-bound journal, a worn copy of *Evelina*. She looked at the other woman. "She tells these girls tales at night, stories supposedly taken from her own life. I suspect they are altered fictions from the novels she reads." She turned and eyed the room, imagining it in the dark. Faithful crept out, and one other. Miss Hopewell was apparently not snoring, though she usually did. Was that because she was not in bed after all? Was she the one who crept out after the student?

She shook her head. She had no reason on earth to think Miss Hopewell was responsible for Faithful's death.

Miss Lee looked at her pocket watch and exclaimed, "Oh! I must retreat, my lady."

"What time is it?"

"It is two in the afternoon. I have commitments."

Anne raised her brows.

"Private tutoring," Miss Lee explained. "I may not teach in a formal sense, but my time is even more taken up as I give individual lessons in topics such as French literature and art history. A schoolroom of girls for an hour once a day would be heaven, but because I have no literary pretensions I must take up the slack and make sure our girls graduate with sense in their imbecilic brains."

"I don't think teaching is exactly your métier, if I may say so."

"No, nor is tutoring, but I must earn my keep. My sisters already do enough for me, as I am reminded constantly when I balk at my obligations. I fulfill my duties."

As the tutor bustled away Anne heard her name being called from below. Osei had arrived, asking if she was present. Her father had sent a request that Anne meet him and Jamey at a shop on Milsom. He wished her opinion on something. The two elder Misses Lee accompanied her to the front door. Both women looked haunted and unhappy.

"Mr. Collier is coming back tomorrow," Miss Sophia said. "He wished to come today, but I said on the Sabbath we expect all to spend their time in worship and quiet handiwork. I told him I would be packing his daughter's clothes, but he insists he will do that himself."

"How odd," Anne said, hand on the doorknob. She thought about it but could come to no conclusion. "I'm sorry I have to leave. I will be back tomorrow morning."

Chapter Seventeen

"What shop owner would be open on a Sunday, Osei?" Anne asked as he handled the reins and set the horse to a trot.

"The shop is not open. His lordship is speaking with a jeweler who is anxious for his trade. They are at the shop to discuss something about which he wishes your opinion."

"I am filled with trepidation," she muttered, huddling into her shawl. "Perhaps you can look into something for me."

"I am at your service."

"Thank you. I'll try not to take advantage." She glanced over at him. "I know how much you have to do, with the marquess in residence, and my father and Jamey now staying with him."

He didn't deny it. "Your request will be an interesting diversion, I'm sure."

"I'm *not* sure. I wish to know more about the Collier men, how often they come to Bath, what they think of Faithful's death."

Osei pondered that. "Such gentlemen may not be amenable to chatting with me," he warned.

"You're right, of course."

"But I know how to get to them."

"How?"

"His lordship may be looking for information on investing in a shipping company in Bristol."

"You'll enlist Darkefell?"

He glanced over at her. "No, *you'll* enlist his lordship. Do it tonight, after dinner. Please give him something to do, for he is rattling around Bath like a bear in a canary cage."

Anne laughed. "He's a restless man, Osei; don't I know it. Too much vigor."

Osei helped her down at a shop on Milsom. Initially built as a row of townhomes twenty-five years before, one of which Lydia and Lord John lived in currently, parts of Milsom had now been given over to shops. It was quickly on its way to becoming a fashionable street, where jewelers, drapers, milliners, cutlers, printers of music and the like jumbled together in a hotchpotch of shopping delight. On a Sunday all was quiet, with a few folk strolling and looking in windows at the arrayed delights.

A lad unlocked and opened the door to the shop. Osei nodded and drove off as she entered. In the dim interior were her father and Jamey, who was exclaiming over a watch that promised to tell the phases of the moon. Anne's father sat at his ease as the shopkeeper, an exceptionally thin gentleman in a powdered wig and elegant blue silk waistcoat, bowed and scraped Anne into the shop. The apprentice, a lad of fourteen or so, bustled about, lighting candles and lamps to illuminate the dull interior.

"Anne, dearest," her father exclaimed. "Come sit with me. This is Mr. Myles."

She nodded to the shopkeeper, then looked about with interest, for it was a magnificent shop, jewels and silver and gold gleaming in the flickering candlelight. The jeweler set a small round table between them, laid a midnight blue velvet cloth over it, and with reverence laid upon the cloth a diamond rivière collar. A rivière piece of jewelry held one type of gem, in this case glittering diamonds. He bowed and backed away.

"I recognize this from Mama's wedding portrait," Anne exclaimed, picking it up and hefting its weight. The painting of her mother still hung at Harecross Hall, in the drawing room. It was an enormous canvas, four by seven feet at least, and presented the countess as she was then, slim and lovely, gowned in sky blue, the collar of diamonds at her exquisite throat, one hand raised in an elegant pose, presenting an urn of roses as if she had grown them herself, and the other touching her slim throat.

"She always disliked it," the earl said in bemusement, staring at the costly jewels.

"Did she? Why?"

"She says it is too heavy, and I think she is right."

"You may have something there," Anne said wryly, setting the jeweled collar down on the velvet. "It is exceedingly heavy."

"I had a brainstorm when I had this brought from Harecross, or rather, *Jamey* had a brainstorm. Didn't you, son?" he called out fondly, as Mr. Myles anxiously followed Jamey's path in the shop, from glass case to glass case.

The earl's son looked up from staring at an ornate snuff box and nodded.

"He saw the collar and said 'crown,' to which I replied no, it was a collar, but he shook his head most emphatically and again said it was a crown. And he is right! Mr. Myles has said it is possible. What say you to having the collar made over into a tiara for Barbara to wear to the wedding?"

"Is it possible? And in such a short time?" She looked over her shoulder at the jeweler.

Mr. Myles darted forth, bowed and murmured, "If I may, my lady? I know your esteemed mother's taste, and I have a suggestion to make, if I may?"

"What is your suggestion, Mr. Myles?"

"Lady Harecross has exquisite taste. This collar is exquisite, but heavy and old-fashioned. Your dear mama is such a fashionable lady! My suggestion is, I could convert it to a tiara, yes, and in a timely manner. I have a man who will devote himself to the task. The tiara I have in mind to design could quite easily be made back into a rivière necklace, albeit one with a lighter modern style. The excess diamonds can be made into earbobs that will complement the tiara. Here, if I may, I could draw it for you." He snapped his fingers and the lad dashed away and came back with a sketchbook and a pencil. Mr. Myles straightened and sketched — Jamey looked over his shoulder in wonder — and in three minutes presented the finished product. Jamey clapped in delight and pounded the disconcerted jeweler on the back, muttering "well done, sir, well done!" over and over.

Anne glanced at the sketch of a lovely tiara with matching earrings, then back up to the jeweler with respect. "You have hit on it, Mr. Myles. Father, I think you should take his advice. I have one concern," Anne said, eyeing the enormous diamonds, a king's fortune in one piece. "There have been robberies of shops on Milsom lately. What kind of security do you have to protect such a valuable piece?"

He smiled and nodded. "Your ladyship is current with the news, I see."

"I am, sir." There had been thefts in Bath of jewel shops, but more of private collections. Tonnish sorts were nervous. Some had hired protection to guard their valuables. Others grumbled that local magistrates were not up to the task of seeking out the wrongdoers. They dare not wear their best jewels to the opera or the Assembly Rooms for fear of being intercepted. At first Anne had written it off as foolishness, but then Alethea and Bertie had been waylaid one night on the way to the theater. Bertie had given the fellow a black eye and he got away with nothing. After that they were careful. He had purchased a German-forged iron safe and was having it installed in their new home. Alethea was having paste copies made of her most valuable jewels. "I ask again, what precautions have you taken?"

Mr. Myles turned serious. "We have a vault, my lady. Among Bath jewelers, we are at the forefront in guarding our customers' valuables."

Anne smiled. "Thank you for allaying our worries. Papa, I think you should proceed. Mama will be most pleased."

• • •

After their business was successfully concluded, Anne and her father and brother eschewed the Harecross carriage, for the day was fine, if cold. She walked on her father's arm, with Jamey sometimes trailing, sometimes ahead of them, depending on his interest in buildings or plants. Up Milsom they strolled, toward George. Her father suggested an impromptu visit to Lydia and John and the new baby, but Anne said a formal planned visit would suit the couple better. She knew Lydia, and spontaneity induced, in her, spasms and panic. The baby consumed her day and night. Even with a nursemaid to attend, the new mother kept to her bedchamber in a robe until afternoon.

At George Street they were about to turn to go up the Paragon, to walk to her grandmother's house, when Anne said, "Papa, could we not walk a little ways out of our way?" She explained what she wished to do. She had told him all about the trouble at the school, and he, an advocate for girls to learn whatever they could in the world, was distressed, fearing it would set the students away from their studies.

He agreed to her planned detour and Jamey was happy, for she promised him a bit of nature rather than the dusty roads of Bath. They strolled along and were almost to the Lee school when she stopped at the path that led away from the street. "Papa, I wish to show Jamey the park down this lane. Would you kindly wait?" She knew her father's stamina was not what it once was. In the country he could tolerate a fair walk, but the town wearied him, and the path sloped downward. Down would be all right, but the path back up would be taxing.

He looked askance at the shadowy path, but Jamey was a stalwart protector of his sister. "Don't be long, my dear child, for I suspect the footpads do not take Sunday off." He smiled.

Anne and Jamey descended the path that led to the park she had seen from the back upper windows of the school. "What do you think, my dear brother?" she said, looking over at his cheerful round face. "Are you willing to have a bit of an adventure with your naughty sister? Like the time I asked you to get me a certain plum from the tree and you climbed to the tippy top and plucked it?" She thought to test access to the walled yard from the park below.

He grinned, his doughy face puckering. "I remember, Annie. You *were* naughty. Mother was angry. She said I could have broken my arm. I said I didn't, so it was all right."

They walked down the path, arm in arm, the day darkening around them as the shrubberies along the path closed in. She had seen the school's yard, but she wished to see how private it was, or if it was overlooked. Could a stranger have gotten into the schoolyard? She was haunted by the smear of Faithful's blood on the flagstone. To where did the assailant intend to drag her? And why?

The path opened out into a green area, sloping away from them, with a wooded area still to the right and the slope up to the school on their left. "Let us walk along this hillside. Find me acorns, Jamey. And pretty leaves to make a dried arrangement."

Given a task, Jamey was indefatigable. He dropped her arm and strode off, gathering into his jacket pockets acorns from a mighty oak, cones from a pine, and plucking great handfuls of plumy drying grasses, identifying them assiduously as he did so. Anne led the way until she saw, above the rise, the recognizable roof window of the school. She was about to move closer to the hill, to climb the slope to the stone wall at the top of the rise, when she saw two figures nearby, on a path at the bottom of the hill below the school. It was a man and a woman. As she approached, she recognized Mr. Augustus Collier and . . . who was the lady? Oh! It was, of all people, Miss Carlotta Dankworth. When she had seen the same two at the Pump Room they claimed to have met by accident. This was no accidental meeting.

Jamey followed her gaze and saw the pair. He stopped, his gaze flicking back and forth from Anne to the pair. He frowned. The couple argued, their voices floating on the cold still air.

Her voice tinged with hysteria, she cried, "You lied to me! How could you say —"

Collier put his hand over her mouth. "Shut up, you ugly ape leader!" He fended off her blows by grabbing her around the waist and lifting her off the ground.

Anne was aghast, but Jamey, with a chivalrous streak, knew exactly what to do. He cast aside the dried grass and lumbered forward, lunging at the man and clouting him alongside the head. Collier staggered back as Miss Dankworth cried out in alarum and fell to the damp ground.

"Help, help, a footpad!" she shrieked.

"Stop it, you *idiot* woman," Anne said, striding over and grabbing her arm, helping her to her feet as Augustus Collier reeled off a few yards and stared at Jamey, whimpering '*my ear, my ear!*' There was blood, Anne noticed, but not much. "Stop blubbering, Mr. Collier," Anne said, tightening her grip on the teacher's arm. "My brother, Lord James, dealt you a blow because you were manhandling this lady. I hope it teaches you a lesson. Now, would either of you deign to explain what is going on?"

Miss Dankworth shrank away from Anne, who would not release her. Jamey stared at Augustus Collier, who gingerly touched his ear, reddening swiftly, a thin trickle of blood staining his white cravat. He was silent now, his blubbering over, his eyes watchful.

"Miss Dankworth, what did Mr. Collier lie about?"

"I don't know what you mean, my lady," she sobbed, her voice quavering, her face blotchy and wet from her tears.

"You accused him of lying. I heard you. Neither of you was being terribly discreet. Perhaps you thought this clandestine place would protect you from view. How unfortunate for you I wished to view the school from this vantage point, while out walking with my brother."

Collier stared at her, his brow furrowed. "Why did you wish to see the school from here?"

"Why do you think, you great dolt? Do you not care how or why your sister died? Or where her broken body was found? Or how her killer got to her?" She released Miss Dankworth. Browbeating the woman would accomplish nothing, and neither would threatening

Collier, though she longed to. As her heart returned to its normal pace, her blood chilled. "Do you make it a habit to linger in the bushes arguing with Faithful's teacher? Mr. Collier, I cannot help but think this all—this argument, the two of you here—has to do with your sister's death. Convince me otherwise."

"How *dare* you say that?" Augustus Collier muttered, though his eyes were clouded with fear.

Miss Dankworth cried out and grabbed Anne's sleeve. "Oh, no, my lady, you have it all wrong. This has nothing to do with Faithful. Or at least . . ." She stopped with her mouth open, her gaze turned inward, her head cocked to one side, like she was listening to an interior voice. "Or at least I don't think it does," she mumbled, her voice fainter.

"You don't *think* it does? Tell me then," Anne demanded, looking between them. "Tell me the truth. Why are you meeting her in secret?" she asked him. "What did he lie about?" she asked, turning to Miss Dankworth.

Mr. Collier's face had reddened, the trickle of blood now drying. He took out a handkerchief, spit on it and rubbed the blood from his neck, glaring at the bloodstained cloth. Jamey made a conciliatory move toward him, saying, "I am sorry, sir, to have hurt you. But you should never hit a lady."

Collier backed warily away, one hand up. "This has nothing to do with Faithful," he said over his shoulder to Anne, echoing the teacher. "We were . . . I was attempting to make love to her, is all. She thought I was proposing marriage and when I said I was not, she said I was a liar." He glared at Miss Dankworth.

Something passed between them. It was not the truth. Why was he lying if their argument had nothing to do with his sister's death? His admission—if that's what it was—came with the risk of being sued for breach of promise, should the law interpret his behavior as a promise to wed.

Miss Dankworth wept into a handkerchief but did not confirm or deny his story. She watched Collier, who stared back in a most unpleasant way. There was a coldness about him. Never once had he—or his father, for that matter—appeared moved by Faithful's death other than an annoyance. This interaction confused matters.

"Shall I ask Miss Lee to intercede, Miss Dankworth, with this unworthy fellow?" Anne asked, flicking a glance at the teacher, who blew her nose unprettily on a handkerchief. "If he has sullied your reputation or made promises he is not ready to keep, we can force him into marriage, if you want him. A court of law will be needed if there has been breach of promise. I will support you in that, I promise."

The woman gasped and staggered back. "No, I beg of you, my lady, please! I would . . . if it got out . . . me meeting here with him . . . I . . . oh *no*! I would lose my position. It would ruin me!" she cried out loud and whirled. Her skirts belling out, she ran to the path, charging up it, huffing and puffing, disappearing up the shadowy rise.

"I don't need to explain myself to anyone," Collier said. He bowed. "I shall take my leave, my lady. Good day to you."

Anne watched him stroll away. What an extraordinarily cold family. Poor Faithful, to be raised in such an atmosphere. However, she must stay focused. She turned and stared up the hill, examining the back of the school through the shadowy thicket as Jamey came to stand beside her.

"Annie, did the gentleman hurt the lady, do you think?"

"I don't know, Jamey."

"Did I do the right thing?"

"You most certainly did," she said, taking his arm and leaning against him. His solid bulk was reassuring. On tiptoe she kissed his fleshy cold cheek and patted it. "If I was in trouble, I would want a knight errant like you to come to my rescue."

He grinned and patted her hand on his arm. She again stared up the hill at the school. The killer had dragged Faithful's body in the direction of the back wall. Why? The only explanation that made sense was the killer intended to drop Faithful's mortal remains over the top. She could easily be carried off by a confederate, or even by the perpetrator who, if he was agile enough, could hop over the low wall to the hillside and be gone.

But again, *why*? She sighed heavily. The mystery was deepening with every discovery.

Chapter Eighteen

They gathered for dinner at the marquess's townhouse. Anne was happy to have Osei as her dinner companion. In a formal setting, as the marquess's secretary, he would be seated further down the table, as would an estate steward or family solicitor. However this was an informal occasion. The dowager viscountess and the countess were seated to Darkefell's right and left and took up all of his time and attention. Even after dinner the marquess was not free, pressed into service as a dutiful fourth at whist with Anne's mother, father, and Lord Westmacott. 'Twas agreed to solely to gain favor in her eyes, Darkefell said in whispered undertones as they left the table, and to ingratiate himself with her family.

She found a corner of the drawing room and beckoned Osei to join her on the settee by the fire. She continued their dinner table conversation, telling him of her day's encounter with Mr. Augustus Collier and Miss Carlotta Dankworth. "I suspect him in his sister's death."

"Why?"

She pondered. "I do not believe in coincidence, or at least, not too many of them. His connection to Miss Dankworth, which he is attempting to pass off as lovemaking, I do not believe."

"Why not?"

"I blush to say it but she is plain and poor. He is vain, expensive and frivolous. What would be the draw?"

"For some men the draw is simply a woman's favor. I do not hesitate to say to you, who I know to be sensible and forthright, that it may be her body he seeks to command."

"Sexual congress, you mean. I don't think she would risk that no matter the temptation. Though I believe she is romantic, I do not believe her to be lustful or stupidly trusting. Her situation is precarious. One moral failure and her reputation and her livelihood would be gone forever. I believe she values her job too much to risk it."

"Perhaps you know too little of their lives to judge what their connection could be."

"What do you mean?"

He frowned across the room as his lordship made a foolish

mistake in whist and received a withering set-down by Anne's grandmother. Osei's expression cleared when the marquess sent them a humorous look that showed he was not offended by the old woman's jibes. He may even have blundered to give her something to twig him about.

"I merely mean there is no telling what attracts two people," Osei said. "He may have a deeper scheme in mind if he did indeed make love to her. But your instincts are generally trustworthy. If you think they were lying, you're probably correct."

"I don't think there is a love affair there, but the fact he claimed one and thought that less shameful or guilty than what they were truly arguing about gives me pause." She thought for a moment. Miss Dankworth would never be an object of love for Mr. Augustus Collier, but was there truth in his claim, though the object was wrong? She thought about Miss Julia Halliday, and her love for the unworthy art teacher. Mayhap she was susceptible in general, and Mr. Collier, brother of her schoolmate, had found a way to attract her. Was an elopement planned? Is that what the tangle was about? And perhaps that is what Miss Dankworth was upbraiding him about when she castigated him as a liar.

"You've given me much to ponder. No matter what, though, why would they meet there, at the bottom of the hill below the school? It doesn't make any sense." She turned a ring on her finger. "I think Mr. Collier the younger capable of murder. He has a coldness to him, a lack of humanity I find troubling. And yet for the life of me, I cannot figure out how he would benefit from his sister's death."

"Half sister, correct?"

"Yes. Different mothers."

"What do you know of Faithful's mother?"

"She died in an asylum. The poor girl has been bullied because of it."

"Did she have money?"

Anne considered it. "I don't know."

"Your description of the gentleman makes me wonder. You called him vain and frivolous. Perhaps he is expensive, too. Could money be involved?"

She nodded slowly. When she put her mind to it, she *could* think of other reasons, ones that may not occur to a man, especially not a gentleman like Osei, who would never dishonor a female, and most especially would never harm his sister. "I'll ask around."

"Enlist Lord Westmacott. He knows more about society than anyone I have ever met."

She smiled. Her mother's reliable and harmless beau was indeed a font of knowledge. He had been valuable in this case already. "The Colliers are from Bristol, though. I can't imagine he knows anything of them."

"As you intend to enlist Lord Darkefell in your investigation into the Colliers, burden him with this additional quest, to seek what the girl might have that the brother might want."

"All right." She sighed deeply and closed her eyes. "I am haunted by the smear of blood, and by the knowledge that Faithful's killer intended to throw her over the stone wall. Why? And why did he not finish the task?"

"Was he perhaps caught at it?"

Caught at it; it was an idea. A bribe would buy silence. "Jonty Thompson is the bribable sort. Or Miss Dankworth. Perhaps what I saw was a meeting of an extortionist and her victim."

Could the teacher have seen something from her window? But no, Anne knew Miss Dankworth's room with the little girls overlooked the front of the school. Maybe she followed Faithful upstairs and saw . . . Anne frowned and shook her head. "I cannot imagine Miss Dankworth having the kind of nerve to witness that and not raise a hue and cry, but be cool enough to extort money. She might be threatened into silence, but I doubt she could be bribed into it."

"We never know what others are capable of, my lady."

The marquess, free at last from the whist table, strolled over to them. Darkefell said, "You are needed at the whist table, Osei. Lady Harecross insists you are a far better player than I am. She sent me to my fiancée and said to fetch you."

The secretary bowed. He retreated to the whist table and took the marquess's deserted spot as Tony sat down beside Anne. He moved close beside her, heat from his body radiating into hers as he put one arm casually over the backrest of the settee. His hand cupped her shoulder, and slid down, touching her back.

She shivered. "You are cruel, Tony," she whispered in a teasing tone. "Trapping Osei there. They will never let him go now, as he *is* a far better card player than you, twice as polite and ten times as patient with Lord Westmacott when our friend prefers to gossip over dealing."

"Shall I distract you from your worries by giving you an interesting tidbit of gossip?"

She looked askance at him, eyes wide, brows raised. "You, gossiping?"

"Your father and I accompanied Jamey on the rooftop last night to examine the stars. There he told me that Lord Westmacott had requested an audience with him. When they met, here in my drawing room, Westmacott, in a roundabout way, sought to reassure your father that absolutely nothing untoward had happened between him and your mother. Ever. He was, he said, the soul of discretion and guarded her virtue like a Borneo tiger. Whatever that means."

Anne bit her lip, then chuckled out loud. "That dear, sweet man!" she said. Perhaps her father knew, or suspected anyway, that Lord Westmacott's friendship with Lady Harecross was indeed innocent in every way because his lordship did not care for women except as his dearest friends and confidantes.

She relaxed back against the marquess's caressing hand. She spoke of all she had already told Osei, about her afternoon in the park. When she and her brother had come back up along the path, her father had been earnestly entreating Miss Dankworth to tell him what was wrong, but the moment she caught sight of Jamey and Anne she hurried off to the school, slamming the door shut, then peeking out the window at them. "What is she hiding?" Anne mused.

Her fiancé, though, was not to be swayed from his determined flirtation with her. He traced the back of her neck with one finger and whispered in her ear, his warm breath sending her into a trance, saying, "I wish I could steal you away."

Fire blazed in her blood. Dangerous notion to her determined rejection of premarital bliss! "I don't think—"

"Come," he said, standing and taking her hand. "Come with me to see the spot where your father and brother and I sit to observe the stars."

She smiled and called out across the room, "Jamey, come show me your new telescope."

"That was not what I had in mind," Tony growled as Jamey

bounded across the room and took her arm solicitously.

"Oh, I know what you had in mind, my lord. And I will not put myself at your mercy. A few more weeks, Tony, and you shall have all of me." To distract him, she set him tasks for the week to come.

Chapter Nineteen

The next morning Anne sat with her disgruntled cat on her lap as Mary fussed with her hair. Irusan batted at the brush as the maid worked and moved about irritably. He scratched Anne, and when she smacked his bottom he got in a feline huff, hissed, and jumped off, stalking to the bed to scratch on the bedpost, digging his claws in the fine mahogany.

"Irusan, stop it!" she cried, trying to stay still with hairpins close to her scalp. To Mary she said, "My grandmother will kill me in my sleep if he ruins the furniture."

"He's powerful put out, milady. You've been gone too much lately, I fear, for his likin', an' he can't go about in the city, for the neighbors don't like it. He digs in the potted plants, yer grandmama was told."

"I'll take him with me today. May I borrow Robbie to hold him when necessary?"

"My lad wouldne mind one little bit, milady. I fear he's a little put out too, as he's not seen you or Mr. Osei lately."

It was true that she had been so busy the people who relished her company most and depended on her for their livelihood were getting short shrift. She'd try to do better by them all.

As Mary finished her hair, she confided her conversation with Tony the night before. She had taken Osei's advice and asked for her fiancé's help to track down information about the Colliers. She had asked the same of Lord Westmacott, who had haughtily questioned why he would be concerned in the affairs of a barrister and his clerk son before admitting he might know someone who knew someone who would have gossip. The older set—his lordship and Anne's grandmother, in particular—seemed intrigued to be helping Anne with one of her scandalous investigations.

Tony had eagerly leaped to fulfill her request for help. They would meet at the Pump Room later in the day, they agreed, unless he sent her a message otherwise by way of Osei. He planned to work with Lord Westmacott to discover anything they could about the Colliers. Osei, too, would investigate, in particular her curiosity about whether the Collier men had come to Bath together the morning Faithful was found dead. It was twenty miles from Bristol to Bath.

Neither could travel it in less than several hours, especially in the middle of the night. If both were in Bristol and traveled together to Bath after learning about the tragedy, then both were innocent in Faithful's murder.

If she had a guess at this moment it would be Jonty Thompson who topped her list of suspects, though there was no logical motive for such a man. This particular murder, by strangulation, seemed more masculine, though his wife, Mrs. Thompson, with her big, strong hands, could easily wring the neck of frail gentle Faithful. Maybe they were in it together, but *why*?

She shuddered as Mary patted her hair.

"What's wrong, milady?"

"I cannot imagine anyone killing Faithful." Tears prickled her eyes. "She was such a sweet child and had suffered already, with her mother dying in an asylum. Her father doesn't particularly care that Faithful is dead. Why would *anyone* kill her?"

"People will do tairible things if they're affrighted."

"Frightened? Of what?"

Mary inserted the last seed pearl and tortoiseshell comb, met her mistress's gaze in the mirror, and said, "Milady, those who work for a living have much to fear. Mayhap Faithful knew something about one of the sairvants or saw something to disgrace one."

That could give the discreditable Jonty Thompson a motive. She explained her thoughts to Mary, then said, "Why, though, would he begin to drag her body to the edge of the flagstone walk, then abandon it?"

"Speaks of haste, milady, surely?"

"Haste, yes, I suppose, or being interrupted." If it was Jonty, interrupted by what or whom? "I still can't understand why Faithful's body needed to be moved in the first place."

"That I canna say, milady. If 'twere me doin' something like that—draggin' a body, I mean—I suppose I'd try, then find myself unable to do it."

"A possibility," she said, thinking again of Mr. Collier's withered arm.

"I'll go fetch Wee Robbie and get a string for Sir Irusan's neck."

"There is no need of that, Mary, the string, I mean. Robbie yes, the string no. Irusan will mind his manners," she said loudly, staring at her cat, "Or I will know why."

He stared at her and blinked, purring with a throaty growl.

• • •

She and Robbie—he dressed in the russet livery of the Harecross family—strolled the streets toward their destination with Irusan prancing alongside of them, well behaved aside from an occasional dash into an alley after a rat. Robbie had been silent for the most part, but when Anne looked down at him, she saw that his brow was furrowed and his mouth turned down. He was rarely downcast.

"What's on your mind, lad?"

"Why would anyone kill a little girl, milady?" He looked up at her, his blue eyes filled with sadness. "Why do grown people act so awful?"

"A good question, Robbie, one to which there is no good answer. She wasn't exactly a little girl. She was seventeen, almost eighteen, an age at which many young ladies make their debut and even marry."

"Was she going to marry?"

"I don't imagine she would have married for a while. She would have stayed at school for this whole year, I would think." Soon she would have finished her schooling. Given her father's middling status, she likely would have gone to a seaside resort town to make her debut and find a husband among the clerks, vicars and shopkeepers of that town. It was a pattern repeated in Bath, Lyme Regis and every spa town. There would be marriage settlements to arrange, financial disclosures and the rest. The bartering and selling of a girl's future was a habit coded into English law, with small provision made for what the young lady might like to do with her life.

"Who would want to kill her?" he persisted.

"I don't know, but I intend to find out."

The school was limestone ashlar, gleaming palely in the brilliant Bath morning sun. It was a lovely building, but Anne could not look at it now without thinking of the turmoil within.

Today she wanted to speak with Mrs. Thompson, and others. The maid—not Kate, but the other maid, Elly, slim, small and pale—opened the door at Robbie's sharp rap and shrieked when Irusan pranced through the door. He took umbrage at her scream, hissed, and chased her through the house with Wee Robbie trailing them, remonstrating loudly that the wee beastie was just a cat. A large one, but still just a cat.

Anne entered and stood waiting. Harriet strode into the hall, skirts swishing like waves about her, looking puzzled. "What in heaven's name is going on?" she asked.

"My cat and my serving boy accompanied me. I'm sorry about the commotion. I thought they'd both behave but, there you have it. Irusan—my cat—startled the maid who screamed. My cat took offense and followed her as she retreated, and my boy followed *her*, to try to retrieve my cat."

"Why on earth would you bring a cat?" Harriet asked.

It would take too long to explain her whim to her friend. "I have come back today to continue investigating. We must solve this awful crime."

"Of course, come along. Besides your part in the tumult, you find us at sixes and sevens today. Kate quit. We have to hire another maid, but it appears that it's the wrong time of year to advertise for a maid, I don't know why." She sighed. "It always seems to be the wrong time of year. Hiring serving staff for this place is our eternal torment."

"Kate quit? Why?"

"I don't know. I never liked her—she is a sly little thing, and I suspected her of . . . never mind—but it is difficult without her. She knew the job, at least, and she was presentable and adept at answering the door. Elly mumbles and is timid. She takes orders, but she's not suitable for anything but cleaning and taking care of the girls. Now I shall have to find and train another."

"What did Kate say when she left?"

"She had found another position."

"It's not that easy, at least not in my household." Servants were required to give notice but seldom left because a good job and reference were vital. Who would hire Kate without a reference? She turned her mind to the task at hand and set aside pondering the maid problem to think about later. "I need to speak with you in private for a moment."

The young woman led Anne to the parlor and they sat. Anne thought for a moment and said, "Try as I might—and I have tried—I cannot place the source of this tragedy anywhere but here. Everyone wants to shrink from the brutality of it, and I understand that, but someone killed Faithful." She leaned forward and enunciated carefully, "*Someone in this building.* It would have been better for your school if it was discovered that the culprit was an outsider with a prior relationship. I'm thinking especially of her father or brother; presumably she would have allowed either inside. Can you think of any possibility that it is either man?"

"I can't imagine it," the teacher finally said.

"Neither can I, which is why I feel the killer must be a servant, a teacher or . . . a student."

Harriet frowned, her gaze turned inward, staring down at her hands as her brow wrinkled. Anne could see it sink in, what she was trying to say. She clasped her hands so tightly in her lap that her knuckles turned white. "This is awful. Her death was a tragedy, but to be blunt, we rely upon the income this school brings us, we three. Without it we starve."

Anne leaned over and gazed directly into the author's eyes. "Your best hope is to rout out the culprit quickly and send them to justice. May I have your sister Anne's aid in this?"

"You find her helpful?"

Amused by the doubt in Harriet's tone, Anne said, "She has imagination, and the right mind for this." Tougher than Harriet, anyway, Anne thought. "She tutors the girls one-on-one and is likely to understand their relationships. She is observant and interested."

"I'll make sure she cooperates."

"Someone saw or heard something and is not talking about it. I'm going first to the kitchen."

She followed the cacophony of voices and an unearthly howl down to the working area of the house. Irusan stood in the middle of the steamy kitchen with Wee Robbie holding his stomach, bent over and laughing while Elly clung to the cook and Mrs. Thompson held a cleaver in one hand, incomprehensible invective streaming from her mouth. Ginny was not alarmed, howling with laughter along with Robbie.

"Stop!" Anne shouted, even as another voice was added to the mix.

Miss Anne Lee entered the kitchen behind Anne, evaluated the situation swiftly, and smiled. "What a fine-looking cat. What are you all howling about?"

"Irusan, you behave," Anne said. "Robbie, laughing is not helpful and you are leading young Ginny astray. Elly, Mrs. Thompson, Cook: Irusan is a cat like any other cat, even if he is big. He most likely saw a mouse. If you let him do his job he will dispatch it expeditiously and be out of your way."

Irusan, as she spoke, had taken to cleaning, assuming the undignified pose that every cat owner knew, foot stuck in the air. Robbie giggled harder and Ginny along with him. Anne Lee grinned. "Let them have their fun, my lady. Everyone has been creeping about like mice in a tomb. It's good to hear laughter again."

The serving staff were already relaxing, seeing Irusan behave like any other cat. Cook tossed him a morsel of chicken. He finished his toilette, snapped up the bit of food, then began to sniff around the kitchen, disappearing into corners and behind cupboards. In moments he had pounced and a smothered squeal, soon silenced, proved his vermin-dispatching zeal. He toted it proudly out to show off, and Robbie snatched it up, putting it in a leather sac he carried.

"May I have all of your attention?" Anne said, folding her hands in front of her. "I have been given permission to speak with each one of you. We all wish this awful tragedy to be solved, don't we?" They all nodded except for Mrs. Thompson, who stared at her through narrowed eyes. "I will speak with Ginny first. Come along, Ginny. Robbie, you stay here with Irusan, then take him on to the storage rooms after. He can do his job."

Her desire to interview Ginny first was born of fear that the child would be bullied into silence by the housekeeper if she knew anything, which she likely didn't. However, she'd make no assumptions. Maybe she was wrong, but Anne didn't trust Mrs. Thompson one little bit. She was a strong woman, with hands like Cook's, large and capable.

Ginny exchanged a look with Cook, who nodded. The girl timidly crossed the room and followed Anne out. She wanted to get the girl away from the others, but a scullery maid would not be comfortable in the drawing room or parlor. Anne Lee perhaps sensed her dilemma, for as they emerged into the shadowy hallways she said, "Follow me upstairs. We can set you up in my office."

She led the way to the top floor. The young woman's office was a small room facing the back, with a casement window overlooking the laundry yard and kitchen garden. Ginny had followed trustingly. A table sat in the middle of the small study, with reference books on shelves and an upholstered settee along one wall.

"This is where you tutor the girls?"

"Good Lord, no," Anne Lee replied. "Well, sometimes. Mostly, though, my tutoring is done in the library downstairs. This is where I do the bookkeeping and my own writing."

Anne cast a sharp look her way. How difficult was it for the lady, sister to two accomplished, energetic and ambitious authoresses and playwrights? "What do you write?"

"Oh, this and that," she said airily. "Nothing important. Ginny, come help me set up the table for her ladyship. Get a chair from along the wall and bring it up to the table, across from it. Now, you'll need a sheaf of paper, ink, a quill, and the rest, if you are to make notes. You two sit, while I round up the necessities." She swished from the room and her footsteps could be heard descending the stairs, echoing up the staircase.

Anne motioned to the chair opposite her across the table and said, "How are you, Ginny? Have you recovered from your awful experience?"

Ginny's eyes widened as she perched on the edge of the chair, her work-roughened hands under her legs. She swung her booted feet. "I haven't had much time to think on it, milady."

"You'd like whoever did this to be caught, wouldn't you?" The girl nodded. "I want whomever did the terrible deed to pay the price." The child, wide-eyed, said nothing. "I would like to take you back to the night Miss Faithful died. You sleep in the room with Cook, Kate, Mrs. Thompson and Elly, correct?"

She shook her head. "Mrs. Thompson has a room to herself, milady."

Good, easy questions were loosening her tongue. "Who do you share a bed with?"

"Cook. It's ever so warm, milady. She snores summat. It don't bother me none, 'cept I don't hear much else. She's big and warm." She sighed. "It's wonderful comfortable."

"You work very hard, don't you, Ginny?"

She nodded.

"So, you sleep undisturbed?"

"Mostly."

"But not always. Think back to the morning you found Miss Collier was dead. Did you sleep soundly the night before? Or did you hear anything? See anything?"

"I . . . I woke up when Cook rolled over and sent me flyin' outta bed. I was afraid I'd a woke the others, but Elly and Kate were asleep."

"You saw them?"

She nodded. "I sat up on the floor. I was about ta go 'round and climb in the other side o' the bed, milady, when . . ." She took a deep breath, then blurted, "I heard voices out in the hall."

Voices! "Did you go to see who was out there?"

She nodded slowly, timidly.

"Who was it? You can tell me, Ginny. Who was it out in the hallway?"

She hesitated, then said in a rush, "'Twas the schoolteacher, and she were arguin' with a man, milady."

Chapter Twenty

A man? A picture leaped into her mind of Miss Carlotta Dankworth and Mr. Augustus Collier arguing in the park. She accused him of lying. Her heart pounded and she felt ill, a pulse thrumming in her temple. If Collier *had* killed his sister, was that how he gained access to the house, by way of the teacher? "Did you recognize him? Did you hear what they were arguing about, Ginny? What were they saying?"

The girl shrank back.

Calm, Anne, calm. "Ginny, you've done well," she said gently. "This is interesting. Did you see the man's face?"

She shook her head.

Eliminate the in-house possibilities: "Was it Jonty Thompson?"

She shook her head again. "I'd know his voice, milady. He swears and spits and talks crudely. This was a gentleman."

A gentleman. Collier? "Did you know him? Have you seen him before?"

She looked helpless and shrugged. "It were dark, milady. I couldn't see his face."

"Miss Dankworth was speaking to him?"

"Not Miss Dankworth, milady, it were Miss Hopewell."

"Are you *sure* it was Miss Hopewell, Ginny?"

"Yes, milady. She's very pretty and kind to me, and she has long *long* hair, very dark. It swung loose, y'know, flowing, like."

Anne sat for a moment, digesting the tidbit of news; Miss India Hopewell, upstairs, with a gentleman, arguing. It still could be one of the Collier men. Given all of the Bristol connections and lies told by the teacher, it made a kind of sense.

That was all the child knew. Frightened and cold, she had scuttled back to bed and shivered herself to sleep. Why hadn't she mentioned this before to anyone? Anne asked. She had been warned by Mrs. Thompson about talking out of turn, she admitted, for she had been condemned as a chatterbox after talking about school business to a maid from another house. Terrified of losing her position, she had become silent as a matter of course. But anyway, finding Miss Faithful dead that morning had rattled the memory right out of her brain, she said, and then she'd been too scared to speak up.

"But Robbie says you're special, and kind to him and his mam," Ginny said. "So when you asked if I saw or heard anything I remembered and had to tell you." She heard no more until morning, she said, when Cook rattled the bed getting out of it and jostled her awake.

"Thank you for trusting me enough to speak," Anne said. "What time was this, Ginny, that you saw the man and teacher in the hall?"

It was a quarter after something, she said, for she heard the clock downstairs in the hall chime the quarter hour when she got up from the floor in her room. She trotted away to resume her exhausting day. Anne Lee brought the writing supplies. She apologized for taking time, but she had been summoned by her sisters to a meeting to decide how to present a united front to the world, in case gossip leaked to the most virulent of mongers.

"Miss Lee, what do you know about India Hopewell?"

She curled her lip and sat down opposite Anne, folding her arms on the table in front of her. "She's a real sly-boots, that one."

"What do you mean?"

"Looks so prim, doesn't she?" Anne nodded. "That's what my sisters think too. When I raised objections at her hiring, I was told I was a jealous cat, envying her because she is pretty."

"I have been accused of that kind of petty jealousy myself once or twice. We point out a woman's failings, or our suspicions of their motives, and are castigated for it. Why, I wonder?"

"We are not as lovely as those ladies," Anne Lee said. She hastily added, "I suppose I speak for myself?"

"No, you have something there," Anne mused. She recalled the years of hurt she had endured, knowing she was not as pretty as the other girls at her debut, her awful Seasons in London. She was too plain to attract notice for her looks, not accomplished in any of the skills she should be—science had always interested her more than the piano—and too proud to let a man woo her for her position and wealth. "I know I am plain, my nose and my bosom too large, my figure not fashionable. For years it made me—rightly, I might add—suspect those who wooed me with extravagant encomiums to my beauty, something about eyes like stars or such rot. When it was my dowry that was most lovely."

"And yet you are to marry a marquess."

"He has never lied to me about my looks, and yet I do think he finds me beautiful." Anne smiled. "He is magnificent himself, like a stallion in a field, bold and handsome and wild. I am the plain mare who has caught his attention, and he has never wavered from me, not for one solitary moment."

"What an exceedingly odd simile to employ, my lady."

"Nonetheless, it's as true as any description can be. He wants my mind and my soul. I'm fortunate, for I have met my match. What about you? Have you never been tempted by marriage?"

"We are not a marrying tribe, us Lee women. Without your advantages of fortune and birth—our father was a poor actor, and what kind of background is that for a respectable suitor?—we are left to make our own way. We are, each one of us, become too independent to surrender to a marriage below our minds and hearts. I have never seen a man of adequate quality for either of my brilliant sisters." Her expression, which had been lighthearted, now sobered. "And so, we must solve this murder, or our school may go under, losing all of Sophia's investment, and we would have to shift for ourselves, doing who knows what? Perhaps as governess in a large household." She shuddered. "Here I have independence of a sort, and my sisters who, despite our differences, I love wholeheartedly."

"And so, we come back to the beautiful Miss Hopewell and your suspicions. You suspect her of what, exactly?" Anne asked, eyeing the tutor.

"Having spent years with all kinds of girls and women, I suppose there is an instinctive recoiling from her. How shall I frame it? It is all bound up in her hypocrisy, her flirtatious modesty, and the pretense she puts on of simplicity, humility, restraint."

"None of those characteristics which she possesses?"

"She is a minx, plain and simple. Women know other women, though men are oft duped. I suppose I should let her minxiness—for want of a better word—pass because it is difficult for women without family protection to make their way in this world, but I cannot. What has made you fasten on her, I wonder?"

"I have information I don't wish to reveal yet," Anne murmured.

"Hardly fair, my lady," Anne Lee remonstrated. "We have trusted her with the education of our girls. If she is involved in any way, if her morals are suspect, or if she is a danger . . . in short, tell us what you know. Surely you can see that is only fair?"

The call to fairness was powerful, and if there was any risk that Miss Hopewell was a danger to the girls, action was required. And yet all she knew was that the teacher was on the third floor arguing with a man sometime in the night. It wasn't enough to destroy her character with her employers. "Please trust that the moment I *know* something I shall tell you immediately. Until then I don't think it's necessary to tell your sisters anything. Do you agree?"

"I wouldn't know what to tell them," Anne Lee said with the faintest of smiles.

"I wonder, can you do me a favor?" The tutor nodded. "I believe your sister has gathered all of Faithful's things. Would you bring them to me? Not the clothes, but any letters or the like she may have had?"

"I can do that now." She disappeared and came back with a cloth sack and set it on the table.

"Thank you. Would you, in ten minutes, send Miss Hopewell to me? I shall wait in the hall. I want to see her come up."

Anne Lee stood, tapping her fingers on the table, her nails rap-rap-rapping an odd rhythm, like time from a minuet. Doubt shadowed her pale, serious face. "I wonder, why do you wish to see her reaction as she comes up to this floor? Do you suspect her of the actual murder?"

Anne didn't answer. She was not about to tell Miss Lee what the young woman was up to that night until she knew more.

"This has the odor of entrapment, my lady. I may dislike Miss India Hopewell, I may even distrust her, but I would not have her snared like a bumbling rabbit."

"I have no wish to accuse anyone of misdeeds unless they are guilty. Would you have me ignore information I have, or rather use it to prove her guilt or innocence?"

She nodded and turned to the door, throwing over her shoulder as she left, "My sisters will remain in blissful ignorance of your dastardly suspicions until you deign to tell us what exactly they are. I'll send the victim up to you in exactly ten minutes."

"Thank you." Once Miss Lee had left, Anne undid the knot on the cloth sack and spread out the contents. There was the brush Faithful used every night. Anne touched it lightly, tugging at a long dark hair tangled in the bristles, recalling the pretty young lady with the lustrous braided hair. Pity for the girl toughened into a renewal of the resolve to find her killer. There were bits and pieces: buttons, handkerchiefs, hair pins, and letters. She sorted the letters into piles and quickly scanned them. They were mostly from friends in Bristol, schoolgirlish nonsense about young men and assemblies and dancing.

There were a couple from her father, too, sternly worded missives admonishing her to be a good girl, behave, learn how to be a young lady. The one dated a week before was different in tenor, anger seething within its lines. Anne read through it, then read it again. What was Mr. Collier responding to with such angry words?

In the letter he wrote:

> . . . you must learn not to question your elders and your betters, daughter, for you are merely an ignorant girl. You may think you know something about this world, but you don't. We men who are about the law and business and the world at large, we are the ones who know what is best. Men carry the weight of all of you frivolous girls on our shoulders. Your concerns are baseless, your questions insolent, and your manner insufferably conceited. Are you saying you are more intelligent than your brother? I had hoped for better from you, after being there with the Lees. Perhaps that was my mistake, given their various dalliances in useless, vain pursuits like the theater and publishing. Perhaps it is time to take you away from there and put you somewhere you can be useful in a real womanly way. Good day. I will see you at Christmastide.
>
> Sincerely and with love, your father, Mr. William Collier.

• • •

Miss Hopewell ascended the stairs slowly, one hand on the banister, the other clutching her skirts. Her gaze darted about the shadowy expanse. She thought she was alone and stood staring at the window that accessed the roof for a long minute, as she topped the stairs. Finally she turned and jumped, screaming when she saw Anne lurking in the shadows. She settled one fluttering hand on her bosom.

"You frightened me!" she exclaimed.

"Did I? Why?"

"Y-you . . ." She stopped and fell silent, watching Anne with a solemn expression. She mounted the last step and approached the window. "Is this where that poor girl fell from?"

"Yes."

The teacher turned and frowned. "Why would she be up here?"

"A most excellent question, Miss Hopewell. Maybe you can help me find an answer. Come along, I am using Miss Anne Lee's office to interview some in the school."

"Why?"

"Come." Anne led the way into the office but left the door open. "Sit." She indicated a chair she had angled so they could both see the window from where they sat.

The young woman was watching her like a mouse might watch a cat, but she took her chair, her fluttering hands tidying her skirts about her.

"How do you like working here, Miss Hopewell?"

"I like it," she said, prim and proper, her voice holding the right amount of warmth. "The Misses Lee are wonderful ladies: kind, considerate, pleasant."

"That's why I'm trying to help them."

"Help them? What do you mean?"

"*You* would wish to assist them if you could, wouldn't you?"

"Certainly, but I don't know how."

"You are this moment by talking to me. Are you and Miss Dankworth good friends?"

"Not particularly. We are colleagues, but not close."

"When we spoke last, you told me a little about your home." She led her back over her history, about her aunt and cousins in Winterbourne, and noticed a couple of interesting details and omissions she hadn't noted before. She never once mentioned Bristol, though Miss Dankworth had said that was where they stayed during the summer holiday break. Anne considered tackling her about the lie but decided to let it be for the moment. Anne leaned forward and stared into Miss Hopewell's eyes. "What were you doing up here with a gentleman the night Faithful was murdered?"

Her eyes widened and she swallowed hard. Her mouth hung

open, but she didn't say a word.

"Miss Hopewell? Did you hear me?"

"I-I-I . . . I did hear you, my lady. Who told you I was up here that night?" She wound a ribbon around her fingers, the pale blue of it reminiscent of her lovely eyes, now clouded with fear. She finally realized Anne was staring at her trembling hands and hid them in her skirts. "They were wrong," she said, her chin tilting up in defiance.

"Who was it?"

Anne watched her, trying to interpret her behavior, the mingling of defiance and anxiety. "Why does that matter? They were not wrong and have no motive to lie. You were up here arguing with a gentleman. Who was he, why were you up here with him and what were you arguing about?"

Silence.

"Did you let him into the house?"

"No!" Her expression calmed. "I-I . . . I heard something. I came up to find out who it was. It was a man. I asked him what he was doing."

Liar! "Who was he, Miss Hopewell?" Anne said, leaning across the table and staring at the woman. *"Answer me."*

"I don't *know*," she cried. "You're frightening me. Please, I don't know who he w-was."

"What did he look like? Was he a gentleman?"

She hesitated, watching Anne's face. Hers went through a subtle pattern of expressions, from thoughtfulness, to fear, and finally to defiant resolve. "He was a rough-looking man." She looked away, and then back to Anne. "Perhaps Mrs. Thompson let him in. Maybe he is a friend of her husband's." Her eyes lit with decision. "I'm sure I saw the two of them together once."

She was digging herself in, laying claim to a false story to which she would be wedded. Anne was virtually certain she was lying. Either she knew who the man was and feared it would be discovered that she let him in or met him upstairs, or she was telling the truth that she *didn't* know who it was and was trying to lay the blame on the Thompsons, who she knew no one would believe if they denied it. A third possibility occurred to Anne; mayhap Miss Hopewell recognized the man but had been threatened into silence. Anne watched her through narrowed eyes until the teacher again looked away, her cheeks pinkening.

Miss Hopewell knew who the man was, she finally decided, and didn't want to admit it. "You said a moment ago you didn't recognize him and now you do and can name him as a friend of Jonty's. Which is it?"

"You're confusing me," she sobbed. "I . . . I've remembered that I have seen him before. I'm sure of it now. He *is* a friend of Jonty Thompson's." She stood. "I've told you all." She turned and fled.

"Miss Hopewell, don't . . ." She was gone, her footsteps echoing and receding as she descended. Anne considered going after her but decided to let her stew in her lies. She would become more and more afraid and may even try to embroider the lie to make it prettier to Anne. Every lying thread she added would weave a rope to bind her.

She went to the top of the stairs, wondering who to speak with next. The sound of male voices floated up the stairs from the entry, Mr. Collier, if she remembered that timbre correctly. They would be wanting to take Faithful's body back to Bristol to inter. Once they were gone from Bath they would be out of her reach to question. She must delay them, but how?

She descended swiftly and discovered that besides the two Collier men, Osei had arrived. He was speaking with the older gentleman as they followed Elly, the timid maid, into the sitting room. Anne joined them. All the men bowed and waited for her to sit, as the maid retreated to find Miss Sophia Lee.

As she sat in one of the chairs she shared a look with Osei, who raised his brows and nodded. He had learned something concerning the Colliers. She turned to the two men, who sat identically stiff, solemn, and without expression. The younger would not meet her eyes. "Gentlemen, I suppose I can guess your sad task today. You have come to arrange transport of poor Faithful's body back to Bristol. True?"

Mr. William Collier deigned to offer a dignified nod. When his son didn't react, he cast him a puzzled look.

"I would not be so hasty as to leave Bath."

"Why do you say that, my lady?" the elder Collier asked.

"There is the outstanding matter of who killed your daughter. Don't you want to stay in Bath until you know? I would be tearing this town apart to find out if I were you."

"You have no children and are not even married. You will have no way of knowing what I should or should not do." His voice held a guttural note of pain and he looked away. "My daughter was important to me. You will *never* understand." Sincerity throbbed in his voice.

He was right; she had no idea what she would do or feel in the same situation.

She turned to the son. Augustus Collier had still not met her gaze, though she kept trying to catch his eye. Maybe she would have to expose him to his father, speak openly about his behavior, demand an explanation. Was he the gentleman who met Miss Hopewell upstairs the night Faithful was murdered? How awful if her suspicions were proved correct, and Augustus had conspired to kill his sister. It still made no sense to Anne; why would a young man kill his younger half sister? She wouldn't expose him until she had thought about it further.

Osei cleared his throat. "My lady, I have a message from the marquess. If we may have a moment?"

"I'll excuse myself, gentlemen, as you await Miss Lee." She followed Osei out to the entry hall. "What have you learned?"

"Various things, some by mail, and some in person. I have found tidbits of information concerning Jonty's habits, what he has bragged about while in his cups, and sundry scandals concerning him and his wife. I shall start with the biggest shock I experienced."

"Tell me!"

"We know the Thompsons owned a boardinghouse in Bristol, which he lost to debtors, forcing them into employment here, at this school."

"What of it?"

"I think you'll be interested to discover how she knew about this position. She is Miss India Hopewell's aunt."

Chapter Twenty-one

Anne gasped, one hand over her mouth. "Oh, that I had known that a half hour ago, while I was interviewing Miss Hopewell. Why did the Thompsons not reveal that to the Lees?"

"Given their rougher appearance, perhaps that was Miss Hopewell's terms for helping them get the position."

"She didn't help if all she did was tell them about it. But it is true that Miss Hopewell is a young lady who seems excessively concerned about appearances." She stood for a long minute, staring blankly into space. Her most recent interview with the pretty teacher had given no hint of her familiarity with the Thompsons. Mrs. Thompson, Jonty and Miss Hopewell would make the perfect murderous triumvirate. She considered the hard-edged Mrs. Thompson and the softly sentimental Miss Hopewell. She remembered the teacher's readiness to blame Jonty Thompson for the man who was upstairs. "It surprises me that those two would be related."

"She lived in Mrs. Thompson's boardinghouse until she came to work here."

"Why has she so persistently lied? She claimed Winterbourne as where she lived before coming here, not Bristol, but I already knew she was lying about that from Miss Dankworth." Her eyes widened. "Oh! Miss Dankworth lied too, by omission if not commission. She claimed to have spent the summer in Bristol with Miss Hopewell, with the teacher's aunt who ran a boardinghouse. She never once mentioned knowing that the Thompsons were related to Miss Hopewell."

"I cannot speak to Miss Dankworth's motive for lying, but as for the other teacher, perhaps her reinvention of herself is understandable. This brings me to more revelations. Miss India Hopewell was, at one time, a companion—more of a maid-of-all-work, even down to scrubbing chamber pots—to an elderly woman who died a little over a year ago, leaving the young lady a tidy sum: one hundred guineas."

Anne gasped. "A hundred guineas?" A fortune, one that, if calculated and spent wisely, could be used to launch a lady into society, or at least buy respectability in the form of appropriate clothes and accouterments to *portray* a lady of means, for a while, anyway.

She could make a splash in Bristol society, pretend to be an elegant young lady, catch a gentleman's eye, and marry into respectability. Miss Hopewell would not be the first nor the last young lady to attempt it. Some succeeded.

Much better than spending her days cleaning an old woman's chamber pot. An ample motive for . . . "Are you hinting what I think you are hinting?"

He pushed his glasses up on his nose. "It is something to be considered, but even if it should be so — let me be blunt and say aloud what we are both thinking, that Miss Hopewell had every reason to wish her elderly employer dead for a legacy of a hundred guineas. Even so, what possible motive could she have for wishing Faithful Collier dead? What did she gain for such a grave risk?"

"We don't know," Anne admitted. But she had the beginning of an idea. If Miss Hopewell had spent much of that inheritance and yet failed at her primary objective, to catch a middling-class young man in Bristol, say a clerk, the son of a barrister . . . she tugged at a loose thread on her glove. It made her think of all the loose threads in any coherent theory that made the teacher a conspirator in Faithful's murder.

It didn't add up. She could not make the threads coalesce into a coherent tale of treachery and murder. "There could be reasons we cannot fathom. What you have brought me is significant." There was something she was missing, a clue that had escaped her but that she knew, in her mind or memory somewhere. Among the various players in this drama — the Thompsons, the Colliers, Miss Hopewell — there must be a motivating force she did not understand. "Osei, did you find out yet if the Colliers come to Bath together from Bristol the morning Faithful's death was discovered?"

He frowned, looking troubled. "I have not yet been able to speak with the man who was working the day the Colliers arrived. I will try again, I promise. As I mentioned, his lordship did indeed send me with a message for you. He needs to speak with you urgently and asks that you meet him at the bun house where you have met before."

"Is everything all right?"

"I believe it has something to do with the request you made of him."

"To look into the Colliers' Bristol connections?"

He nodded. Perhaps the answers were that close to hand. Perhaps Mr. Augustus Collier would yet turn out to be the villain of the piece. It all hung on what possible motive he could have for wishing his half sister dead.

"If I am correct — and his lordship would not tell me too much, for he wanted to tell you in person — he has been working with Lord Westmacott, and together the two of them have discovered something of importance."

She looked over her shoulder toward the drawing room, from which the murmur of conversation could be heard. "And yet, do I dare leave? I need to be sure they will not take Faithful and leave Bath. Osei, is there any way to keep the Colliers in town?"

"Let me handle that," Osei said, his dark eyes gleaming with mischief. "Dr. Fothergill has influence with the other magistrate and may be able to delay Mr. Collier from taking his daughter's body back to Bristol."

"I hope I'm not imagining things, Osei. I would not like to be the cause of compounding a father's heartache."

Osei's expression hardened and his mouth twisted. "We are not imagining the mark from a ligature around the poor girl's neck, my lady. Dr. Fothergill is making inquiries, so I will indeed request his help in delaying the removal of Faithful's body. You're asking that everything be examined carefully, not an unreasonable request given the gravity of the matter. A girl has been murdered. You do right."

"Thank you, Osei," Anne said, reaching out and placing one hand on his arm. He patted it, bowed and left to visit the doctor.

Anne returned to the drawing room and found that Sophia had joined the Colliers. They were discussing removal of Faithful's possessions. There was not a moment to lose. "May I speak with you privately, Miss Lee?"

They moved to the room beyond the drawing room. Miss Lee stopped, but Anne retreated further, tugging the instructress's elbow to guide her to the back window, where pale light from the cold day gave a wan silvery brightness to the space.

Sophia met her gaze with barely concealed impatience. "What is it, my lady?"

"I know you care about your students and are devastated by what happened to Faithful within your walls."

The woman's eyes clouded. She was not one to shed tears, though. She dashed them away with one finger before they could spill. "I'm appalled. I cannot believe it, and I want it all to end." Her tone was stern, emotion given away by a tremble. "The quicker those two men take that poor girl home and remove her belongings, the sooner we can get on with things."

It sounded cold, but Anne understood a desire for terrible times to be swept away. "Imagine, please, that you get your wish." She paused, examining her expression, letting the woman think. "You're picturing a return to tranquility. Yes?" Miss Lee nodded. Anne peered directly into her eyes. "That's not what is going to happen. I'll give you a glimpse into your future," she said urgently. "I'm sure you've already experienced a few sleepless nights of worry and fear, have you not?"

Reluctantly, the woman nodded her head. "If it is murder, who did it? I can't believe it, and yet I suppose I must."

"Because it's what happened. Let me tell you, the girls are also having sleepless nights, but together, they will talk. Fear will grow among them. Some will have fun with it, tormenting the others, as girls do."

"Surely—"

"I'm not done," Anne said, her voice hard and tone bleak. "Who did this terrible deed, they'll ask each other. Is the murderer even now lurking about, looking for another victim? They will write letters home. Parents will become alarmed and some will remove their girls. Gossip will spread about how the women who run the Lee school can't safeguard their precious charges. Women in our society must guard their reputations with vigor. Even the parents who don't remove their daughters will talk to other parents. Others will justify leaving their girls here, but you won't get any new girls, not a single one. If this is not solved, it will hang over your school forever. Ask your sister Anne. She understands what I'm talking about. She sees it if you will not."

Miss Lee paced away, then turned. "All right, enough. What would you have me do to prevent this dire occurrence?"

"Don't let the Colliers take Faithful's belongings, not yet. Don't encourage them to take Faithful's body. Delay, if you can. I'm hoping I have made sure they cannot and will remain another few days at least, but if you have the opportunity, encourage them to be patient and to trust that everyone wishes to discover the truth."

Miss Lee regarded Anne, her head tipped to one side. After a moment she said, "You think the Colliers had something to do with Faithful's death, don't you? Her brother and her *father*? Surely not!"

"I don't know."

"You are enjoying this . . . this *spectacle*!" the woman accused. "I cannot help but think, my lady, that you are looking for scandal where there may be none."

"I am not!"

"I won't believe the Colliers are involved."

"Then who did this? She was murdered, there is no refuting that. If it was not the Colliers, we are left with your staff or your students. Would you prefer one of them to be the culprit?"

With an unintelligible exclamation, the schoolmistress turned and glared out the window, wringing her hands together. "I don't know. My preference has nothing to do with it!"

"You're right about that."

"I want the truth."

"As do I," Ann insisted. Should she disclose what she had seen of Miss Dankworth and Augustus Collier? Should she say what Ginny saw, Miss Hopewell and a gentleman on the top floor the night of the murder? Not yet.

She stepped up to the schoolmistress, who turned toward her, and addressed the obvious suspicions about her motives. "Miss Lee, I am not a dilettante dabbling in crime solving. This is not entertainment for me, whatever you may think." She saw in the other woman's eyes that she had considered it. "This is no rich woman's frivolity. I met Faithful. I liked the child. I want her killer to be punished, to be hanged by the neck until dead."

Miss Lee gasped at the extreme language.

"Yes, I wish him — or her — *dead*. I do *not* want an innocent person to suffer suspicion, and that too is a possibility. I want Faithful avenged. I'm not asking for forever, just a day or two. I have narrowed the field to a few suspects."

"May I know who they are?"

Anne considered it and reluctantly shook her head. "I respect you and your sisters immensely, but if I tell you what I fear, I worry you wouldn't be able to treat my suspect with equanimity."

"That implies that one of my household or staff—or even one of the students, I suppose—is on your list of suspects. And to tell me whom you suspect, you would need to tell me *why* you suspect them." She frowned and looked away, faint lines on her face revealing the wear that time and trouble was taking. She was a businesswoman, but also an artist, who felt things deeply. "That would, perhaps, leave me with information about their lives I have little interest in, but once revealed, I cannot un-remember it. It would color my opinions. We all have those secrets that, if revealed, would change how others view us." She turned to Anne. "I cannot swear I would be able to separate suspicion and doubt from what I know of them. Two days, my lady. I make no bones about it; you have *two days*. I will cooperate and do my utmost to keep the Colliers here."

"And say nothing about what we have spoken."

She nodded.

• • •

Having determined that Wee Robbie and Irusan were still performing their valuable task—the giant cat had a most promising mousehole staked out—and were welcome to stay for luncheon and a few hours after, Anne walked swiftly away from the school toward a small pastry shop at which she and Tony had met a couple of times. They sold the best Bath buns Anne had ever tasted, and she was furiously hungry. When she entered the steamy, delicious-smelling establishment, she saw Tony and Lord Westmacott at a table by the window. Both men rose as she entered and sat when she took her seat.

A pot of chocolate and a plate of Bath buns was set on the table. The light sweet buns, made with lavish amounts of egg and cream, were warm from the oven. Anne tore one into pieces, dipping it in her chocolate. As a luncheon it was cloying, but the brain required such rich food, or so she would say if anyone mentioned it.

Her delicious fiancé was being stared at by every lady in the place. Lord Westmacott, too, watched the marquess devour his food with an indulgent smile, while he sipped tea with lemon. His waistcoat was already too tight, he complained. His stays creaked when he moved.

Finished and ready to share theories, Anne said, "Shall we talk now?"

Tony glanced over at the table next to them, where two matrons with fractious little lads sat gossiping. "I think it is best if we walk and talk in private surroundings."

Anne rose and tugged a shawl over her spencer. "We can walk toward the Royal Crescent. Today is moving day for Alethea, Bertie and the others and I said I would drop in. I got a note from Alethea this morning that accused me of neglecting my social duties in favor of scandal and murder."

"Let us walk that way."

Lord Westmacott bowed out, saying his aging legs would not carry him so far. Anne knew he would end up in the card room at the Assembly Rooms, where he would discreetly gamble and win against those who mistook his bonhomie for idiocy or even frivolity. Westmacott was never frivolous where money and cards were concerned.

Anne and Tony walked together away from the pastry and chocolate shop. "What have you learned?"

"What, no soft words of longing or impatience for me?"

She looked up at him with a smile and took his offered arm. "You're not the kind of man who requires reminding. I have displayed my eagerness most immodestly at times. Now, stop teasing. What have you learned?"

"Some of this is from Lord Westmacott. He is a remarkable man, Anne. His knowledge of society is vast and threads through every layer like tree roots through the earth. He discovered information on certain debts one of our subjects had accrued. I learned more after a brief visit to Bristol, from men who know all of the interested parties."

"You mean the Colliers?"

"Mr. Collier the elder is known as a particularly sharp fellow, who specializes in the law as it pertains to business partnerships and lawsuits resulting from them."

"And the son?"

"He is a failure no matter how you look at it. He began training as a solicitor, but his mentor died during his training. Young Mr. Collier declined to begin again, as would be required. His father became weary of supporting him and found him a clerkship at the Hawkins Africa Shipping company, where he is nominally employed."

"Nominally?"

"He's not terribly good at his job. It seems his father is paying an apprenticeship fee, so he retains his position." Darkefell shrugged. "He is an expensive wastrel who still requires his father's support. If his family was wealthier, that would go unnoticed, I suppose, for there are any number like him in government offices throughout the empire. He has been embroiled in several scandals. His father is, from Bristol reports, becoming weary enough of his son's mischief that he may send him away to the colonies in the New World, or India. The young man does not wish to go anywhere. He'd rather be rich and has been attempting for some time to attract a wealthy bride, though the ladies of Bristol have been too intelligent so far to accept his elopement proposals."

"These scandals of which you spoke, what are they?"

"He attempted to abscond to Gretna with a rich young lady. He was stopped, and his father paid a fee to help him escape unscathed. Having been in that situation with my own ward, I suspect the father did not want it bandied about that his daughter was compromised and so declined to press charges. Even worse in the eyes of some, he has incurred gambling debts in excess of his means."

"Has his father paid them?"

"Lord Westmacott was unable to answer that question, and my trip to Bristol did not illuminate it. I suspect there are debts beyond what the younger Collier has confessed to the elder."

"He is an inveterate and unlucky gambler and a fortune seeker, but that doesn't make him a killer. As much as it makes a kind of sense that Faithful's murder was a family affair, I can find nothing to support the theory. How does Faithful's death benefit anyone?"

"One cannot prove a negative, Anne. There are still areas of investigation within her family. Did she know a secret and threaten to tell it?"

"She was not that sort of girl, Tony. She had no malice, even though she did not appear fond of her brother."

"Revealing a family secret may not have even been malice, it could have been because she didn't know she was not to reveal it."

"I suppose."

"I began to wonder about all of the Bristol connections in this mystery, and while I was there I also asked after the mysterious housekeeper and her slovenly husband."

"Yes?" she said, her interest quickened. She nodded to an acquaintance as they strolled past.

"Nothing much beyond what you already know, most likely, from Osei."

"He was able to tell me some interesting information."

"It seems they were virtually run out of town after losing the boardinghouse. Thompson is known as a fellow not above a bit of petty larceny. He has been picked up before for various charges including public drunkenness and lewd behavior, has been charged with theft on occasion, and spent time in jail, a few years in one stretch. More often a month or so here and there. He has been fortunate not to hang or be transported."

Neither magistrate mentioned having Jonty up on charges in Bath, and surely Brereton would have. It didn't mean the thief had stayed out of trouble, though, just that he had not been caught.

"I do have a promising avenue of investigation," Tony said. "I am going to shock you now, my lady, and speak of indelicate matters."

His tone was mocking, and she picked up the gauntlet of humor he had laid down. "Oh, do tell me, my lord! I like to be shocked and sent all aquiver." She shivered dramatically, hugging his arm to her side.

He chuckled. "Mr. Collier the younger had a lady friend with whom he was known to cavort."

"Not one he was willing to marry, if he was looking for an heiress?"

"No, the kind of girl you don't marry. But more on that in a moment. Where was I? Oh, yes . . . the lady friend. This could be another expense he incurred; imagine if she fell pregnant, or incurred debts in his name."

"Still has nothing to do with Faithful."

"I have not told you all. You know that Faithful and Augustus are half siblings."

"Yes."

"Did you know that the second Mrs. Collier came to the marriage with considerable money?"

"She was the daughter of a viscount. Her family may have had money. Faithful's poor mother died in an asylum. What does that have to do with Augustus Collier?"

"This is where it gets messy and hazy, my dear. Patience, if you please. The second Mrs. Collier's family is wealthy, even, it appears, the distaff branches. There was a maiden aunt, sister to Faithful's late mother. She had money."

"Had?"

"She died sixteen months ago."

"I still don't see—"

"She left money—a lot of it—to Faithful."

Anne chewed on the news. It tangled in her mind, threads becoming snarled. There was something there, but what? "I don't understand what this has to do with Faithful's death."

"Think about it, Anne. Who inherits Faithful's bequest?"

"Her father," Anne replied slowly.

"If he is struggling for money because of his expensive son, the money might come in handy. I'm not saying that's the solution, but it is certainly possible."

She considered the situation. "Tony, if her aunt died sixteen months ago, who has been looking after Faithful's bequest until now?"

"Likely her father, who was also the aunt's barrister, I might add. It would certainly be customary for her father to look after Faithful's bequest."

Anne recalled Susanna's problems getting her inheritance from her father and her suspicions that he was delaying because he had misappropriated the funds and would now need to account for them. Had Faithful's father done the same? "Perhaps Mr. Collier, with an expensive son and gambling debts—"

"A motive for murder?"

"Rather than having to account for missing money, yes."

"He would not need to account for the money until she was about to wed."

"True," Anne said. She told him of her other suspects, the Thompsons and Miss Hopewell, then sighed. "They do all seem to be tangled up with each other, do they not? The Colliers, the Thompsons, Faithful. The tangled roots go even deeper, it seems to me. I've told you about Augustus Collier and Miss Dankworth's meeting in the Pump Room and argument in the park and her calling him a liar. I have told you about Miss Hopewell's upper-floor nighttime excursion the night Faithful died. What if . . ." She stopped walking and thought. "No, that wouldn't work."

"What wouldn't work?"

"I thought perhaps Augustus Collier and India Hopewell conspired to kill Faithful for her inheritance."

"Neither of them will have access to it, I don't imagine."

"You're right. The family angle may not work. I am left with Miss Hopewell and the Thompson husband and wife as suspects."

"We shall explore on."

"My head hurts," Anne said crossly.

Chapter Twenty-two

There were movers at the Crescent location, but the family was not there. Their harried butler informed them that the family had departed to the comfort of the Pump Room, where Quin was having his daily treatments, accompanied by Dr. Fothergill. She stood undecided.

Tony awaited her next wishes, but when she didn't speak, he said, "I must go, Anne. Your father and Jamey are to visit a lecture at the Assembly Rooms this afternoon. There is a famous astronomer visiting, and I promised to accompany them. I may be able to help your investigation even there."

She smiled up at him and reached up, touching his hair, pushing back one unruly lock. She felt him shudder at her touch, a shiver of desire that caused a pulse in his forehead. Perhaps once they were married that desire would calm. She hoped not. "I love how you call it my investigation. And yes, please, pluck grains of information for me. What will you do there?"

"I understand that the magistrate, Mr. Brereton—my landlord, as it were—will be in attendance and I expect he will try to ingratiate himself with me. I have heard from those who know local politics that he is always looking for a leg up in the social circle, even ignoring legal peccadilloes of the rich."

"You mean people bribe him to look the other way?"

"I didn't say that, Anne. No, I think he is reluctant to press charges on those who can afford to defend themselves against them."

"How shoddy a legal practice our country is prone to."

"Shall I speak with him and see if he has made any progress on the investigation?"

"What investigation?" she said caustically. "He would rather the whole thing disappear."

"I suppose that's natural for any peace-loving man. I have felt that way myself in his shoes."

"You didn't let it guide your actions, Tony. You did what was necessary to keep safety and peace in your household and community," she said, referring to his past actions to catch and convict a murderer at Darkefell Castle.

"I am an exceptional man, in case you did not realize it."

She took his arm and hugged it to her. "I fully realize it, my lord, or I should not be marrying you. An exceptional man deserves an exceptional woman."

"On that we are agreed."

"I have no sense Brereton is in any way extraordinary. He is a brewer who inherited his wealth and expanded it by his judicial purchase of land. He is a magistrate because here all it takes is to be a local landowner and businessman." She grimaced. "Like you said, he is a social climbing fellow and will likely bend a knee to you because of your eminence. I don't like him, but by all means talk to him. Make him ashamed, if you can, by telling him your intended wife is indefatigable and will stalk the killer into submission. Tell him I have several new insights and expect to produce the culprit imminently."

He chuckled and squeezed her arm. "I shall relay the message, you can be sure of it, and shame him into acting if I can. Shall I walk with you back to the Lee school?"

"Perhaps that would be best. I can see what havoc Robbie and Irusan have wrought."

They walked in companionable silence and bid each other a warm farewell. She wished what she told him in jest to pass on to the magistrate was true, that she had a killer in her sights. There were threads she felt sure were part of the mystery, but none would fit tidily. If Osei could discover if both Colliers came together to Bath from Bristol, that knowledge would help immeasurably. It was hard to imagine that both men would be involved in a plot, but not outside the bounds of possibility, she supposed.

She entered the school, where all was quiet. She sought out Anne Lee, who was in her office upstairs with a student, tutoring her in English history. Miss Henrietta Greerson was clearly struggling with a question Miss Lee leveled at her about the Reformation, and escaped happily when Anne asked the tutor to talk.

Closing the door behind her escaping pupil, Miss Lee motioned for Anne to sit, and sat down opposite her.

"In your opinion," Anne said bluntly, "who among the staff or students would be most likely to go along with a plot to kill Faithful?"

The tutor gaped, then regained her equilibrium. "I can't think of any single one of the girls, and neither of the teachers. Miss Dankworth is too painfully principled, and Miss Hopewell—who I do not like, as we have confirmed — is too stupid."

"It doesn't take intelligence to go along with a plot. She could be a cat's-paw."

"True, but I maintain she would have given herself away a hundred times if she had been involved."

Maybe she already had. Ginny seeing her with a man that night, and the teacher's shifting account of who it was, were points in favor of that theory. "What about the male teachers? Can you see any of them involved in an intrigue?"

"Those men have too much to lose and absolutely nothing to gain. They had little contact with Faithful except as a student, a half hour at a time."

"True. I'd like to see Miss Dankworth again, this afternoon, as well as Alys Edisbury and a couple of the other girls. It may seem like I am stumbling about in the dark, but I do have questions to answer."

"I'll summon Carlotta and have her meet you upstairs." Anne Lee swept from the room.

Anne ascended to her borrowed space, and a few moments later Miss Dankworth entered the room, staying close to the door. Anne motioned to the chair opposite her. They sat in silence for a few minutes. "If I were you," Anne said, taking a shot at what she thought might be behind the teacher's frightened demeanor, "I would not want to protect someone who had shown no regard for me."

"I beg your pardon, my lady?"

"Miss Hopewell says she barely knows you. That you're not friends." She watched the other woman's face as she said it and knew she had landed an arrow in her breast.

Wounded, Miss Dankworth's eyes watered and she sniffed. "I . . . I can't say why she said that, for we spent our vacation together, and that is what friends do."

"I have finally made a connection, Miss Dankworth. You spent the summer in Bristol, at Miss Hopewell's aunt's boardinghouse. Correct?" She nodded. "And you knew that she was spending time with Mr. Augustus Collier, correct?"

She looked like a frightened rabbit caught in a snare. She wasn't sure whether to admit it, deny it, or stay silent. Her eyes slewed right, her eyes slewed left, but she ultimately chose silence.

"May I call you Carlotta?"

"M-my friends call me Lotta," the teacher stuttered.

"We are not friends, though, are we? I don't make friends with anyone who protects people who do bad things. Maybe you didn't know at first what you were involved in," Anne suggested. "Or maybe you thought the person in question innocent. Why did you tell Mr. Augustus Collier that he was a liar?"

"Because he is."

"What did he lie about?" The woman stared but stayed silent. Maybe she hadn't asked quite the right question. "Miss Dankworth, what did he lie to *you* about?"

She bit her lip, which was trembling. "He told me he loved me, but that India was holding something over him and he needed me to carry messages to her. I told him India and I were friends, but he said she had spoken ill of me, and that I should . . . should do what he asked, and maybe we'd . . . maybe we'd marry someday."

He was using Miss Dankworth to facilitate correspondence with a possibly reluctant or angry Miss Hopewell, but to what end? "What made you realize he had lied about being in love with you?"

She was silent, looking down at her hands, as tears dripped from her eyes.

"Miss Dankworth?"

She looked up and closed her eyes. "He said he was negotiating to get out of her grasp. I believed him at first, but India was once my friend. In the summer we were as close as sisters. She even asked me to keep silent about Mrs. Thompson being her aunt." She gasped, wide-eyed, and put her hand over her mouth. "Oh, I should not have said it!"

"I already knew, though I didn't know why you told no one. I could understand why Miss Hopewell did, but your motive was a mystery. Now I know that too," Anne replied dryly. "Carry on, Miss Dankworth."

"I still have not told the Lees about it. Poor Mrs. Thompson needed a job after she lost her boardinghouse."

"Why *did* she lose her boardinghouse?"

"A speculator talked Jonty into investing money. It was supposed to be a lottery, guaranteed money."

"Guaranteed money?" Anne frowned. "Miss Dankworth, the words 'lottery' and 'guarantee' do not belong in the same sentence.

And if it is investment you are speaking of, it is called speculation for a reason; nothing is certain in investments. Those who consistently earn money in speculation are those who set up the fund. Hoaxers, cons and tricksters prosper."

Chastised, the teacher remained silent as Anne thought it through. Was it possible that Augustus Collier had, through India Hopewell, encouraged Mr. and Mrs. Thompson to "invest," or rather speculate? Many speculated by investing in shipping—in which business Mr. Collier was employed—then when ships went down, losing all the cargo, human or otherwise, those investors lost everything. Insurance was expensive. Perhaps investors were hoaxed into thinking the investment safe because of the insurance, should the ship sink?

Maybe. Maybe not. Regardless of any of it, the Thompsons lost their boardinghouse and local magistrates were hinted that Jonty had best leave Bristol, for if he was caught one more time on the wrong side of the law, transportation was in his future. She shook herself; time to think about that later. Right now the instructress was staring at her with trepidation. "You were vacillating between believing him or Miss Hopewell?"

She nodded. "I looked at myself in the mirror one day and thought, what would make him choose me over India?" It was a painful admission. "The answer was, *nothing*! He saw nothing but a fool to use. I became suspicious and opened a note I was supposed to take to her."

"What did it say?"

"It was a note between lovers, that was clear, or at least between two who *had* been lovers." Once the floodgates were opened, Miss Dankworth told Anne what she knew about Mr. Augustus Collier, Miss India Hopewell, their relationship, and what it all had to do with Faithful. It was a revealing recitation, with money at the heart of it, as gold would inevitably intrude into love affairs gone wrong, or even those going right.

Collier was aware of and resented his half sister's inheritance. She would come into her money when she turned eighteen—her maternal aunt did not believe in strictures on women when it came to money—but that would be hastened if she married. Collier apparently had a scheme with Miss Hopewell where he thought to influence Faithful to marry a friend of his, to elope to Gretna Green, in fact, and that friend, in exchange, would make sure Mr. Augustus Collier was compensated when he got his greedy hands on Faithful's money.

It was a dastardly plan, but to effect it, Faithful had to stay alive. Augustus Collier got nothing from her death. But in any case, the scheme did not go off. Miss Dankworth indignantly said she would never let an innocent girl like Faithful be used that way.

Anyway, perhaps, Anne speculated, the father learned of the scheme and it inspired one of his own; rather than have the money go to a husband he would be better off if Faithful died, leaving the money to him. She didn't say any of that last theory out loud, thanking Miss Dankworth for her honesty and dismissing her, after an admonition to say nothing to Miss Hopewell of their conversation.

Anne had intended to speak to others of the students, but her mind was whirling after her conversation with Miss Dankworth, and it was getting later in the day. She now had more questions than before, and things she had been certain of, she no longer was. She descended and went to the back garden, staring up at the upper-floor windows. She had so many questions.

Jonty bumbled into the garden from a gate to the street but stopped dead when he saw her.

"You!" Anne said. "Mr. Thompson, I have questions for you. You saw something the night Faithful fell or was pushed out of the window."

He shook his head. "Didn't see nuffin," he growled around the pipe clamped in his teeth.

"Heard, then; you must have heard something. I speculate there were at least two people involved." He stubbornly stared off at the back garden wall and shook his head. He was frightened, Anne thought. She tried another couple of questions, but he made a disgusting noise in the back of his throat, spat on the ground and scuttled into the garden shed, slamming the door shut.

Discouraged and confused, she told the Lees she would return in the morning, as she had engagements she could not get out of. It was almost the truth. She was going to see her father and brother. She retrieved Robbie and Irusan and left.

• • •

After depositing Robbie and Irusan back at her grandmother's house, she walked to Upper Church Street. A late afternoon visit to her father and brother was the refresher she needed. They were full of excitement at the fascinating astronomer whose talk they had attended at the Assembly Rooms. Miss Caroline Herschel gave a rare lecture on her discovery of comets using the telescopes she helped create for her brother, William Herschel.

"We were privileged to hear her! She is the littlest miss you ever have seen," her father said, holding out one hand at chest height, "and very German, don't you know—I wished terribly to have a discussion with her about the German dialect from . . . but never mind—and terribly fascinating. Wasn't she, Jamey?"

Her brother nodded vigorously. "Annie, Annie, oh! I said my sister was a famous investigator, and she was kind to me. I wished to put her in my vest pocket and carry her about, but I could not, I know that. She is not a mouse or a hedgehog. She did not look frightened of me like some ladies do, you know, for I become excited and talk too much and too fast. She stayed afterward. We spoke of our telescope, which new brother bought for us."

Anne smiled over at Tony, who sat a ways away writing a letter. He smiled back, warmly. She mouthed *thank you*, and he nodded gravely, dropping a wink. She stared; he was becoming playful! An extraordinary development she had begun to witness of late.

"Miss Herschel was interested in Tony's rooftop observatory, as I called it, but the marquess made sure she knew it was no such thing, just chairs for an old man and his son, and a table for tea things." Her father smiled. Sitting back, a look of surprise widened his eyes. "I never knew Bath had so much to recommend it! There is a farming society that Darkefell has joined and promised me a spot in, and the astronomers' club. And bookstores! Osei, darling fellow that he is, has given me a list of all the best places for me and Jamey to explore."

"Mother always said you had an unreasoning prejudice against the place."

"Perhaps we shall stay on into the new year while you and your new husband travel north."

Anne took a deep breath. Was there a possible rapprochement between her father and mother? She would accept it for what it was, a tentative hand extended, a truce. Along with the gift of the reset diamonds, it showed her father's intentions to mend their damaged marriage.

"Back to the lecture. There were many of Bath's leading lights there, my dear. Even Mr. Edward Collibee, the last mayor! Merchants, magistrates, businessmen, all gathered to listen to this tiny little German lady! Astounding."

They had a late luncheon together, then the earl and his son retired upstairs to write notes on the lecture, which they would compare that evening.

Anne stayed at the table and spoke to Tony. "It was kind of you to accompany my father and brother. It is not necessary, you know. If you have business that takes you elsewhere, my father along with Dorcas and Alf are accustomed to dealing with Jamey on their own."

He nodded. "It is my pleasure. I find myself fascinated with your brother's astounding mind. He is a lot like your father in his singlemindedness on a subject. He has already learned enough from the book I gave him that he and Miss Herschel were quite able to carry on an interesting conversation, except that your father was fascinated by her accent and quizzed her on the dialect of German she was most familiar with, speaking of his planned book on comparative language. He is not even aware when he does it, you know, when his thoughts run on. I'm convinced he thinks they did not speak of it, but they did. There was a real possibility that the two gentlemen would monopolize her time to such an extent that she might never get away, and I could see she was wearying."

"Oh, I hope they did not put the poor lady out of countenance?"

"Not at all. She was kindness itself, but I saw in her my own discomfort at long periods exposed to too much humanity. I drew the fellows away, letting her escape." He smiled. "As I hinted, I was there on a mission for you, too. I was hoping Brereton would be in attendance so I could quiz him on the investigation into Faithful Collier's death, but he was not there at first."

"At first?"

"More on him later. First, I spoke again with Lord Westmacott at the Assembly Hall."

"We are engaged to him this evening, my mother and I. Surely he was not attending the lecture?" Her mother's dear friend was a vain man and he would be the first to say it, more interested in ballroom slippers than heavenly nebulae. That frivolity hid a heart of gold and a sharp wit, when he chose to employ it, along with a bottomless curiosity about people that made him both a gossip and a secret doer of good deeds. Nevertheless, he would not risk his reputation by being seen attending a serious astronomical lecture.

"He was in the card room, where he had been watching Mr. Augustus Collier lose. The young man is, it seems, exceptionally bad at cards, but with the confidence of a much better player."

Osei joined them, bringing with him fresh air from his day of exploration. A maid brought him tea, curtseying and blushing when the secretary thanked her, with his grave politeness. Osei was a favorite belowstairs in every household because of his kind demeanor and calm disposition.

Anne caught him up on their conversation, and the marquess continued.

"Westmacott had more information for me. He relayed what gossip he had gleaned around the card room, much that is a repetition of what we already know, that the elder Collier is respected in law circles in Bristol, but his son is a scapegrace, leaving a trail of broken promises and gambling debts behind. Even his position at the shipping company is hanging by a thread."

"On that topic *I* have fresh information," Osei said after a long draught of tea. "Having searched exhaustively, I can tell you with certainty that the Colliers came to Bath from Bristol together, in the afternoon on the day Miss Collier's body was discovered. That fits with the indication we have from the Lees that a messenger sent to them in Bristol found them at their homes or lodgings. After receiving the dreadful news, they gathered their things and traveled by carriage together."

Anne slumped in despair. "I don't like losing my favorite two suspects, but that washes out that theory, I suppose. Unless I surmise nefarious machinations between the two Collier men and can suppose the father and son conspired to kill poor Faithful—which fits with none of my pet theories—it looks like both may be cleared of wrongdoing."

"Now, not so quickly," Tony said. "Who told you that they came together?" he asked his secretary.

"The ostler at the livery stable," Osei replied. His spectacles gleamed in the candlelight. "I finally found the one who was working that day."

"And is he not bribable?"

Osei appeared to think on the topic. Anne watched his face. On occasion he withheld his opinion judiciously, when to give it meant contradicting his employer. Tony was a good man and an excellent employer, but he had been raised knowing his word was absolute. He did not like to be crossed. He was not petulant, nor was he vengeful, but he occasionally was irritated by contradiction. Would this be one of those times?

"That's not likely, sir." Carefully, Osei explained: "I don't think you can appreciate how vital an unimpeachable record of employment is to a working man. The ostler has been at the livery for three years. He has a wife and child. A bribe, as tempting as it would be, would not feed his family until they are grown. His job will." He paused, then added, "I asked about him in the tavern nearby where he takes his dinner. He's a steady sort."

Tony nodded. "Perhaps you judge rightly. There may be other explanations. From my inquiries in Bristol I was able to confirm the elder Collier received the message of his daughter's death. He lives in the house alone, other than his servants, of course. His son has lodgings. Is it not possible that the son was somewhere in Bath already when the father arrived? The elder Collier could have picked his son up, and they could have traveled together to the livery."

"You make a good point, sir."

Darkefell turned to Anne. "Brereton did finally come to the Assembly Rooms and I spoke with him briefly. He had nothing to report, or at least nothing he would tell me, except all was being investigated most closely. I gave him the subtle message you wished, Anne, about the Colliers and etcetera. Perhaps even now he is taking action."

"I hope so. He has the right to ask questions we cannot and is a familiar face in this city. I hope something comes of it all."

"But I did not tell you all that Westmacott told me about his examination of Mr. Collier the younger. He was seated quite close, at the next whist table. Mr. Augustus Collier was boasting quite loudly—in his cups, I imagine—and saying that he would quite soon be flush with money. I found that interesting. What do you suppose that means?"

Anne, in shock, stared at the wall, her mind churning. "What indeed?" she murmured.

Chapter Twenty-three

The day had been long. Anne sat on a chaise in her room reading a letter. Irusan, after his busy day, was curled up on her bed in a contented ball of fur. Wind rattled the windowpane and the candle's flame flickered in the chill air that found its way in. It would soon be time to get dressed for a dinner engagement with Lord Westmacott, but she had almost an hour.

There was a tap at her door. "Come in," Anne answered.

Wee Robbie entered with a folded wax-sealed note. "Milady, this came by hand."

She set her letter aside and held out her hand. "Who is it from?"

"The magistrate," he said, giving her the note.

She glanced down at the seal, *TB* with a handsome profile featuring Brereton's beaky nose. News, perhaps! Mayhap Tony's encouragement was paying dividends already. But with a frown, she glanced up at Robbie. "The magistrate came to our house? Is he here now?"

"No, milady, pardon. It's a *messenger* from the magistrate. He's a'waiting downstairs. Said to put this message in your hand, and your hand *only.*"

"Even if he has news, why would he bring it to me?" She broke the seal. It was a short note in a wonderfully legible hand.

> "My lady, I pray this letter finds you in glorious health. I have discovered something of great import concerning the . . ."

She stopped reading aloud and read further in silence.

> . . . concerning the fate of poor Miss Faithful Collier. I suspect you and the good doctor Fothergill — with whom I am this moment discussing this latest finding — have been right all along and those low-born Collier men are behind the child's murder. Your fiancé, the Marquess, today had a few questions for me that I could not answer, but it made me curious. I have taken his advice and made inquiries that are yet to bear fruit. I can say no more on that matter,

though I have been assured I will know more soon.

The case is become desperate, though. I'm afraid my inquiries have made their way to the father and son, who, alive to their imminent arrest, and are about to abscond.

Anne sat up straight, alarmed. But how far could they go?

. . . They are, I've been reliably informed, packing their bags and will abandon their claim to Miss Collier's body. That seems to me to be the last assurance that one or both are guilty of the poor girl's murder. If they make their way to Bristol I despair of capturing them, as there is a packet headed to Spain departing on the next tide.

A ship! Anne had not considered the Colliers' familiarity with shipping and the benefits of knowing the sailing schedule and sea captains willing to take passengers.

. . . Once they are in Bristol, who knows if we will ever find them? Lost to us forever, that poor child's death will go unavenged. Who knows what she suffered at the hands of her father and contemptible brother? Please accompany my trusted assistant with this letter in hand to the Saracens Head, for I have a question to ask, one I dare not commit to paper, as it is of a delicate nature. I would not ask a lady to do such a thing under any but extreme circumstances, but your information will give me the last piece of this puzzle and allow me to detain the despicable pair, who I am watching this very minute. Thus have I provided you with an escort and safety. I beg of you, for little Miss Faithful's sake, do not fail me.

Dr. Fothergill sends his respects and bids you hasten, milady. There is no time to waste! Please, if you wish to see justice done, meet me.

Your servant,

T. Brereton — Magistrate

She frowned and stared at the note. What could he possibly need to ask her that he could not write in a private note? She could guess what was meant by a "delicate question," though she might be wrong. Had Mr. Augustus Collier taken advantage of his sister? Did Brereton think she might have insight into it, as she had met Faithful before the girl's death?

Common sense would command she stay home and send her driver to meet the fellow. Or send a note to Tony and Osei. It would be ridiculous to go out herself to discover what he had to say. No lady in her right mind would do it. And yet, if the answer to this awful puzzle was close at hand, she would give much to know the truth.

He said he was watching the Colliers at the Saracens Head and dare not leave. He also said he was with Dr. Fothergill. Could he not leave the doctor to watch them? But the doctor did not have the authority to make an arrest, should it become necessary. Perhaps this vital information he thought she had was the last piece of the puzzle needed to arrest the pair.

It was such a tangle, for she had no such information, and yet if he did not arrest them, they would flee. She chewed her lip and read the note again. "Robbie, what is this fellow like, the man at the door?"

"Big feller, milady. Been in a few punch-ups, I'd guess. Got an ear like a cauliflower, been hit so often. Boxer, likely, and a big jaggy scar along his jaw, and a nose that's bent to the left." His description was given excitedly as he hopped on one foot, for every lad loves a boxer, and the more beat up the better. "He seems right pleasant," he added, settling down. "Cook is givin' him cake and ale. Says a big feller like that needs cake. She's actin' all moony, milady, red in the face and smiling at him and feeding him cakes." His tone was aggrieved. "I asked her, I said how could I grow to be a big fellow if I don't get cake?"

Anne smiled. That was Robbie's constant complaint, not enough cake, even though he was indulged to a shocking degree. She sobered. If it were true that the Colliers were about to leave Bath, the magistrate was right, they needed to do something immediately. How she could help was a bit of a mystery, but she always wished to be in the thick of things. "I'll go." She got up, tucked the note in her pocket, then hesitated.

What if this note was not from Brereton at all? She believed it was, but still, better to be safe, or as safe as she was willing to be while doing exactly as she wanted. She took it out of her pocket, sat back down, took out her desk, and wrote a note. She sanded it and folded it with Brereton's note enclosed, then melted sealing wax and pressed her personal seal into it. "Robbie, will you do something for me? If you do it swiftly, I promise you a cake. A lot of cake. And a whole dozen Bath buns."

"Yes, milady!" he said, eyes shining as he hopped from foot to foot.

"Take this to the marquess and Mr. Boatin. You know where they are, correct?"

"Upper Church Street, milady." It was farther away than the Saracens Head, and in the opposite direction, but not far for a nimble lad like Robbie. He stopped before darting away, though, and stared at her. "You're not goin' out alone, are you, milady? It's dark out."

The faint Scottish brogue of his mother came out when he said words like *out*, and she smiled, swiping a curl off his forehead. He didn't know the note had said she was to accompany the man who brought it, and she wouldn't have been able to explain her failure to comply anyway. Common sense said either she trusted the magistrate and should accept the company of the messenger, or she *didn't* trust him and she shouldn't go to the inn at all. Or perhaps the note was not even from the magistrate, but from a desperate criminal luring her into a trap. And yet, here she was, at a fork in the road and about to take neither path, but forge one of her own, straight ahead. She'd do things her own way. "That's why I am sending you to his lordship and Mr. Osei. They will meet me and see me protected."

Still, he hesitated. "Mama would go with you, milady."

"I know she would, but I sent her to bed an hour ago with a fever. I would never have her come out in wet weather. It could be the death of her, and she is too important to both of us to let her suffer."

His mother was his world, and he loved her with a ferocity that was gratifying and sweetly funny. And yet he still hesitated.

"Go!" she commanded. "I will be back here within the hour to have dinner with Lord Westmacott, but only if we get moving now."

"Will you at least take Sir Irusan with you, milady?"

She smiled at the notion that he thought a cat good protection. But if it would soothe his worries . . . "I will."

"What should I tell m'mother, milady? She expects me to go to bed soon."

"You may tell her what is going on . . ."

He looked relieved.

". . . Once you get back from the marquess's. This task should take you forty minutes if you move smartly. Remember: cake is the reward, with Bath buns if you're extra good! Now, be quick and do not say anything to the messen—" She stopped. If they didn't tell the messenger anything he'd start asking questions. "Will you tell the messenger I'll be down in a moment?" The boy nodded. "Don't let him see you leave the house afterward though, and don't tell him about the note you carry! Discretion, Robbie! And dress warmly in that new coat your mother made you."

She shooed him on his way, donned a dark cloak, beckoned her sleepy cat—a promise was a promise—and slipped along the hall toward the stairs. She could hear the faint murmur of her mother's criticisms as her maid worked on her hair, and her grandmother loudly complaining to a footman about a loose spot on the rug. She took up a candlestick from a table in the hall, slipped past their rooms and to the stairs, then descended, waiting on the landing until the entry hall was vacant. Heart pounding, her mouth dry, she pulled her cloak tight about her and emerged into the gathering gloom, followed closely by Irusan, now thoroughly awake and ready for an adventure.

Her cat relished the dark, though he was seldom allowed out alone in the city. It was damp, as she had feared, but not raining at this moment. She sheltered the candle flame from the breeze as Irusan followed her in his own way, slipping from hedge to hedge, bush to bush, a dark streak in lamplight at times, at others, leaping out at her from the shadows.

She knew how to get to the Saracens Head, straight down the Paragon to Broad Street—a block over from Milsom—past Saracen Street, and there would be the tavern. She had passed by it many times. It would be busy this time of evening, with the damp encouraging thirsty men to order port and mulled cider, and food to go with it, mutton or eel pie, turtle soup, ragout of beef. The kitchen would be a hum of activity, the tables full. To go there *should* be no more dangerous for her than to go to a pastry shop in the afternoon, she told herself, and yet she could not go in, nor even allow herself to be seen lingering close by. She must be wary and canny.

Would Brereton be awaiting her outside the tavern? What did he expect her to do once there? She exclaimed in exasperation as her candle guttered in the breeze and went out. She halted in her tracks, pinching the wick between her thumb and finger, and tucking the candlestick in the capacious pocket Mary had sewn into the cloak lining.

She was being a damned fool, she thought, halting in her steps. Irusan crept out from along a doorstep and looked up at her. Maybe the note wasn't from Brereton at all. Perhaps the Colliers had gotten wind of her investigation into their actions and wished to put an end to it.

She shook her head in disgust. That would be a ludicrously complicated plot. She walked on, Irusan prancing at her side, then darting down an alley into the shadows. As a carriage passed Anne crept into the shadow of a gate and waited until it was gone. She moved on, becoming increasingly relieved that she had sent off the note to Tony. Adventure was exhilarating, but there was every potential for danger this night.

Robbie was probably with Tony by now, being swifter than she was. She would look about the Saracens Head premises to see if the magistrate was there while awaiting her fiancé and Osei. It struck her that she was merely a street away from John and Lydia, on Milsom. She could go there and beg his help, but of all the people in the world who *might* help in a dire situation, Lord John would not be her choice. He was good-natured but dull, as unlike his older brother as chalk is to cheese.

She slipped past lamplit pools of light, staying in the shadows, and finally passed by Saracen Street as her thoughts tumbled about her brain like circus performers. How did Brereton propose to stop the Colliers? And what had made him decide that one or both men were Faithful's murderer?

What did he need to ask *her*?

Doubt again assailed her. Wouldn't Dr. Fothergill, the soul of manly discretion, come to see Anne himself instead of send a messenger? He had not seemed too fond of the magistrate previously. Perhaps they had mended fences.

There was the tavern ahead, the sound of laughter erupting whenever the door was opened. She hesitated. Past the tavern loomed the shadowy bulk of St. Michael's church, a domed structure built on the site of a medieval church in what was still referred to by older residents as Bath New Town, outside the old Northgate, torn down thirty years before.

The church offered shadowy protection. Light glowed in one of the windows; late work by the caretaker, or a minister finishing his sermon. It was surely a better place to be idling about if she was discovered. She slunk swiftly past the tavern, between customers coming and going, followed by her feline shadow. There was a protected porch near the street, and she slipped into the shadows of a church pillar, her heart pounding, wondering what in heaven's name she was doing. She could have gone to Tony, or she could have roused her coachman and taken him as a companion. She could have done a half dozen more sensible things than this, but the plain and simple truth was she wanted to do exactly what she wanted to do despite the danger. Over the last months she had taken countless risks and the feeling of her blood thumping through her veins had become a thrilling antidote to the stifling boredom of a woman's life.

With each successful foray into danger she was becoming more daring. Where would this enthusiasm for jeopardy end? All her life she had felt the pull of freedom, and had found a measure of it beyond most women. Wealth eased her way, though the wealthier a woman's family was, in general, the more restricted her life and movements. She had freedom because she was single, her father was taken up with other concerns—her brother's care, among others—and he believed as she did that women, as rational creatures, should be given the same freedoms men had.

Was this rational, what she had done? It was a conversation she must have with herself.

But not this moment.

She slipped out to the curb and stared at the tavern. Tony must by now have her note. She'd wait for him.

Tony. How she loved him and longed for marriage, and yet, at the same time, knew that it was going to change everything. Maybe that's why she was here, torn between acting and being sensible and awaiting her fiancé. Why *did* she have to wait, after all? If society was different, she could confidently walk where she wanted as men did, with no one questioning their presence. If she was a man, she could walk right into that tavern and meet with Brereton. But she couldn't. It would disrupt social convention and she would be in grave danger. Assumptions would be made about her, and liberties taken.

The tavern door opened and a man staggered out, took a few steps, then leaned against a wall, where he relieved himself. She turned away and took a deep breath.

Drunken men were dangerous men. Even sober men were dangerous if she was a woman unprotected, fair game, like a trembling sheep out of the care of a watchful shepherd and in peril from the wolf. The sot ambled peacefully away, weaving and singing on his path.

She stared at the door of the tavern, a low little establishment, two floors plus an attic nestled close by the church property. Shivering, she wrapped her cloak around herself more securely and considered her current dilemma. The impulsive decision to forge her own path to the Saracens Head had been tempered by the rational decision to send Tony the note. Now she was bound to stay and wait for him, rather than make her own decisions.

The tavern door opened again. She slid back into the shadows and ducked down, while keeping her eye on the door. Magistrate Brereton emerged, looking about, a puzzled expression on his gaunt face. Beside him was a tall brutish-looking fellow, looking exactly as Robbie had described, his ear like a cauliflower, the scar along the jaw, the nose bent out of shape. He must have crept in through the tavern's back door. Why was he not still waiting in Cook's warm kitchen? He must have realized she had slipped out without him.

Something was not right with Brereton. What was it? She shivered, huddled in her cloak. Should she come out of the shadows? Call Brereton over to her?

No, not yet. Something was very wrong. Must she accept that the Colliers, either severally or together, killed Faithful? If so, why? To hide some family disgrace? Family. Anne considered Faithful, the intelligent and observant daughter of a barrister. As much as Anne had suspected Mr. William Collier of killing his daughter, perhaps she had been prejudiced toward him by his cold and heartless appearance. As despicable as unfeeling lassitude was toward the memory of a dead child, it did not mean he killed her.

She peeked again toward the tavern. She had seen no trace of Dr.

Fothergill. Her initial instincts — that the good doctor would never have her summoned to a tavern in the evening — surged back to the fore, with the additional surety that therefore the doctor was not there, and therefore Brereton's note — now that she'd seen him and knew he was awaiting her, she knew the note was from him — was a lie meant to lure her out alone.

Why?

The men glanced about and spoke to each other in low tones. The magistrate had not, at first, wanted the murder investigated. His granddaughter was Faithful's bully and had, Anne suspected, hoaxed her and yet appeared distraught and frightened after her death. Frightened and *guilty*, but guilty about what? As unpleasant as the girl had seemed, she was not a murderer. Anne had considered it briefly, but dismissed it as impossible. Maybe the guilty look was not about what she had done, but what she knew. Or . . . Anne's eyes widened; maybe the guilt was over what she figured out afterward *about her grandfather!*

Intelligent, imaginative Faithful had stayed in his home for several weeks. What had she learned while there?

Anne pulled her cloak hood up and huddled into the garment, thinking over clues that began to cling to each other, forming at first into a nebulous shadowy glob, then taking shape in a pattern. The increase in theft lately, both in Bath and the highways around it: *noted.* Laxity in sentencing: *noted.* The other pleasant magistrate was a fellow full of bonhomie, who liked nothing better than a warm brandy by a blazing fire on a December evening. He *was* willing to let things go, a trait she and her friends had been happy to exploit in the case of the menacing mystic: *noted!*

Magistrate Brereton had, she *thought,* been the other kind of magistrate, astute, busy, probably assiduous in enforcing the law, and yet . . . there was no corresponding rise in sentences against thieves on his watch, except of the petty kind: *noted.*

Faithful, an intelligent girl surrounded her whole life by the law, might notice things other girls would not. Staying in a magistrate's home for weeks with Henrietta, had she overheard conversations? Seen shifty or suspicious people come and go?

Was Brereton what had come to be known as a "trading justice," not merely lax in following up the increase in jewel thefts lately in

Bath, but perhaps even encouraging them and taking valuables in exchange for looking the other way? Bath was overflowing with the wealthy and elderly who loved to display their jewels in the Assembly Rooms, concerts and balls. A few had been waylaid on their way home and robbed. Homes had been broken into while owners were away.

And all the while in their midst, had Brereton been plotting and conniving against their security? It all made sense. How had Faithful threatened that business, and had Brereton actually killed the girl? Had he conspired with someone else to do so?

Who, in the school, was involved? She prayed it wasn't Henrietta. It was more likely to be Miss Hopewell. India Hopewell, who was upstairs that night with a gentleman! She shivered, trembling through her whole body, the damp sinking into her bones. She had seen enough to know that Dr. Fothergill was not at the Saracens Head awaiting her arrival. Brereton had given his name knowing she would trust the doctor.

She was leaving. She'd walk in the direction from which Tony would be approaching and tell him about her suspicions, that Magistrate Brereton was not only a trading justice but a murderer, too. "Irusan!" she hissed, looking about in the shadows. Her cat had been at her feet moments before but was now gone. She peeked out from her hiding spot and gasped in fear as she looked toward the tavern. Brereton and his brute were no longer there, but in a faint pool of lamplight was her courageous cat, prowling along the front of the Saracens Head, looking for an opportunity to slink in, perhaps?

"Irusan!" she hissed again, in the tone she knew he could hear. His ears pricked, he sent a glance over his shoulder and his tail flicked, but he did not return to her. "Pestilential cat! You'll be the death of me!"

She slipped along the church wall and into the open, along the front of the tavern. She crept up on him and reached out to grab him about his middle. He wriggled out of her grasp, circled her and trotted into the shadow of the looming church. She chased him into the dark, felt a crack to her skull, and then . . . oblivion.

Chapter Twenty-four

Anne groaned and shuddered, nausea taking her over as pain shot through her head. She opened her eyes and tried to sit up, but her stomach roiled so she stilled to let it pass. Where was she? It was dark, and foul odors assailed her nostrils. All she could see were dim shapes humped close by. Gingerly, she touched her head, feeling a smear of blood and a lump.

Outside the room men argued, one wanting in, another demanding the speaker go away. "Give us a couple o' minutes, willya?" a rough voice commanded. The other voice whined, the rough voice answered, and silence fell.

A door opened, hinge shrieking in protest, letting in a faint slice of light and cold air. She could make out that she was in a shed in a loathsome back alley. She felt rather than saw the presence looming over her and was about to scream when a rough, smelly hand was clamped over her mouth. She was levitated, lifted by a man so strong there was no buckling of his knees despite her weight. Her head hit the wooden doorframe and she exclaimed with a muffled expression of pain. She bit the hand, tasting dirt and something even more foul, but all she got for that was a slap and her hair pulled, then the hand clamped over her mouth again.

"You shut yer mouth," a rough voice muttered. "I'll set you down in two ticks."

She struggled for a moment, but the fellow was powerful. She'd save her strength. It was not the first time she had been in a dangerous position; choosing her opportunity for freedom carefully would be vital. He carried her outside and along a narrow passageway, cold wind hitting her bare neck and cheeks, then down a lane, and from there into a building. The odor had changed from filth to the grainy scent of an alehouse, a brewery storeroom, perhaps. She was plopped down and her assailant left. Her head still pounded with pain, a trickle of blood oozed from the corner of her mouth. She took a deep breath and felt around. She was on top of a burlap sack holding grain. She was right, this was a brewery storeroom. The door screeched open again. She heard rustling and murmuring voices in an anteroom. A heavy sigh, whispered remonstrance. Two men entered.

The uncouth fellow — he of the cauliflower ear, she thought, from what little she could see in the dim light — asked her, "So, what do yer know, milady?"

Anne hesitated, but what was the point of prevarication? "I know the magistrate Mr. Brereton is with you, directing the questioning."

A murmured argument, querulous imprecations, commands.

"It ain't 'im, though," the fellow said woodenly. "'Tis Mr. Collie with me, y'see."

"Collier, you idiot. Brereton told you to say *Collier*, not *collie*."

The hood was raised from a lantern and Anne blinked at the sudden light. Brereton perched on a bag of grain, one long leg crossed over the other as he observed her dispassionately, his dour expression indicative of irritation. "You are a handful, aren't you? I wonder at the marquess's taste, for you are no beauty. Of course, you are rich and well-born. For some men that is enough. My own tastes run to a more agreeable lady."

"Aren't we both lucky that I have no need of your approval?"

"Defiant to the end," he muttered.

The end; that didn't sound good.

"I hope you are comfortable, my lady?"

She struggled to sit, licking blood away, the iron tang on her tongue unpleasant. Her lip, swelling now, stung. "I've been better. What are we to do now, Mr. Brereton?" Her voice sounded odd, mumbly past the swollen lip.

"I wish I knew. I don't *want* to kill you. Of course, *I* won't, to be completely clear. Duggan, here, will do the deed."

"I never will," the other fellow protested, rearing back. "Don't you go tryin' to pin shite on me like the last time. I'd 'ang!"

"You won't hang, you idiot. I am the magistrate. I'm hardly going to turn you in, am I?"

"Don't listen to him, Duggan," Anne said, her voice trembling with fear and cold. "He *will* blame it all on you, like he will with Faithful's murder. Of course, maybe you *did* kill the poor girl yourself?"

"I never did!" Duggan said, outraged. "Mr. Brereton 'ere did it. First 'e snuck upstairs in that school and pushed her out o' the winder, then 'e coom down an' choked her to death wiv 'er own ribbing while I 'eld the other one."

The other one?

"I ain't no child killer," he growled.

"Shut up, you lout!" Brereton said. "Or I *will* see you hang. Go away. Keep watch, and make sure no one comes along."

Godspeed, little man, Anne thought of Robbie. How was she going to get out of this? She shivered in fear, took a deep breath, and determined to defeat the terror. She'd keep Brereton talking until help arrived, if it would, or figure a way out of this herself if it wouldn't. "However did you get Faithful to come up to the attic, I wonder?"

"Shut up, my lady. I need to consider."

Her mind teemed with questions, foremost among them, had anyone seen a large, fluffy, angry cat? She hoped her feline companion was all right.

But back to the problem at hand; maybe if she could keep Brereton talking and taunt him enough, he'd brag and explain, using up some time so help could arrive. Men like him did not like to be underestimated. "I have it all figured it out, from start to finish," Anne said in as snide a tone as she could manage around a swollen lip. "You haven't been very clever about it, have you? You've played your hand too openly. You will hang. How embarrassing for your family."

"There is nothing in any of this that will lead back to me."

"If you thought that was true, you would not have taken the risk to summon me here tonight. My message by way of my fiancé got you worried."

He eyed her with distaste.

She watched him, her mind reeling as she shivered in fear and cold. Her body felt icy, her nerves fretted, fear making her breath come in short gasps. *Focus, Anne,* she admonished herself. *Focus on the crime.* How did they get Faithful to go to the attic? Brereton must have been the man in the attic who Ginny had seen with Miss Hopewell, but why didn't the teacher turn him in? "I hope you've realized if I've figured out your part in all of this, others will, too."

He grunted, eyeing her through narrowed eyes, but not responding to her taunts.

"You killed Faithful, and I have a notion why. She was a bright and brave girl, wasn't she?" Anne's anger burned as she glared at him. "She was worth ten of you. She figured out who was behind all the thefts in Bath lately. She saw or heard something when she was staying with you in the summer."

"Stupid girl."

"Ah, but that's the problem. She wasn't stupid. Because she grew up with a father who is a barrister and a brother who was studying to be one, she listened and learned and read. Where her brother failed in his attempt to become a barrister, or even a solicitor, she would have succeeded, given the chance. She saw what you were doing. You had to kill her."

"She, like you, did not know how to keep her female nose out of male business," Brereton snarled. "She fancied herself a righteous do-gooder, one of those who would advocate for reforming the law." He gave a loud exclamation of disgust through his teeth. "The law works perfectly as it is."

"For men like you," Anne retorted.

He ignored her. "She planted suspicions in my granddaughter's mind. She had no business doing that," he hissed with sibilant malice.

"You're nothing more than a trading justice, getting paid by thieves to turn your eyes away unless the thief is a child stealing bread to feed his infant sister." She stared at him, her throbbing head angering her. "You've done *more* than turn your eyes away from thieves, am I not right? You've encouraged . . ." She paused. "No, you've *organized* the thefts. Who else knows these householders? Who else has pushed himself into the society of the wealthy citizens of Bath? *You* have. And you used what knowledge you gleaned to arrange the thefts."

Silence.

Something else occurred to her. "Ah! Jonty Thompson; I'll bet one of your henchmen nabbed him for thievery, am I right? You saw his usefulness to you and told him unless he cooperated, you'd have him up on charges. He's a shifty sort, but I don't think he was a part of your plan to kill Faithful. I do believe he let you into the house that night, though, after stealing the key from his wife, then scuttled off to his shed and pulled the curtain. You were the gentleman Miss India Hopewell was speaking with upstairs. Was she your helper? But no . . ." She paused and thought. "You wouldn't have needed her, because you had Jonty to let you in . . . unless she delivered Faithful to you?" Something didn't make sense. She looked away and considered. If her head didn't throb so much, she felt like she'd have the answer.

Bemused, he almost smiled. "Like all other women, you don't understand how the world works."

"Why, because I think justice should be evenhanded and convict actual criminals rather than penny loaf thieves and street urchins?"

"This world is a hard place, my lady. No place for weaklings, and no place for those who would *coddle* weaklings. Let them succeed or fail on their merits, like I did."

"As the son of a wealthy brewer. Quite the struggle. Bath society may not care about those thieves and street urchins, but I would wager that when they learn what one of their magistrates has perpetrated against them, they will howl for your blood, a pint for every diamond stickpin or brooch you have stolen from their homes. You will not, I think, be coddled."

He glared at her, a nerve jumping at the corner of one eye. "What you say, my lady, tells me you must not leave here alive. You would be far better to shut your *mouth*."

Who did he think he was fooling? He was never going to let her live. She'd prolong this discussion until Tony got there, or find a way out of it herself. She swallowed hard, trying to stamp down the fear roiling in her gut. "How did you discover that Faithful had figured you out?"

"She tried to turn my granddaughter against me," he said heatedly. "Henrietta was upset and came to me crying. She's not a clever girl, but she is loyal."

"You didn't think she was clever because you don't think any female is. She's smart enough to know, now, that you're a murderer. She would likely have been your next victim. But her questions of you told you the jig was over. That's when you concocted the plot to make Faithful kill herself, or at least to make her seem a lunatic."

"Weak family, the lot of them! Collier is all right, but his son is a wastrel, his first wife died, and his second wife, that girl's mother, died in an asylum."

"Collier is all right? Pleasant praise for the man whose daughter you killed."

He smiled, a cold, soulless expression. "I wasn't going to let her ruin me and my family. If the rumors are right, he will benefit. He'll get the money his weak wife's family left her daughter and be able to pay his idiot son's debts. I doubt he'll worry overmuch about a burdensome daughter's death. I saw a path forward, a way to work on Miss Collier's spirits."

Despicable man! Anne's eyes widened. "Ah! I understand. Even if she didn't die by her own hand, the attempt and her wild tales of ghostly perturbations would make her veracity suspect. If you couldn't handle her before she spoke of her suspicions you could dismiss her as a feeble, or an imaginative dolt. And her 'suicide' would be explained by her unbalanced behavior and her mother's instability."

He was silent, eyeing her with dislike. She could tell he was trying to decide what to do, and her stomach again clenched. "I think I understand," she said slowly. She saw a movement behind Brereton. Irusan's reflective eyes glowed in the shadows. Of course! Grain storage in a brewery would attract mice and rats, and her cat would have followed the scent. He was working his way up to shelves above the grain bags. She looked away, afraid of drawing attention to the big cat, and hurriedly said, "You know about Faithful's inheritance, and that her father will now receive it. It figured into your plans; if things went poorly and it was discovered that she did not die by suicide, the suspicion would fall on her father, who inherits."

He smiled, a ghastly, cadaverous look. "You're guessing, but it *is* amusing, and you're right, so far as it goes. Those two have made it easy to fasten blame upon them. I think you were on your way to believing it yourself, were you not?" He sat up and straightened his waistcoat, tugging it down. "I think the Colliers will be blamed for *your* death, once I decide how best to implicate them, how to kill you, where to leave your body."

Shivering with cold and fear she rushed into speech. "How did you get Henrietta to go along with your plan? The ghost tale was your invention, yes?"

"Of course," he said with a dismissive wave of one bony hand. "Faithful and my granddaughter read ghost tales all summer when they weren't writing them, and then performing silly plays with ghosts and villains named Gustav and Alphonse. Henrietta is easily manipulated. She loves her grandmother. When she came to me, asking about what Faithful had said, I told her that Faithful appeared to have it out for our family and had also threatened to spread unsavory rumors about my wife about town."

Unsavory rumors . . . Anne gaped. Aha! It was falling into place now. She had nothing to lose by saying aloud what he preferred to intimate. "That is why you don't like Alethea. There is a *tendre* there, a softness of your wife toward my friend."

Duggan had returned and chuckled but stopped when Brereton glared at him. The magistrate's cheeks suffused with red and his eyes darkened. He lifted his hand as if to slap Anne but defeated his fury and let his lips twist into a grimace. "What a disgusting mind you have. My wife is soft, yes, but not in that way. They were friends, and my foolish wife would not turn her back on Alethea, not even when these rumors started last month, not even when I told her she *had* to, for my sake. She valued her friend over me, her husband!"

"How did she feel about you using Henrietta to frighten poor Faithful?"

"My wife is too stupid to *ever* figure it out," he said. "And you can leave my granddaughter's name out of this. Henrietta is a delightfully gullible girl, so easily manipulated she even wrote a note — at my direction, of course — to that awful girl inviting her up to the attic for an apology."

That's how he got Faithful up there! It wasn't Miss Hopewell at all. *That* was the note Fanny saw Henrietta give to Faithful. "Henrietta didn't know that Faithful was being lured to her death."

"Of course she didn't. I said Miss Collier was going to be frightened into leaving us alone."

When she discovered that Faithful was dead, she must have suspected, but she couldn't be sure. She would be loath to think her grandfather, a respected magistrate, was a killer. "How vile to make your granddaughter into a tool to kill her schoolmate," Anne said in disgust. "You are evil incarnate. That girl will bear the scars of this for a lifetime. Where is your wife, pray tell? Does she know what you've done?"

"Of course she knows nothing, suspects *nothing*. Even if she does, she will keep her mouth shut if she enjoys her jewels and a box at the opera." The magistrate chuckled, a humorless sound, but sobered and said, "I sent her to stay with our son in London. Said she needed a rest. She'll have nothing more to do with Mrs. Birkenhead, or she'll be shut into an asylum and never see the light of day or her granddaughter again." He stood and loomed over her. "Thank goodness your disgusting independence made you so easy to manipulate, as I supposed it would. One can never go wrong by overestimating someone else's stupidity. And now I need to decide what to do with you. Give me the note I sent to you," he said, holding out his hand.

"Why do you think I still have it?"

He blinked. "I told you to bring it. Where is it?"

She smiled.

He roared in fury, yanked a rope up from the grain sacks and threw it at Duggan, saying, "Tie her up. We'll have to take her away from here while I think what to do."

"Why?" Duggan said, standing slack-mouthed and staring.

"She has sent the note on to someone, you fool! I don't know who, but I'd hazard a guess it is that confounded terrifying lumbering fiancé of hers."

Duggan hefted the rope and started toward her. What happened next happened swiftly. Irusan screeched and leaped on Duggan, fastening his fangs on the man's cheek. Duggan roared in pain and staggered, flinging his hands up in the air. The looped heavy rope flew from his grasp and hit the magistrate, who staggered sideways, tripping over a bag of spilled grain, and fell, hitting his head on the flagstone floor. Anne gathered her cloak and skirts and ran for the door, but Duggan, who had thrown Irusan aside, grabbed her around the waist, roaring in pain and anger, blood streaming down his face.

Irusan launched himself at the man's leg and wrapped himself around it, digging those fangs in again, this time holding on so the man could not shake him off. Duggan, flailing, let go of Anne and she made it to the door. "Irusan, let him go and come!" she yelled, yanking the wood door open, running out into the cold air, needling rain pouring down on her and soddening her skirts. She started yelling, stumbling about in the dark, and did not let up until a man grabbed her in his arms and held her close. "Let go of me!" she screamed, flailing.

"Anne, it's me!"

"Darkefell! Thank God! Let go of me and get Brereton and his confederate, Duggan."

A man surged past Darkefell, someone bulkier. In a moment, from the dark, came a shriek of pain and terror. Jamey, grinning, dragged Duggan out of the alleyway and threw him down at his sister's feet in a pool of lamplight. "Is this him, Annie? Is this the man who hurt you?"

"Oh, Jamey, my hero!"

"Why do I never get to be the hero," Darkefell grumbled, but he was almost grinning.

Duggan tried to get up. Jamey kicked him in the side of the head. "Never hit Sister!" he shouted. *"Never!"*

"There are villains enough for all, Tony. Magistrate Brereton is behind all of this and, by his own word, is the one who killed poor Faithful. You would oblige me greatly, my lord and husband-to-be, if you would lay hands on *him* none too gently. He should still be in the storage room yonder."

"Your wish, my lady, is my command." He kissed her bloody lip, then bowed elaborately and strode off into the dark shadows of the alleyway. When he came back he had the magistrate slung over his shoulder like a sack of brewer's grain, and the man was howling in fury.

Anne dissolved in laughter and plunked down on the pavement as Irusan climbed into her lap. The scene, lit in weak lamplight, was farcical. It was over.

Chapter Twenty-five

"I look dreadful," Anne said, staring into her looking glass. She touched her lip, still swollen but beginning to heal now, three days later. It would heal more quickly if Tony didn't insist on kissing her every time she stopped long enough for him to grab.

"You do," Alethea, visiting Anne in her chamber, said with a grin. "I wonder if you will still be bruised on your wedding day?"

Anne groaned.

Mary came in and stiffly said, "Visitors, milady. In the drawing room."

"Who is it, Mary?" Anne asked, but her maid was already gone.

Alethea stared after her. "I've never seen her act that way before."

"She still hasn't forgiven me for sending Robbie out in the cold and damp to take that message to Tony. Thank goodness he did, for I may have been the late Lady Anne if he hadn't. Tony stormed over to the Saracens Head, with Jamey not willing to be left behind if new brother, as he charmingly calls him, was going to save his sister. Robbie caught cold—likely from her!—and she has used that excuse to keep him in the house. He is in perfect health but dreadfully gloomy and complains constantly. Poor lad. I've been taking him copious amounts of cake and a dozen Bath buns to make up for his confinement."

"I'll bring him Quin's old toy soldiers. Do you think he would like them?"

"*Would* he?" Anne exclaimed. "Even more so if Quin would visit and explain army campaigns."

"Done."

"That will be a novelty for Robbie." She sobered. "Poor Mary is taking her unhappiness out on me. I will endure it and hope she forgives me. I can't bear it when she's angry at me."

"Only you would be cowed by your maid."

"You've never seen an enraged Scotswoman. I suppose we must go down and see who is visiting."

It was the Lee sisters, all three of them, sitting in a row on the settee, stared at by Anne's grandmother. As Anne and Alethea entered, her ladyship was saying, "You write plays? And translate novels? Whyever would you do that?"

"To make a living, my lady," Sophia said. "The same reason we run a school."

Anne introduced the Lee ladies to her grandmother, who subsided in silence in her favorite chair, examining the visitors with a bewildered expression. That they had no man to look after them and yet seemed refined and of a genteel class puzzled her. Some gentleman *should* have stepped in, her doubting expression implied. They made polite conversation until the elder lady summoned her favorite footman and toddled away on his arm to her boudoir, where she would spend most of the afternoon napping and writing letters.

Sophia Lee took the opportunity, once she was gone, to say, "Lady Anne, we wanted to express our gratitude. You have saved our school from destruction."

"Please, don't tell anyone else that," she said with a smile. "I'd prefer it remain a mystery how the magistrate was caught, for my behavior will irrevocably mark me as a madwoman if the truth gets out."

Sophia nodded. "We can never repay you."

"Repayment will be seeing that man hanged," Anne said savagely. Brereton had tried unsuccessfully to blame Duggan, Anne, the Colliers and anyone else he could point a finger at. His fellow Bath magistrate had failed to be swayed and had gone through the almost unprecedented steps required to strip the other man of his legal standing and put him in jail.

"He is a foul beast," Alethea said. "I never liked him."

Miss Anne Lee smiled and said, "You make me proud to be an Anne." She eyed her bruised face and her smile died. "I'm happy you're alive. You're so brave!" she said with fervor. "I have hope that even after marriage you will stay as fierce as I now know you to be."

Irusan strolled into the room and allowed himself to be adored as his due, as Anne explained his part in her triumph, the hero of the hour. "My brother, too, took part and was most gallant."

"I still don't understand how you hit on Brereton as the villain of the piece," Harriet said, leaning forward.

"I didn't. I was incredibly stupid through the whole thing," Anne admitted, even as the others protested. "No, it's true. I didn't figure it out until the last moment when it was almost too late. I was swayed this way and that, suspecting everyone in turn. They all gave me plenty of reason to suspect them, I will say."

"Who all did you suspect?" Sophia Lee asked.

Anne considered it for a moment. "In order? First, Mr. Russell."

"The art tutor?" Anne Lee exclaimed. "Whyever did you suspect him?"

"He is the kind of man one must suspect of something. He is not above flirtation, and he had been meeting Miss Julia Halliday at the Pump Room and market for strolling and flirting."

Harriet exclaimed, "He is not a proper tutor, I said that all along. He dismissed the girls with ability as much as those without."

"I found he had been flirting with Faithful, too, and I worried he had learned about her inheritance. One swift trip to Gretna Green and she would be committed for life to a man unworthy of her."

"That isn't murder," Alethea said.

"Exactly. Even if it was his plan, Faithful was only of use to him alive. I most strongly considered the Colliers, either separately or together. Augustus Collier is as slimy an individual as ever graced the surface of our fair planet. A clerk at a shipping company engaged in the slave trade, I already knew he had not a whit of honor. The case against him alone was involved and two-pronged. First, I knew for sure that he had compromised Miss India Hopewell."

The women protested.

"No, it's true. I don't know where she stands with you, but I will tell you the truth, and you can tell me how it affects you. You may not know that before being a teacher she was a dogsbody for a rich old woman."

"Not a sin," Harriet said stoutly.

"Of course not, but that rich old lady died, leaving her a hundred guineas."

"You're not saying she killed her employer?"

"I don't imagine so. If she did, it may not have been for the hundred guineas, but for the love of a man who promised to marry her. Augustus Collier."

"What? Why would he want an old lady killed?" Sophia asked, frowning severely and adjusting her lace mittens.

"That old lady was Miss Faithful Collier's maternal aunt, the one who left her a considerable fortune. This is pure speculation; please give it as much credence as you would any wild tale based on supposition. Killing her would have been stage one in a convoluted plot. More people would need to die to accomplish it. The money would go to Faithful, Faithful would die and the money would go to her father, but if her father died, the money would go to Mr. Augustus Collier."

"So, he'd have to kill his sister and his father?" Anne Lee said.

"That's why I thought it unlikely. Too involved, too risky. Many of the clues fit it; the one requirement of the plot was that it involved two people, one upstairs and one down. It's why I could imagine the Thompsons as assailants; the fact that they were from Bristol, and that Jonty Thompson was running from the law, added plausibility. Perhaps Mrs. T. tipped Faithful out the window, I thought, and Jonty could have taken it from there."

"How cavalier you are, Anne, in relating such horrid possibilities!" Alethea cried, eyes wide.

The three Lee sisters exchanged glances and Anne noted it to follow up on later. "Whyever would our housekeeper and her husband have killed Faithful, though?" Miss Anne Lee asked.

"The Thompsons didn't have a motive alone," Anne admitted. "I dismissed them as a pair rapidly. Augustus Collier lasted longer. I thought he could have involved Miss Hopewell, with his promise of marriage if he had enough money. She would have pushed Faithful to her death, and he could have attempted to take his sister's body away. I couldn't imagine why he needed to take the body away, but there it was. In the end, it took too much imagination. The Collier son is venal enough but too stupid and lacking in ambition to accomplish such a feat. I moved on."

"To the Collier father," Sophia said.

"Yes, you have me there. The father is almost as unsavory as the son, but looking back, I was misled by my own prejudices. He never seemed to care one whit that his daughter was dead. And I suspect it was his cruelty and indifference that sent his wife to die in an asylum."

"We know more of that now," Harriet said, sharing a look with Sophia, who nodded regally, giving her permission to tell the tale. "Mrs. Collier had been depressed and anxious, yes, but she was not a danger to Faithful, and she never posed a threat to anyone. Collier sent her to the asylum because he didn't want to see her mopey face anymore, an acquaintance of theirs wrote to me when I inquired."

"Poor woman. Poor Faithful, to have such a father."

"Mrs. Collier did not kill herself as has been implied," Harriet said. "There was a fever that went through the place, and it took several women, her among them. Faithful should have been told the truth. I wish when we knew she was being teased about her mother that we had taken the steps to find out, but it seemed an intrusion into matters not our business."

Anne nodded. "Sadly enough, my ill opinion of him was such that I could see Mr. Collier doing it, with the help of an insider. The one thing in its favor was, he is lame in one arm."

The ladies looked puzzled. "What does that mean?" Harriet asked.

"I suppose I haven't explained one of the sticking points; the drag marks in the blood on the paving stones."

"Someone wanted to take her body away," Alethea said.

"Yes, but *why?*" Anne said, leaning forward with urgency. "It didn't make any sense. Why take away her dead body? First, I'll tell you why the body needed to stay there; to establish that she had fallen or jumped to her death."

Anne Lee stared into space and her eyes widened. "Except she wasn't dead!"

"Right!" Anne jabbed her forefinger at her. "She was *not dead.* The assailant strangled her to death with her own ribbon. Once he did, he realized that it could no longer be explained as a suicide. He didn't want it to be a murder because of the inevitable investigation and furor if a sweet schoolgirl was murdered, so he decided to take the body away and perhaps toss it into the Avon. *That* could be written off as a suicide, and the action of the water would explain the bad condition of her body. Faithful's father is lame in one arm; if he tried to drag her away it would be difficult for him."

"It wasn't him," Miss Anne Lee said.

"No. I know from Duggan's confession that it was all Brereton; the magistrate lay in wait up in the attic, then pushed Faithful out of the window, descended, found she was still alive and strangled her, poor girl, and all because she knew him for what he was." She had told all of this to the other magistrate of course, and both Brereton and Duggan were being held for the next assizes. "I suspect Jonty bullied his wife into giving him access to the key, or maybe he stole it, because Brereton told him to cooperate or be up on charges. I'd bet Jonty had continued his larcenous ways here in Bath and had been caught at it by Duggan, Brereton's lackey."

"Why then did Brereton abandon the idea of dragging her away?" Alethea asked.

"I don't know for sure," Anne said. "Perhaps they were making too much noise?"

Harriet said, "Those Thompsons have absconded with what little silver we had. I would bet Jonty became frightened of what had happened and what he knew. I would suggest, if you're wondering why Brereton gave up on taking Faithful's body away, that Mrs. Thompson may have interfered in their plan."

"You may be right. She *must* have been uneasy about her husband, rotter that he is. Perhaps she had hoped their move to Bath would begin a new idyl for them, but it was never to be, not wed to Jonty. If they're gone, we may never know. Anyway, Brereton's guilt was the theory that fit all the facts. I hope I would have come to it sooner or later, because I *did* suspect him." Too late, of course, but that was true.

"I don't understand," Harriet said. "Why and how did he do it?"

Anne explained about Faithful's knowledge of the law and of trading justices, from listening to her brother's lessons. "She would have made a good barrister, if women were allowed such a profession, and perhaps an even better judge. She had a strong sense of justice." She explained further how Henrietta's tearful questions of her grandfather, inspired by Faithful's assertions about his practices, told Brereton the danger he was in. He liked the money his schemes gave him and put it to use buying Bath properties that were far beyond his capability or status in the town.

"That was what came between the girls. Faithful kept asking Henrietta questions, and finally—recently—told her friend what she believed. Henrietta's loyalty to her grandfather led her to tell him what Faithful was saying. She believed him when he told her Faithful was a spiteful girl out to destroy their family. He even threw in that she might be behind scurrilous rumors going about town concerning Henrietta's grandmother," she said, with a glance at Alethea, whose color rose. "And he wanted her help to distract Faithful, to use a 'ghostly visitation' from her mother to warn her away from hurting the Brereton family."

"Despicable!" Anne Lee teared up and looked away, a gleam of water dripping down her cheek to her lace collar. "Faithful was a clever girl, even if she did believe in ghosts, but beyond that, she was kind and sweet. I miss her."

"At first, before I learned anything much, I suspected Henrietta," Anne admitted. "Her spite was clear, her emotions powerfully wrought up. But I saw she was a cat's-paw. The only one with that much influence over her was her grandfather. It took a while for all the facts to cling together: the thefts in Bath lately, the non-capture of the thieves, and everything else I learned along the way." She sighed. "If I'd reasoned it all out in time, I could have avoided this," she said, indicating her own bruising and scratches. "How are the other girls?" Anne asked. "How is your school faring now?"

"We have prayed about it and talked about it," Sophia said. "Parents were alarmed, but we made much of the fact that Faithful died because she had figured out what was going on outside of our school and was about to do something to stop it, thus bringing the violence to within our walls. Not her fault of course," she hastened to add. "But still."

"The Colliers took her home to bury. Mr. Collier allowed us to distribute Faithful's belongings to those closest to her, especially Alys," Harriet added.

"I'm surprised at that," Anne admitted. "He did not strike me as particularly sensitive, and the son is loathsome."

Anne Lee primmed her lips. "I may have said something to him."

"What did you say?" Alethea asked.

"I may have said that if he had paid a bit of attention to the letter Faithful sent home—"

"Ah, yes, the missive to which I read his reply," Anne said. She related what she had read in Mr. Collier's letter to his daughter. "I am curious what exactly she asked him that warranted resentment. At one point it made me suspect him and his son, he was so defensive about the contents of her last letter to him."

"She wrote to him asking him questions about trading justices," Harriet said. "And asked what to do if she suspected there was such a one in power."

"That explains much," Anne exclaimed. "He resented that she was asking about legal questions, and she a mere woman. In the letter he asks her if she thought she was smarter than her brother—of course, she was—and told her to stop thinking she knew better than adults."

"Meaning men, of course. She must stop thinking she knew better than *men!*" Anne Lee, pink-cheeked, exclaimed. "If he had paid a little bit of attention, he would have made the two-hour ride to Bath to make sure she was all right."

"How would confronting him about that convince him to disperse her belongings to the girls?"

"I pointed out that those girls were her family for the last year and a half. Alys was her confidante, Julia her big sister, and we . . . we were her mothers." Anne Lee clasped her hands together, agonized. "If we had delved deeper *we* may have saved her."

"You couldn't have known what she was thinking unless she told you, and she didn't." Anne paused. "What about Henrietta?" she asked with a swift look to Alethea.

"She is with her grandmother in London," Sophia said.

"We are friends, Mrs. Brereton and I, and I've heard from her," Alethea said. "I don't expect either of them to return to Bath."

"She would be welcome at the Lee school if she came back," Harriet said, her cheeks coloring. "The girl was wrong to do what she did, but it was her grandfather who pushed her and lied to her. I'd like the opportunity to help Henrietta understand what she did wrong, and how to find her way again."

Sophia put her hand on her sister's and the three Lees exchanged significant looks. "I'm sure her grandmother will help her."

"We are grateful, anyway, that we survive," Anne Lee said.

"What about Miss Hopewell and Miss Dankworth?"

"Miss Dankworth has been promoted," Sophia said. "She is passionate about some subjects and will now teach geography and science to all the girls, as well as helping to write the lesson plans. We are adding much more science and mathematics instruction in future."

"I'm happy that you are being compassionate toward Miss Dankworth," Anne said. "Despite her failings and the intrigue within which she became entangled, I believe she has learned a valuable lesson, to value herself more highly than to fall for such a stupid fool as Augustus Collier. She has a romantic heart that in her life has found little food. Collier played on it and made her feel chosen, preferred. That is a wonderful thing when you find it." Anne thought of Tony. He had chosen her when there were more beautiful ladies who would have thrown themselves at his feet. But he wanted her, and she wanted him.

"I don't understand why he did any of that," Alethea said.

"I have thought of it a lot," Anne said. "Let me tell you what I think but I'll warn you, some of this is supposition."

Chapter Twenty-six

"Augustus Collier met Miss Dankworth last summer when she stayed at the Thompsons' boardinghouse in Bristol with India Hopewell. Young Mr. Collier had met Miss Hopewell through his sister's great-aunt, the one who left Faithful the bequest. India Hopewell was working for the elderly woman until her death sixteen months ago and had to deal with Mr. Collier to receive her bequest of a hundred guineas. The younger Collier had already found out that Miss Hopewell — who was far too susceptible to his charms and his promises, but had become disenchanted with both — left Bath to become a teacher at the school his sister boarded at. He knew from Faithful that there were some moderately wealthy young women going to your school. Sixteen- and seventeen-year-old girls are highly susceptible to rogues like Augustus Collier. He planned to induce Miss Hopewell with threats of revealing her past to introduce him to the more susceptible of the older girls, heiresses in particular."

"What an idiotic plot," Harriet Lee cried. "But why would he not take advantage of his sister to do that?"

"She knew what her brother was and never would have done it."

"True," Anne Lee said.

"He is an unscrupulous, lazy scoundrel, too stupid to concoct a coherent plan, dimly making moves he thinks will benefit him. When Miss Hopewell disappointed him in that regard — she was certainly not going to introduce him to any girls who would replace her in his so-called affections — he hoped to convince Miss Dankworth to help him find a rich girl to take off with him to Gretna Green."

"I thought you suspected our art tutor of that," Sophia said dryly.

"I did but he, as far as I can tell, confined himself to pleasant flirtation. When Miss Halliday became too attached, he made sure to break her heart. Anyway, I don't think Miss Dankworth would have helped Collier to find a victim. He flirted with her and used her to take letters to Miss Hopewell, who he claimed was threatening him. But she got suspicious and opened one of the letters and gleaned enough to figure out Miss Hopewell was castigating him for not fulfilling his promise to marry her. She had finally decided he was a wretch and a schemer. Which he was."

"Oh!" Harriet exclaimed. "I forgot to say this: there is one mystery solved. Kate, the maid, came creeping back to us, weeping and frightened. Augustus Collier seduced *her* with promises, all while trying to get her to tell him what girls at the school were wealthy heiresses."

"Bounder!" Anne exclaimed. "What an idiot he is, so sure of his attractions, so stupid in his schemes, so devoid of any intelligence."

"He put Kate up in a boardinghouse while trying to convince her to help him in his scheme to marry rich. To her credit, she would not do it."

"Or at least she *says* she wouldn't," Miss Anne Lee, the cynic, said. "But more to the point, how could she? She's a maid, for heaven's sake."

"Regardless, we need a maid, and as long as she behaves herself, we have taken her back on a probationary basis. As for Miss Hopewell, we have not yet decided what to do about her," Sophia said with a steely tone, which softened when she added, "She did nothing so wrong, at least . . . not in my eyes. She fell for an unsuitable fellow."

"Why ultimately did she come as an instructress to Bath?" Harriet mused.

"I suspect she knew she could not do so in Bristol," Anne said, "for her reputation had been damaged by Augustus Collier's attentions. She had spent her whole inheritance on him, you know, because of his promises to her. She gave him all the money she had left after her clothing and accouterments purchases."

"That was a mistake," Alethea said sharply.

"Truer words were ne'er spoken," Anne replied. "Once that well was dry, Collier had no further use for her. I suspect the reason he tried to employ Miss Dankworth—a susceptible young woman, unfortunately—to carry notes to her from him was that he wanted to speak with Miss Hopewell, to soothe her anger. She knew too much about his schemes and he saw the danger too late. As I said, he is not very bright."

"Why *did* India stay silent, I wonder?" Harriet said. "I would have told anyone who listened about him."

"I think she was afraid of being caught up in his schemes. It would not reflect well on her, after all, and women's reputations are easily lost. She's a pretty and nicely behaved young woman, but has made a lot of mistakes," Anne said. "Word got about in Bristol of her dalliance with Collier, and her reputation there was ruined. Collier is indiscreet and a braggart. Every man in Bristol would have known her easy ways. She would have been much better to have taken her inheritance and gone to Lyme Regis to capture a rich, sickly widower. If she had perfected her helpless act . . . however, as for not having done much wrong, Miss Sophia, she *did* conceal her coming upon Brereton in the attic, you know."

"True," the schoolmistress said. "We would have known the truth about Brereton immediately if she had just told us. Why *was* Miss Hopewell up there? How was she involved?"

"Brereton made Henrietta write a note, luring Faithful up to the attic. He told his granddaughter he was going to scare her, to keep her from talking about her suspicions, but he was locked into that method of killing her because of her previous attempt to jump. He really thought he could make it look like suicide." She shook her head. "But then the fall didn't kill her. She may have lived.

"After giving Faithful the note, Henrietta was asleep that night," Anne continued. "I think India Hopewell suspected something was going on and followed Faithful upstairs." She frowned. "Or it's possible that she didn't go up until she heard the poor girl cry out as she was pushed out of the window, and caught the magistrate up there when she investigated. We know the two—Brereton and India Hopewell—were up there from Ginny's account. Perhaps he threatened her, hauling her downstairs and outside with his hand over her mouth. He's very strong for his age. Once outside he would have put her in Duggan's care while he strangled poor Faithful."

She looked away, her voice clogged as she said, "You know, if I had put two and two together, I would have realized her involvement, or at least her knowledge. I saw the teacher with the ribbon, you know, the blue satin ribbon Faithful wore in her hair and that was used to strangle her. Miss Hopewell had it in her hands, winding it around and around her fingers. She hid it in her skirt when she saw me looking at it. I imagine Miss Hopewell picked up the ribbon from the scene of the murder. She was afraid, certainly, of the magistrate and his power over her. And with such an example of cold-blooded murder before her, she knew if he caught her alone he might do away with her too. I'm surprised he didn't kill her right then and there. I can only imagine he had his hands full. And he knew things about her past from Jonty's connection to her. He could threaten her to stay silent, if necessary. Would anyone listen to a schoolteacher against a magistrate anyway?"

"Not likely," Anne Lee muttered.

Anne nodded. "I think I'll write a note to the magistrate suggesting he question Miss Hopewell. What to do about her may depend on what the magistrate says about her fate."

"Meanwhile, Anne is stepping in to teach classes," Sophia said in a steely tone, as she looked at her younger sister.

The Lee ladies stood, extending their hands one by one.

"We congratulate you on your coming marriage, Lady Anne," Sophia said.

Harriet reached out and pulled her into a hug. "Be happy," she whispered.

Anne Lee rolled her eyes and folded her arms. "If you can," she said, in response to what her sister said. "That man, the marquess, is a bruiser. I've seen him, you know. I prefer someone a little gentler."

• • •

Later, Anne walked with Tony along the Avon with Jamey and her father. Lord Harecross had been told by Dr. Fothergill that he must get more physical exercise and he was taking the advice to heart, using the time to explore Bath with his son. "You have never remonstrated with me that I went out into the night alone." She had expected him to upbraid her, as Mary had.

"We are not wed yet. I will give you no reason to back out."

She looked up at him in alarm. "Tony, are you going to become a controlling brute once we are married? I won't stand for it, you know. I'll run away."

He looked down at her with a solemn expression and put one hand over his heart. "I promise to never do anything to make you want to run away from me."

"Oh, Tony, you know you can't promise me that. You're bound to do all kinds of things to make me angry, as I will you. But I promise that once we are married, if I'm going to do something foolish, I'll tell you first. You won't stop me, short of locking me up, but it would be hypocritical of me to promise to love you and honor you, and then treat you shabbily."

"I am grateful, my lady," he said with a mocking bow.

And that was all they said on the matter. There were ducks to feed, and fresh air to breathe, Christmas to plan for, and a wedding to look forward to.

• • •

Thursday, December 21, the first day of winter, the shortest day of the year. Anne stood at the altar of St. Swithin's opposite Tony, who was garbed magnificently in dark blue velvet breeches, creamy clocked stockings, a silver embroidered waistcoat and over it a dark blue velvet frock coat with silver embellishments and buttons.

Anne had fussed at her mother and grandmother, but finally acquiesced to the best output of her seamstress, who had made for her a gown of sky-blue watered silk frilled with silver and snow-white lace, in the Polonaise style. It was lovely. Her face had healed, so she looked the best she possibly could.

A sumptuous wedding breakfast awaited them back at her grandmother's home, and to crown the event an enormous layered wedding cake created by a Bath baking genius in the shape of the Assembly Rooms — why, Anne did not understand. That was her mother's doing. Her dear mother had gone quite mad in the last month with frenetic plans that had become more elaborate by the day. Thank goodness the day was here.

She glanced away from Tony as the minister droned through the marriage rites — words like *carnal lusts* and *fornication* drifting absurdly to her ear on such a solemn and yet happy occasion — to her family, her father jubilant, her mother teary-eyed, wearing the lovely tiara that had been fashioned from the old-fashioned rivière collar. Jamey looked pleased and proud of himself, sitting with Dorcas and Alf Carter, craning his neck, waving happily at friends and fancied friends. Lolly Broomhall sat with Anne's grandmother, comforting her. The dowager viscountess kept swatting her comforting patting hand away, but Lolly smiled radiantly. And there was Tony's family, Julian, who had made it after all, John and Lydia, and, his smile for her one of true friendship, Osei Boatin.

Other friends attended them. Alethea, Bertie, Quin and Susanna, Lord Westmacott, and even the Lee sisters. After all they had gone through, Anne was happy things had settled down for them, with the magistrate deciding that not a one of them had done anything wrong. They could not have foreseen poor Faithful's murder within their walls.

Mary and Wee Robbie sat with Irusan, whose magnificent bow was made from remnants from the making of Anne's gown, with blue velvet bits from Tony's suit of clothes. He looked cross and put out because he could not wander this new place and hunt mice. Anne smiled tearily at them. Mary dropped her a wink and Wee Robbie raised Irusan's large paw in a gesture of salutation. The cat bit the boy and he yelped, drawing the attention of the gathering, through which a wave of muted laughter and dismay rippled. Lord Westmacott chuckled and Osei moved, discreetly, to sit with the mother and son. Irusan was handed over and curled up in his second favorite person's lap and went to sleep.

Her attention was demanded by an echoing silence. The minister had asked her something. Tony looked down at her, his brown eyes twinkling from . . . was it the light? Or was it moisture? The candlelight made it hard to see. The day was gloomy and raining, but no one inside the walls of St. Swithin's cared.

Anne looked up at Tony. "Did you already say it?" she whispered.

"What?"

"Did you already say you'd have me? Did I miss it?"

He quelled a smile and looked to the priest. "Sir, would you repeat that solemn section again so my wayward bride can hear my answer?" he said, his voice echoing, rippling laughter following his teasing pronouncement.

From there, Tony loudly proclaimed his intention to be wed to her so long as they both should live. The minister turned to her, and asked, "Wilt thou have this man to be thy wedded husband, to live together after God's ordinance in the holy estate of Matrimony? Wilt thou obey him, and serve him, love, honor, and keep him, in sickness and in health; and, forsaking all others, keep thee only unto him, so long as ye both shall live?"

"I will," Anne answered, trembling, her voice quavering. "Wait . . . obey? Oh, I won't do *that*."

Laughter again echoed, as her mother wept in scandalized horror. What had she done? Anne thought. What had she agreed to? Her breathing quickened, her chest expanding against the stays. This was it. No turning back. She was now one with Tony, and forever after. A moment of dizzy panic overwhelmed her.

Maybe there was a way to take it back. Should she run? Feign madness? She met his warm gaze. He wasn't exactly smiling, too full of emotion, but he was intent. She took in a deep breath, pushing against the stays, relaxing as her father affirmed that he gave her to the marquess in holy matrimony. She focused on Tony's gaze and let the ceremony wash over her.

She made a vow, yes, but their deepest promises to each other had been whispered passionately in moments of desire, ardently in moments of calm, and without the need of words in all the moments they had spent together.

Finally it was over. They walked together down the aisle and to the doors and exited into the gray gloomy day. The rain had stopped, leaving the world shimmering in chilly wetness. The world would, in a few months, awaken again, and it would find them at Darkefell Castle, man and wife, forever.

Tony turned her toward him and embraced her. "Everything all right?" he murmured. "I saw a moment of panic."

She leaned against him, his warmth flooding her. "It surprises me every time, but then I remember . . . I'm marrying you. Or rather now, I've *married* you. I'll hold you to your promises, you know."

"Your freedom?"

"To make my own choices."

"To make your own choices. I knew it was the only way I could have you."

"Did I bully you into it, Tony?" She smiled as she said it.

"No, you freed me from feeling I'd need to coddle you. When first I knew I wanted to marry you, I didn't understand you completely, but you have been so open and free with your thoughts—"

"And opinions," she muttered. "My mother and grandmother would be appalled."

"I hope other women do as you do, Anne. Men keep an iron grip on power, mistaking that grip for their birthright as men, and mistaking their sense of control as necessary. I know. I've been that.

You changed me. They would be happier if they could learn what it is to love a woman who does not *want* their control, does not *need* their guidance."

"Don't expect other men to agree, Tony," she said dryly. "You're one in a million, an exceptionally strong and confident man. You know, I almost dashed for the door when I realized I had agreed to obey you."

"You immediately took it back," he said, a rumble of laughter in his chest. "We should have had it written out of the vows."

"What, and scandalize my grandmother?" She smiled.

"She didn't look terribly scandalized when you took it back, though your mother did. A while longer and we'll be alone."

"Or as alone as you can be in a townhome in Bath surrounded by servants and shared by the bride's father and brother."

"Your father is taking Jamey to stay with your mother and grandmother. They'll come back to stay the day after Christmas, to see us off on our journey."

Anne's heart thudded and she turned her face up to him. The soft calm gray light of Bath, reflected off the warm yellow stone of St. Swithin's, bathed his face in a glow. "I'll love you forever, Tony, I can promise you that. And I also promise you, no murder investigations for a while."

"There had better not be," he growled into her mouth as he kissed her.

They lost themselves in the kiss until her grandmother snorted, "Wait until you're alone, Anne, if you please."

Tony laughed and looked over at the elderly woman, standing stiffly upright, supported by Anne's father on one side and her mother on the other. "My lady, I think you know how I have used my time alone with Anne before now. I would have you all witness this; I will love my bride, Marchioness of Darkefell, for all time. She is my wife, my marchioness, and my companion. Every one of you is welcome to visit us at Darkefell Castle." He looked down at Anne as he put his arm around her. "But give us a couple of months first."

Epilogue

Christmas was merry, with gifts exchanged, church attended, and food consumed.

Love was made, frequently and thoroughly.

Once the marquess and marchioness of Darkefell had departed Bath, Jamey and his father were moving back into the marquess's rented townhome. In an interesting (to Anne) development, Lady Barbara had hesitantly agreed to consider living there with them. Perhaps. As a trial.

A rapprochement? Anne wasn't sure she quite believed it, but she was happy nonetheless.

Osei had departed with Dr. Fothergill and his wife for London.

And now finally, Anne and Tony, ensconced in a capacious carriage, warmed by bricks at their feet, and huddled under rugs, held on to each other. Mary and Robbie had been unexpectedly held up when the boy came down with a malady Dr. Fothergill named as a childhood disease that would clear swiftly but was still contagious. Tony had promised to be Anne's abigail on the journey, at which Mary snorted and rolled her eyes. She and her son would travel directly to Darkefell Castle in a couple of weeks.

"Alone, finally. I have longed to have you all to myself!" he said. He pushed the robe away from her neck and pressed his warm lips to the pulse point.

They had indulged themselves scandalously since the wedding, but she was not yet sated. As he murmured sweet words and she sighed ecstatically, she lost herself in desire, happy they had miles and miles to travel before they arrived at the inn where they would spend their first night on the road north.

Afterword

For those interested I can tell you that, as in *Lady Anne and the Haunted Schoolgirl*, there really were sisters, the Misses Harriet and Sophia Lee, eminent authors and playwrights, who ran a school for girls in Bath from the late seventeen hundreds into the eighteen hundreds. And they did indeed run it out of buildings that still exist in an altered form—now split up into separate residences—the Belvedere (occasionally spelled *Belvidere)* Villas in Bath, England.

Miss Sophia Lee, the eldest, made a home for her writer sister Harriet, but also another sister, Anne, about whom I can find no information, and apparently another sister, though I cannot even find her name. Their brother—younger than Harriet—became a wealthy cotton miller, but in 1786, the time of this book, he would have been a clerk at Mr. Drinkwater's cotton mill in Cheshire. He worked his way up until he owned a mill that he designed as an architect.

The two Lee sisters are fascinating. You can read all about them and their school on Wikipedia, of course, or read their varied works, still in print over two hundred years later. They were writers, playwrights, and talented translators. They ran the school successfully for years.

And that is where I take fictional licence. I make certain assumptions in my literary portrait of them. Miss Sophia Lee, the elder, sunk her entire savings earned from *The Chapter of Accidents*, a successful Drury Lane play, into starting the school in Bath. So, I extrapolate, how would Harriet, a talented writer in her own right, have felt? My assumption is, because of her older sister's investment, she would have felt obligated to make of it a success, even at the cost of time she would rather have devoted to writing.

That is purely my speculation, as is Miss Sophia Lee's occasional forceful manner. I make the additional assumption that anyone who would take the bold step of sinking all of her money into starting a school must have been what some would call pushy, or domineering, in a woman. She had responsibilities and, as the elder, would have felt a natural leadership role in her relationship with her sister Harriet.

About Miss Anne Lee I can find little but her name, and that she, too, lived at the school. So I have taken liberties, making her a kind of sleuthing accomplice to my Lady Anne, the two women alike in name and sly intelligence.

Perhaps it goes without saying that I have created out of whole cloth the roster of teachers, arts masters (art, music and dance were generally taught by male "masters" who came in for lessons), and students who attend and board at the school. I have also created the death of Miss Faithful Collier. My apologies to the Misses Lee, because to my knowledge there was never a murder there.

I hope history lovers forgive me my historical trespasses.

To write this book I did a lot of reading about schools for girls in that time period. Much has been made of the fact that the curriculum included French, because a lady should be able to sprinkle her conversation with a few *au courant* phrases, as well as penmanship, sewing of the fancy kind — embroidery — piano, voice, art and dance. All to prepare a lady to take her place in society as a wife who would lend credit to her husband with her grace, wit and charm.

However, we often overlook the real academic and artistic accomplishments these students attained. Girls and women of the Georgian age were not dolls, manipulated solely by the men around them, though because of the constraint of laws and social mores of the time they did have to behave in a manner that kept their reputations intact. To do otherwise would have left them ostracized and even impoverished. They were, like women today, intelligent and fierce, capable of matching wits with the great minds of the age.

The Lees were successful in their endeavors, showing the resilience of women in a time when they were not considered wholly adult, with no ability to run for office or even vote. Girls of the Georgian era were taught much more than the art of pleasing a gentleman. They were encouraged to read and even to write.

In fact, it is believed that the eminent Gothic writer Ann Radcliffe (née Ward) was a student of the Lees. If so, being taught and mentored by two such remarkable women would surely have had an effect on her vocation as the preeminent writer of fiction of her day, admired by Jane Austen and Sir Walter Scott.

I do speak briefly about another Bath, England, personality from the day, Miss Caroline Herschel — sister of famed astronomer William Herschel — who was in her own right a leading luminary in the science world, discovering comets and nebula and ultimately cataloguing so many discoveries that in 1787 she was able to realize her wish to be granted an independent income, fifty pounds annually granted by King George III. She was a remarkable woman and long outlived her more famous brother, garnering numerous awards and commemorations over and beyond her lifetime. An asteroid and a crater on the moon are named for her.

In *Lady Anne and the Haunted Schoolgirl* I have Caroline Herschel giving a lecture at the Bath Assembly Rooms, but by the time of this book she no longer lived in Bath, having moved — reluctantly on her part, for she much enjoyed the company and culture of Bath — with her brother four years earlier to a small town near Windsor Castle so her brother could entertain royal guests.

There is another important thread in *Lady Anne and the Haunted Schoolgirl*. Anne discovers that Magistrate Brereton is what was referred to as a trading justice. That was a real term indicating a magistrate who was corrupt, looking the other way and failing to prosecute thieves, but who also at times benefited by receiving stolen goods, or even encouraging and giving information to thieves, telling them who had what jewels, and who was gone from town and when. This did happen, on occasion, though Brereton is a completely fictional character. I have absolutely no reason to think any Bath magistrate was crooked.

Bath . . . what an amazing and historically important city in England! As in *Lady Anne and the Menacing Mystic*, the city is almost as much a character as the people, and I have enjoyed "living" in the city for two books.

But now it is time to move on, to Anne's honeymoon journey north which, taken in winter, is bound to be exciting. Watch for the next adventure in the series, *Lady Anne and the Winter Witch*, coming soon.

With best regards,
Victoria Hamilton

About the Author

Victoria Hamilton is the pseudonym of nationally bestselling romance author Donna Lea Simpson. Victoria is the bestselling author of three mystery series, the Lady Anne Addison Mysteries, the Vintage Kitchen Mysteries, and the Merry Muffin Mysteries. Her latest adventure in writing is a Regency-set historical mystery series, starting with *A Gentlewoman's Guide to Murder*.

Victoria loves to read, especially mystery novels, and enjoys good tea and cheap wine, the company of friends, and has a newfound appreciation for opera. She enjoys crocheting and beading, but a good book can tempt her away from almost anything . . . except writing!

Visit Victoria at www.victoriahamiltonmysteries.com.

Made in United States
North Haven, CT
10 June 2024

53438015R00146